Intoxicated by You

KC McCormick Çiftçi

In memory of a dear friend

A note from me

Dear Reader,

Thank you so much for picking up this book. Writing it was therapeutic for me and brought up a lot of challenging memories and feelings, and it is my sincere hope that these pages will be helpful to others navigating loss and grief. However, I feel it's particularly important to let you know what to expect in these pages so that you can decide for yourself if this is the book for you.

This story contains an in-depth exploration of grief, the previous death of a loved one in a car crash, an on-page but not serious car crash, and themes of addiction and alcoholism. Please take care of your mental health when deciding if this is something you're ready to read. While it does hold true to the definition of a romance novel (in that the ending for our two main characters is a happy one), the journey to get there may not be for every reader.

Love,
KC

One

A premonition was nothing to trifle with, Maya Jefferson knew that. Now, if only she could convince her friend that the "bad feeling" that had been plaguing her of late was a result of her sixth sense and not just her everyday anxiety, then maybe they could move off this topic and actually enjoy happy hour together.

"I'm telling you," she pleaded. "This is different. This isn't like Luisa stressing out about winning a new client—which we all know she's going to end up with, anyway." How could she explain this to them when the two of them couldn't possibly fathom the stakes? "It just feels like...well, like something bad is waiting around the corner. I don't know. Just...just promise me you'll both be careful, okay? Look both ways a couple of extra times before you cross the street or whatever."

Luisa huffed a sigh in her direction. "Don't even joke about me not landing a client, Maya. It's not funny."

Maya rolled her eyes. "Bad example, sorry. It's just that things have been...well, they've been pretty good lately, haven't they?" She shrugged. "All the more reason to keep a lookout over your shoulder, in case some bad luck catches up with us."

"That's not the way it works," Andie chided, shaking her head fervently. "Life isn't going to punish you because you've been *happy*, for Pete's sake. You're always looking over your shoulder, Maya. I know you're kidding, I get it. But you've got to stop joking like this. I'm saying this in all love...you know that, right?"

Luisa jumped in before Maya could respond. "I think what Andie *means*, Maya—" She shot a stern look at Andie. "—is that we're worried about you. And...I have to ask. Have you actually been happy lately? Like...is it worth worrying that something terrible is about to happen when you've been just midline content, anyway? Or are you ecstatically joyful and just keeping it to yourself?" Her eyebrows climbed with her question, her hazel eyes conveying the depth of her concern and love for her friend so intensely Maya had to look away.

Maya shook her head. "I thought this was supposed to be a light-hearted happy hour. It's not fair, you know. And we don't even have the excuse of having a drink or two and that loosening up our inhibitions." She nodded towards the table, where their glasses sat. None of the women drank alcohol, each for their own reasons. It was one thing that normally made Maya feel safe with her friends. She could order her usual ginger ale or iced tea without bracing for the cajoling and wheedling that came afterward. But today, she felt like a wire with its insulation stripped off, a live copper line just waiting to zap anyone who dared touch it, even by mistake.

Luisa sipped her kombucha and smiled at Andie and Maya in turn. "You know, speaking of light-hearted happy hours...when was the last time either of you had some fun?" She lifted an eyebrow, giving her friends a moment to think. "I got asked that on a date last week, and I couldn't remember the last thing I'd done that wasn't for work. All my hobbies have either become potential sources of side hustles or gone by the wayside." She looked intently at Maya. "It's not just you, friend. And I don't want you to feel like we're ganging up on you."

"I know," Maya said. She forced a smile as she worked to shove the foreboding feelings this conversation had brought to the surface back down below where they belonged. "But don't think you can skip right over talking about your date like that. Who? What? Where? How?"

"Uh huh," Andie agreed. "I caught that, too. She thinks she's sneaky, but that doesn't fly with me. Spill!" She pointed the neck of her root beer at Luisa, who laughed and shook her head.

"Well, I'm afraid you're both about to be very disappointed," she said. "Apart from that question, the entire date was forgettable. I met him online, we had lunch, and it was all very average. I think we were both clear on the fact that it wasn't a love match or anything, so I have no intention of calling him again, and he seems to be thinking the same. So in that way—and only in that way—we are perfectly in tune with each other."

"Sorry, you met for *lunch*?" Andie asked. "On a workday?"

"Of course!" Luisa answered. "I have a 45 minute lunch break, and you know I don't believe in giving up my rare free evenings for just *anyone*." She gestured to her two friends.

Maya and Andie made meaningful eye contact and choked back laughs before Maya spoke up. "Luisa...please tell me you didn't tell your date that."

Luisa threw her napkin at Maya, but she was laughing. "You know I do have *some* tact. I didn't tell him he wasn't dinner-worthy or anything like that. I just told him a lunch date would be efficient. What?" Her friends' laughter was descending into out-of-control cackles. "What is so funny about that?"

Andie was the first to regain control of her faculties and respond. "Nothing. Nothing at all. But I think you're on to something with the idea that we might need a little more fun in our lives. Let's come up with some ideas and really set the intention of making it happen."

"Oh, I'm way ahead of you," Luisa said. She pulled out her phone, tapped a few times, and then turned it to her friends. On the screen, there was a spreadsheet full of different colored squares, each filled with text. "I took an inventory of how I'm spending my time currently. I found the gaps, where there is an opportunity to fill in a blank space with something enriching and fun, and I started to work on a list of potential activities to incorporate into those white spaces."

Andie raised her eyebrows but said nothing. She turned to Maya. "How about you, then? What's on your mind?"

Maya took a long drink from her glass to give herself more time to think. Her friends' questions about her current level of happiness had struck a nerve and made her think about something she hadn't thought of in a long time. Maybe not even since Nina had died.

"I'm not really sure," she admitted. "How do you even begin to know what's missing from your life? Is this like a spiritual or philosophical question, Andie? Am I supposed to ask my inner child, or what?"

"I think the less thinking you do, the better," Andie answered. "Go with your intuition or with a feeling you get. When something occurs to you, like an idea that you should try something, then do it. Try something different the next time. We don't all have to make spreadsheets." She turned her intense gaze on Luisa, who was typing away on the screen of her phone again. "What did you enjoy doing when you were a child?"

"Playing businesswoman," said Luisa, at the same time that Maya answered, "I don't know."

Maya's childhood memories were full of after school play dates with Nina, and they'd had so much fun no matter what they'd done that it didn't seem possible for Maya to separate the activities from the wonderful friend that she had shared them with. Whether they were pretending to be veterinarians, building forts in the woods, or reading on her parents' cozy living room couch, there had always been laughter, fun, and a lightness that Maya hadn't noticed until it was taken away from her.

But she couldn't get into all of that with her friends right now. They knew about Nina, of course, but that didn't mean she wanted to have a public cryfest in front of all the unfamiliar hipsters who were sharing the patio with them. She'd save that for another time. For now, it was enough to brainstorm without getting into the nitty-gritty details.

"I spent a lot of time outside," she said. "Reading books, playing pretend. I always loved art, no matter what kind of project it was."

"I loved art, too," agreed Andie. "I started painting again recently, after things were so hard at work. It seemed like it might be a good way to process all the grief, and so far it's been really helpful." Andie was an end-of-life doula, guiding people who were near death to and through that final transition and supporting their families as well. She often talked about how rewarding it was with tears in her eyes, and Maya knew that some days weighed heavily on Andie. She was glad to hear Andie had another tool in her tool belt when she needed to process all the emotions she brought home from her work.

"I liked painting," added Luisa. "I stopped when I realized I wasn't very good at it, but until that point, I had a lot of fun."

Maya shook her head. "I did the same thing. In middle school, I decided I wasn't one of the naturally talented artistic kids, so I never took another art class again after that. And of course I never did it on my own either, because what if I wasn't any good?"

"I think that happens to a lot of us, maybe even most of us," Andie said. "But what is 'good,' anyway? If we aren't trying to win a contest, if we're just trying to process our emotions and get out of our heads for a damn minute, isn't that all that matters?"

"I guess so," said Maya.

"I mean, I'm not crazy about the idea of not being good at something," said Luisa. Off Andie's expression, she continued. "But yeah. You're right."

An idea occurred to Maya, and she piped up before she could talk herself out of it. "Why don't we make a painting date together, then? No judgment, no rules, just the three of us, a few canvases, and some paints. What do you think?"

"I love it!" Andie exclaimed. "And I'm happy to host it. We can use my living room, or maybe the balcony. And I've got a lot of paints. We'll just need to buy some canvases. And make sure you wear ratty clothes in case you accidentally paint yourself. Sound good, Lu?"

Luisa looked hesitant, but she nodded. "Let me check my schedule to see when I could do it."

Within ten minutes, they had settled on a date and time—Thursday at seven o'clock—and Maya had offered to make a run to the art supplies store to pick up canvases before then. Excitement and anticipation tingled within her, almost—but not quite—extinguishing the anxiety she had been feeling when the evening began. The sense that something was about to happen followed her home, refusing to leave her no matter how focused her attention was on ignoring it.

Two

Maya set her travel mug of herbal tea down on her desk at ten to nine the next morning. She had worked at Andersen Marketing Consulting for three years, and she prided herself on the fact that she had never been late. She'd never missed a day either, unless you counted the week she had been sick with a nasty case of food poisoning. Even then, she had come back to work sooner than any of her coworkers had expected, staying close to the bathroom in case she had made the decision to come back so quickly in vain—it turned out she had, but that was a story for another day.

"Good, you're here," a voice sounded from behind Maya. Maya turned to find Chris, assistant to her boss, Catherine Andersen, smiling at her. "Ms. Andersen requested a meeting with you first thing this morning. Once you're settled in—" He nodded towards her mug and backpack. "—you can head into the conference room."

"Thanks, Chris," she said, feeling anxious bubbles warring in her stomach. Maya was good at her job, there was no doubt about it—there was a reason she was reporting directly to the CEO now, despite starting in an entry level marketing assistant position three years ago. But regardless of the accolades and promotions her work had earned her, she still felt like she was about to get into trouble for something she had—or hadn't—done every time her boss requested a meeting with her.

She positioned her backpack underneath her desk, extracting her work laptop from it and placing it on her power station as she connected it to her large desktop monitor. She picked up a legal pad and a pen, scribbling on the corner of the top page to be sure she'd chosen a pen with a good ink flow. Satisfied, Maya walked out of her office and down the hallway to the conference room.

Andersen Marketing Consulting's offices occupied one floor of their downtown high rise, and the staff was small enough that Maya knew everyone by name—the local staff, at least. There were countless more remote employees, the majority of them in vastly different time zones, who were largely responsible for the graphic design end of things. Communication between the local and remote employees was asynchronous and free-flowing, with emails and direct messages taking up a good portion of everyone's work day.

The conference room was at the end of the hallway, opposite Ms. Andersen's office. Chris's workstation was outside the closed door of the CEO's office, and he nodded to Maya as she walked into the conference room. She heard Chris pick up his phone, connecting directly to Catherine to inform her that her meeting was ready to begin.

While Maya waited for the boss to arrive, she busied herself arranging her notepad and pen on the table in front of her. Keeping her hands busy kept her anxiety at bay—or at least that's what she told herself. She pulled her phone out of her pocket, checking for the third time that it was on silent mode and her meeting with Catherine wouldn't be interrupted by an untimely call or text message.

"There you are!" crowed Catherine Andersen as she floated into the room. Her larger-than-life presence filled any space she occupied, and the cavernous conference room was no exception. Catherine glided across the room, making her way to the chair next to Maya. Her movements were graceful, her appearance immaculate, and raw confidence oozed from her pores. "Good morning, darling Maya!" She leaned down to air kiss both of Maya's cheeks before sitting down next to her.

"Good morning, Ms. Andersen," Maya responded. "How are you?"

"Oh, fine I suppose. I had the most exciting news last night, but of course that meant I didn't sleep a wink. You're lucky I didn't call you in the middle of the night just to bend your ear."

"I should thank you for that, I think," Maya smiled. She looked down at her own outfit, noticing a stray wrinkle on the front of her blouse she had missed while ironing. If Catherine looked as put together as she did after a sleepless night, she probably thought even one of Maya's hairs out of place was unacceptable. "I'd love to hear this exciting news if you're ready to share it."

"I thought you'd never ask!" Catherine beamed. "I had a call from Conley Corporation. Can you believe it? They want to retain our services."

Maya worked to keep her expression neutral, afraid of giving away that she had never heard of Conley Corporation before, that she had no idea what was so special or exciting about it. Was she supposed to know what that meant?

Thankfully, Catherine plowed on. "Conley is so hot right now. They got a lot of attention after their CEO was on Shark Tank a few months ago. He invented a new water filtration system, cutting-edge technology, really. The sharks didn't bite, unfortunately, but their product still got a lot of attention. Now Tom—that's Thomas Conley, the CEO—wants to be sure to keep the momentum going. He's coming to us for a fresh perspective on their marketing, a real way to keep their brand top of mind. Isn't that exciting?"

"Yes, it is," Maya agreed. "What sort of water filtration system is it? Something for campers to use, or something to send to people who don't have access to clean water in their villages? I'm not familiar with it..."

"Hmm, multipurpose, I'd say. There are in-home units, portable ones for campers or people on-the-go, and they're working to spread the product, the technology worldwide. I'm sure, once we start working with them, we'll get the device in here to see it for ourselves."

"That's great," Maya said. "So, what can I do to help with this new project?"

"I'm so glad you asked!" Catherine exclaimed. "That right there, that initiative you show...that's exactly how I know you're the woman for this job."

Isn't that a natural question to ask when you've been called in for a one-on-one with the boss? Maya wondered.

Regardless, she smiled and nodded, waiting for her boss to continue.

"Mr. Conley is a bit unorthodox, I'd say. He specifically requested to work only with one person on our team. He doesn't want one person doing the graphics while another writes the copy—he wants someone who can do it all. And he wants that person focused solely on working on his project. It's all a bit funny, all a bit particular...but it has the potential to be a big account, so I certainly don't mind any demands he makes."

"Are you saying...?" Maya trailed off, waiting for Catherine to confirm her suspicions.

"...that you're just the woman for the job? Of course I am! You've shown yourself capable of all the skills Mr. Conley needs, and your loyalty to the company hasn't gone unnoticed. Maya, this opportunity is perfect for you. And it could be just the thing to really cement your position in this company, set yourself up in a career you can retire from one day."

Maya's eyes widened. At twenty-eight years of age, retirement wasn't exactly on her radar. And while she liked the work she did at Andersen, she wouldn't say she *loved* it. But those were concerns for another time; for right now, all she had to ask herself was if she wanted to take on this project or not.

"That sounds great, Ms. Andersen. Where should I get started?"

Catherine beamed and clapped her hands together. "How wonderful! I'll have Chris bring all the information to your desk. Mr. Conley is coming for a meeting this afternoon, so you'll have time this morning to brush up on all the information you need to know before then."

As Catherine bustled out of the room, Maya focused her energy on keeping her face neutral. Underneath the surface, her mind was going a mile a minute—she had the image of a duck cruising peacefully along the top of a pond, while underneath the murky water, its little feet were paddling frantically. A mixture of emotions played at once—excitement about the opportunity, doubt that she could handle it, anxiety about it all happening *so soon*, and that ever present foreboding feeling that something was about to Happen with a capital H. That feeling had been her companion for years—ever since she had gotten that fateful phone call that changed everything. Upon learning about Nina's car accident, something had clicked into place, some sort of knowing. She couldn't look backwards to the last time she had seen Nina without the memory being colored by the horrible thing that would happen later. It added a weight and gravity to every anxious feeling that came up—could this, too, be a premonition of bad things to come?

Just a few hours later, Maya was back in the conference room preparing for Tom Conley's arrival. She was twenty minutes early, of course, and it was a good thing. Hank, one of the senior associates who had been at Andersen since the beginning, was retiring today and his retirement party had just finished in the conference room. Maya didn't know Hank well enough to exchange more than a handshake and a few well wishes, so she set to work clearing away the napkins and cups that had been left on the conference room table.

Maya placed a pitcher of water and a few clean glasses on the table. Her ever-present notebook was there, too, reserving a chair for her with a prime view of the conference room door. Once everything was in its place on the table, she'd seat herself in that perfect spot where she could flip through her calendar, jot down notes, and read emails on her phone, all while keeping an eye on the door so as not to be caught unawares by the arrival of her guest.

As she crossed one leg over the other, her foot clinked against something under the table. As she spotted the half empty whiskey bottles under the conference room table, Maya shook her head and chuckled. Leave it to Hank to go out with a bang—this was definitely not standard practice at Andersen Consulting. Maya ducked under the table, finding an even larger stash of hidden alcohol than she had expected and groaning as she began to gather them in her arms.

"Bad time? I can come back if you're busy," a deep voice with a melodic Irish lilt called into the room. From under the table, Maya could just make out a pair of shiny leather shoes, topped by tailored trousers, her eyes wanting nothing more than to keep traveling upwards if not for the conference room table blocking her way.

"Just a second," she said, struggling backwards with the last of the bottles, the very picture of grace in a pencil skirt, huddled on the floor.

"Take your time." His voice rippled with humor, and her pulse increased as she imagined the man who would match that voice.

In too much of a hurry, Maya jolted to her feet, smacking her head on the edge of the table as she did. She winced with pain, barely managing to stop herself from uttering a very unprofessional word.

"Are you alright?" The man stepped forward with concern, worry creasing his brow as his eyes—his gorgeous, deep eyes—searched hers. Maya nodded, words failing her, as all her brain could comprehend was that this man was like a work of art, better even than she had imagined upon hearing his voice. But as his eyes traveled down to her arms and took in the bottles there, his demeanor changed completely. It was as if he had frozen, all warmth seeping out of his expression, as his own arms crossed over his body.

She set the bottles down on the table and reached to shake his hand. "Mr. Conley, is it? I'm Maya Jefferson. It's very nice to meet you."

Tom's gaze was still fixed on the bottles Maya placed on the table, but he returned her handshake with a smile that didn't quite reach his eyes. "Nice to meet you too, Ms. Jefferson." He tore his eyes from the bottles and up to meet hers. "I take it you're the poor unfortunate soul who's been tasked with dealing with me and all my demands?"

"I certainly don't see it that way, sir," Maya smiled and gestured to the seat across from hers. "Can I get you a drink before we get started?"

As Tom settled into his seat, he winced with visible discomfort—physical or emotional, Maya couldn't be sure.

"A bit early in the day to be offering the Irishman a drink, isn't it?"

Maya felt the color rising to her face. "I meant coffee...or water?" Her voice raised with a question as she pushed the pitcher across the table toward him with a little too much force. Gesturing to the bottles, she hurried to explain. "These aren't supposed to be here. There was a retirement party, and I think they got snuck in to send the honoree off in a memorable way. Let me get them out of here..."

"It's alright," he replied, holding up his hand to stop her from standing. "Let's just begin." Tom sat down and opened the leather organizer in front of him to a clean page to take notes, and began clicking his pen repeatedly.

Caught off guard by the abrupt change of manner, from warm to cold to cordially polite, Maya balked. "Er..." she began. "Well, I've got a few ideas—"

"Why don't we start with me telling you about the initiative, eh?" Tom cut in. "I imagine that'll be the more efficient way to go, since I can give you more information than what you were probably able to find online in the hours you spent preparing for this meeting."

Maya's blush was deepening now, she was sure of that. It was a rookie mistake, jumping in when she should have been listening. Despite her rapidly deepening distaste for Tom and his abrupt nature, this was an opportunity she couldn't let slip through her fingers. Stuffing down her pride and embarrassment, she raised the edges of her lips in a tight smile. "By all means, go ahead."

Three

"Oh, come on, it couldn't have been that bad." Andie's voice came through the phone. "I'm sure he doesn't think you're—how did you phrase it?—'completely inept and devoid of all talent.' Is it at all possible that this is just the story you're telling yourself? And the story of what actually happened is nowhere near this dramatic or exciting or worthy of end-of-the-world feelings?"

Maya sighed as she flopped onto the couch in her apartment, switching the phone to her other ear as she picked up the cup of tea on the side table. "Sure, it's possible. But you weren't there, Andie. And no offense, but like...do you even know what you're talking about here? You've never seen me at work. How can you be so confident I'm good at my job, anyway?"

"Let's just call it intuition. The intuition of a friend who sees how much—ahem, some might even say *too* much—care you put into everything you've done for this job. How much sleep are you getting these days, anyway?"

Maya rolled her eyes. "What does that have to do with anything? Looking for another area where I'm failing at life to put it all into perspective?"

"I'm just starting at the base of the pyramid, love. You've got a roof over your head, and for that we are thankful. Now we make sure you're eating, hydrating, sleeping, moving your body once in a while...if all those things are in order, *then* we can take your existential crises seriously. So, spill. How much sleep are you getting?"

"Probably four or five hours a night lately." Maya winced as she said it. "I know, I know...I'll work on it."

"I'm not going to chastise you. Don't you know me better than that by now?" There was a smile in Andie's voice that warmed Maya's chest as it reached her ears. "Why don't you try winding down early tonight? Maybe instead of working in bed—don't start with me, I know you do it—you could read a novel, take a bath, drink something cozy, smell some lavender..."

"Okay, okay," Maya laughed, then glanced at her phone as it vibrated in her hand. "Luisa's calling me. I gotta go. Love you!"

"Love you, too." Andie said, "And don't let Luisa rile you up again—"

But Maya didn't hear the rest of Andie's words, as Luisa's clear voice was ringing out of the phone. Maya put the phone on speaker and placed it on the table, settling back into the couch with a smile on her face.

"That dick!" Those were the first words of Luisa's rant that registered on Maya's radar. "What absolute nerve he has, and at your first meeting! And why would he even think you were offering him alcohol? Did he think you were being culturally insensitive to Irish people? He'd have to think you were a total fool to think that was intentional, and that's yet another reason to hate him." She sighed dramatically. "Anyway, hopefully it wasn't entirely a bust. Did he have a cute accent, at least?"

It was Maya's turn to speak at last, but the question caught her off guard. Reflecting on her meeting with Tom, memories of her feelings of embarrassment, of being chastised, filled the screen of her mind. When she swept them away, there was a glimmer of something...that first moment, before the humiliation began. Tom had walked into the room and his presence, his smile, and yeah...that voice. It had all been impactful, for sure. Whether it was charming or presumptuous was hard to say now. But he had made an impression.

"Maya?" Luisa's voice interrupted her reverie. "Whatever you're thinking, you aren't saying it out loud. As you know, I'm not a mind reader, busy gal, places to go and people to see, time is money, et cetera, et cetera."

Maya laughed. "All right, all right. The accent was charming, I'll admit. That's a silver lining, at least to being forced to work in close proximity. When he's ridiculing me or shaming me, I can just focus on the way he's saying the words and not the words he's actually saying, and that's bound to help me get through the moment."

"That's the spirit," Luisa said. "Keep your nose to the grindstone, or whatever the expression is. I'm sure you'll do an amazing job with whatever Catherine has given you. And if you need me to come down there and kick some Irish ass, you know you just have to say the word, right?"

"It definitely won't come to that, Lu," Maya smiled, "Though I do appreciate your fierce loyalty. Why don't you just direct that energy my way instead of his and pour it all into pampering me or taking me shopping or something fun like that?"

"There's that F word again," said Luisa. "I'm afraid I haven't discovered the meaning of the word since we last spoke about it. Oh! I *did* attend a rather entertaining exercise class during my lunch break today—does that count as fun?"

"Hmm, that depends, I suppose. Were you there for the pure joy of it, or were you just doing it because you know it's good for you and you wrote 'exercise' on your to-do list last night?"

There was a pause. "Damn it. All right, you caught me. I still haven't figured out how to have fun. On that note, I've got a stack of papers here with my name on them. See you tomorrow?"

"See you tomorrow. And get some sleep!"

The next morning came sooner than Maya had expected. Her anxieties about the previous day's meeting with Tom Conley getting off to a rough start hadn't made it easy to switch off her brain and float into dreamland. She had tried to remember everything Andie had suggested she do to ease her way into sleep, but by two o'clock in the morning she was still wide awake. She had resigned herself then to the fact that sleep wasn't coming for her, and she had scrolled through the various social media sites on her phone for longer than she cared to admit.

A few minutes before six o'clock, while Maya braced herself for the fact that her alarm was about to go off, her phone pinged with the alert of a new text message. Pulling her phone out from under her pillow, where she had shoved it after an unexpected wave of frustration and discomfort had overcome her, she saw the message was from her mom.

"Thinking of you today, hon. Nina's birthday. I love you. If you want to talk, I'm here."

Maya groaned and pulled the blankets over her head. Of course she knew it was Nina's birthday today. As if she needed an excuse to think about her, today or any day. Still, it was comforting to know that her mom was thinking of Nina, too. She should text her back and tell her that...but the thought of picking the phone back up, of translating the messy ache in her chest into words on the screen, so neat and clean in their sans serif style...it didn't work. It wasn't enough. And it was exhausting.

"That's my cue to get up, I guess," Maya said to herself. God, it was tempting to call in sick today. Calling in heartsick wouldn't be a lie, but she was pretty sure Catherine Andersen wouldn't consider it an acceptable excuse. Andersen Consulting wasn't exactly on the cutting edge when it came to promoting or even acknowledging the importance of employees' mental health. Maya had certainly never seen a chink in the armor Catherine Andersen wore to work every day—from her designer wardrobe to her ever-immaculate hair and makeup, she strode into the office with the confidence of a general whose army had never lost a battle.

Maya wished she could be like Catherine. Carrying around this much pain, this much anxiety couldn't be healthy, could it? It kept bubbling up to the surface lately, and she missed the days when it had stayed put. That was all before Nina died, of course. And in the years since that had happened, Maya knew she had been irrevocably changed. Once it was out of the tube, you couldn't put it back in. She couldn't un-know that it was possible to lose the people you love. She couldn't relate to the previous version of herself who had never known loss, never grieved from the depths of her soul.

Maya sighed as she swung her feet over the side of the bed. "That's enough of that, now. We've got an Irishman who vastly misunderstood us to make a second impression on today, self. Let's do this thing."

The building housing Andersen Consulting was still dark when Maya arrived, or at least the floor their offices occupied was. Maya was early, clearly, and she was glad to have taken the time to memorize the access code for the floor. Otherwise, turning up this early would have been pointless—she'd be waiting in the corridor until someone else arrived.

She let herself into the office and flipped on the light switch next to the door. The fluorescent lights hummed to life, and Maya shivered off the last of the cold from outside. Her workstation was a short walk from the entrance, and she found her way there through all the empty cubicles. Glancing at her watch, she noted it wasn't even eight o'clock yet. She had plenty of time to get some prep work in before the day began—or before anyone else arrived, for that matter.

It wasn't easy to think at home sometimes, especially not when the day began with her thinking about Nina. Maya rubbed a finger against the necklace she had chosen today. It was a single pearl, Nina's birthstone, with an understated silver charm with the word "Embrace" on it. Her aunt had given it to her at Nina's funeral as a reminder to, well, embrace. Embrace the moment, embrace your loved ones while you had them...Maya supposed it also was telling her to embrace the feelings she was experiencing—had been experiencing since she got that fateful phone call—but she wasn't going to act on that anytime soon. Who had time for messy feelings like grief and despair?

"Despair. There's a word I never used to describe my feelings as a child. So dramatic! And yet so fitting, at a time like this." In the empty building, Maya was talking out loud to herself. If she didn't, the quiet of the cavernous rooms might give her the creeps or make her think she was hearing things.

But she definitely *was* hearing things now. She heard a faint sound, like flowing water, and Maya felt herself tense. Why had she insisted on coming in before anyone else? Now, she was either about to confront a squatter who was literally living up to his title and peeing in the corner of the office or come face to face with a ghost pouring water on the conference room floor.

A voice rang out from the same direction as the flowing water. "Despair is a strong word. Take heart, love. It can't be that bad, can it?"

Maya stopped in her tracks. The ghost, or the squatter, whichever one he was, had a delightful lilt to his voice, an accent that sounded familiar and sent a thrill of electricity up her spine.

Tom Conley rounded the corner with a mug in his hand, stirring as the spoon in his other hand clinked against the sides of the cup. "Now tell me, what's got you so out of sorts this morning?" He greeted her with a devastating smile, any hint of the ice that had appeared in their first meeting long thawed.

"I...I'm sorry," Maya sputtered, "But what are you doing here? Don't you know it's—" She glanced at the clock on the wall behind him. "—7:40 in the morning? Oh God, did an early meeting get added to the calendar...?"

While she fumbled to pull out her phone to check her calendar, Tom reached out and put a hand lightly on her forearm to stop her. She looked up into his eyes, and the smile he gave her was sheepish.

"You haven't forgotten anything, Maya. It's my fault. It's the jet lag, I suppose. It's been waking me up at all hours, and I couldn't fight it any more. Catherine graciously gave me the access code to the building when I told her about my odd hours after our last meeting. Plus, the coffee here—" He held up the cup in question. "—is significantly better than the shite in my hotel room." Tom shuddered at the mention of it, and Maya couldn't help but laugh.

"I'm glad we could help with your coffee problem." She smiled, "And I've heard nothing but good things about our coffee machine. I can't vouch for the coffee or the espresso myself, but the way it steams milk is just—" She made the gesture with her hand against her lips. "—chef's kiss!"

Tom's expression and delivery were deadpan when he spoke again. "You...don't drink coffee? But how do you get out of bed in the morning? Especially at an ungodly hour like this?" He looked at her travel mug meaningfully. "Black tea? That shouldn't surprise me. God knows half of Ireland runs on tea."

"It's tea alright, but...no caffeine." Maya laughed. "I'm an herbal tea kind of gal. No caffeine for me—well, apart from however much is in a chocolate bar, but even that I'm careful not to eat too late in the day. It just doesn't work for me. I feel nervous and jittery when I drink it, and the thought of *having* to have it every day in order to feel like a human—well, that scares me if I'm being honest."

Tom shook his head. "Damn. You're right, you know. It *should* scare you to be dependent on any substance, and it should scare me, too, as the one who's drinking the stuff every day." His expression had sobered, and he looked like he was deep in thought, reevaluating his life in the context of coffee and caffeine.

It was all getting a little too serious for Maya, and she knew it wasn't exactly her place to talk her clients out of their caffeine addictions, so she put on a cheery tone and spoke up again. "Anyway! It's not like caffeine is an illegal substance. And we're all allowed our vices. Though it seems like you and I share another addiction—work, maybe? Why else are we here when the sun has barely risen?" She laughed and gestured around them to the empty office.

Wow, two strikes. Again, Maya had made a joke, and again it had landed about as well as an egg tossed off a high rise. Tom looked even more anguished than he had a moment ago, something Maya hadn't imagined possible until just this moment when she saw it creep across his face.

"God," she muttered, "I sure am good at the small talk today." Then, directing her voice back to Tom, she asked, "Could we start the morning over, perhaps? How are you? Anything in particular you're looking forward to today?"

Tom's smile was pasted over the clear discomfort he was still feeling, like wallpaper used to cover a massive crack in the living room wall.

"Absolutely," he smiled—or grimaced, if Maya were accurately describing the look on his face. "I'm very well, thank you. It's looking to be a beautiful day, and I'm feeling very confident about this project of ours. How about you, Miss Jefferson?"

"I'm doing well, too. Just in the office early to get a head start on a few things before a busy day of meetings. Are you all set up with a space to work, or would you like me to help you find a desk?"

"Erm." Was Tom blushing? "I'm actually going to be working in Catherine's office." He held up a keycard in his hand. "She insisted, though I told her I'd be fine at any old desk."

"Well, all right." Maya smiled. "Please let me know if there's anything I can do to help in the meantime. I'll just get out of your hair now." She turned on her heel and made her way to her desk, mind racing with Tom's last words.

Was there something more than just professional courtesy going on between Tom and Catherine? Not that it was any of her business, of course...but it would be helpful to know, wouldn't it? Tom was a VIP client no matter what, but if he was also Catherine's significant other, well, then that would make him a VIP with an extra V—a very, *very* important person. With even more power to influence the future—or lack thereof—of Maya's career.

She pulled out her phone and fired off a text to her group chat with Andie and Luisa.

"Help! I came to the office super early and guess who's here? Cranky Irishman!! What's he doing here? And super weird...Catherine told him to work in her office. What if the two of them are hooking up? Is that important? Significant? Do I even need to know?"

The first response came immediately, and it was from Luisa, who was no doubt also at or on her way to the office.

"Keep it profesh. What you don't know can't hurt you! And who cares if he's hooking up with the boss? Nose to the grindstone, remember?"

Luisa wasn't wrong, Maya knew. Separating the personal and the professional had always served her well in the past. There was just something that wasn't sitting right with her, and now wasn't the time to figure out what that was.

"Good morning to you two beautiful souls, too. It's going to be a gorgeous day, and I'm so grateful to have both of you in my life."

Andie was nothing if not consistent. And wonderful. Maya felt herself smiling despite herself as she read the message. It *was* a beautiful day, and she knew how lucky she was to have these two friends by her side.

Before she could capture any of that in a text message, another ping sounded on her phone. Andie again.

"Now that we've covered the important stuff, we can get down to business. So tell me, Maya. Why do you care about a personal relationship between Tom and Catherine? Don't overthink it—go with the first reaction that comes to mind, the one your subconscious throws out, not the one your conscious mind hems and haws over. Is it because you think it's inappropriate? That one of them can do better? Or is it jealousy? And if so, of whom? Jealousy of Tom for being in Catherine's inner circle? Or of Catherine for being in Tom's?"

Damn, Maya thought. *I mean, damn. It's too early for deep dives, doesn't she know that?* Her first reaction was to set the phone down and get to work, but she felt a prick of discomfort low in her belly. Something Andie had suggested had resonated, probably. But now wasn't the time to question which particular comment had done the damage.

Four

"**G**ood mooorning!" Catherine's voice sailed through the office, creating ripples of awareness in every direction. The cubicles had filled up in the hour since Maya had arrived, no doubt full of new employees eager to make an impression on their renowned boss. Catherine Andersen was famous in the marketing world—the local universities, at least, often cited her success in their business classes and the number of applications for internships grew every year. The bullpen, the area of the office Catherine was currently striding across, held a mixture of first-year employees and the (unpaid) interns who aspired to one day be first-year employees. Maya could feel their nervous energy permeating the environment as they clamored for Catherine's attention.

Alas, their efforts were in vain this morning. Catherine walked as if she were wearing horse blinders, directly to Maya's desk, where she stopped and cleared her throat. Maya looked up, startled to have been graced by such a presence—undeservedly, it seemed, as she hadn't received any emails or text messages from Catherine since she arrived at the office nearly an hour and a half ago.

"Good morning, Catherine." She smiled. "How are you? Is there anything I can do for you this morning?"

Catherine smiled back. "Is he still here?" she asked. Off Maya's expression, she continued. "Tom, of course! I heard the two of you were here working this morning, and I just wondered...did he leave? Is he still here?"

Maya resisted the urge to roll her eyes at the excitement in Catherine's voice and expression. She reminded herself again that personal drama had no place in the office and that she was definitely *not* going to be the go-between for Catherine and Tom. She looked up at Catherine and responded, "As far as I know, he's still in your office. I haven't seen him since I arrived."

Catherine's face clouded with an expression Maya couldn't read. "You...what? Maya, this is a very important client! You *are* aware of that, right? I'm not asking you to babysit him, Maya. But at least showing the barest of interest in ensuring his needs are met would go a long way to keep him from walking out the door and going straight to one of our competitors."

"I...I'm sorry, Catherine." Maya could feel the blood rushing to her face. "I didn't mean...I just figured he was here to get work done, and he seemed perfectly comfortable making himself coffee, helping himself to your office...I didn't want to get in his way, I guess."

"Good grief, Maya," Catherine's expression softened nearly imperceptibly. "You deserve to be here, you know that, don't you? I hired you because you're incredibly capable, and you've moved up the ranks for the same reason. But that means you can't get scared every time some *man* shows up and acts like he knows his way around the place."

"That's...that's a really good point. Thank you, Catherine. I didn't even realize that was the problem, honestly."

Catherine sighed. "We never do. But it's a nearly universal experience for women in the workforce. It happened to me, too, until one of my supervisors started mentoring me. She told me to stop apologizing for taking up space, and I took it to heart. And I tried to pass that message on to as many women after me as I could." She winked at Maya.

"I appreciate it, I really do. And I'm sorry this happened today. It won't happen again."

"Don't be sorry—there's an epidemic of sorries among women in the workforce, too. Unless you run over my cat or punch my mom in the face, don't apologize."

"I...you're right. Okay."

"You're learning quickly, Maya Jefferson. Now, go march right into my office and ask Tom Conley if he's available for a status update meeting this afternoon."

"Should I at least knock?"

A hint of a smile played at the corner of Catherine's mouth. "You can knock as you're already opening the door. How about that?"

"I can do that." Maya smiled back.

As Catherine departed for the kitchen, no doubt to prepare her own morning beverage, Maya headed in the opposite direction, to Catherine's office, where Tom was waiting.

In front of the door, Maya steeled herself. "You deserve to be here," she said under her breath. "Shoulders back, chin up, open the door, and ask your question."

And then she did just that. With her posture in a perfectly powerful pose (shoulders back, core muscles supporting lower back, chin raised) and her hand poised to knock on the door, it suddenly swung open, the handle colliding with her soft stomach.

"Oof." Maya stumbled back, all efforts at confidently taking up space forgotten as she tried to stay upright.

"Sorry, love!" Tom grabbed her elbow and kept her on her feet. "It's after nine, and I had lost track of time. I imagine Catherine needs her office at some point, so I best get out of her hair." He let go of her elbow, and she felt the loss of his warmth immediately.

"Er…" Maya began. "Status meeting! Today…I mean, could you…would you be available for a status update meeting this afternoon?"

"With yourself?" Tom asked. "Absolutely. I've got a few things to take care of downtown this morning, but I can plan to be back here by, say, half two?"

"Half past two?" Maya asked. Off Tom's nod, she continued. "I'll reserve the conference room. See you then, Tom."

At lunchtime, Maya left the office. She had sent Andie and Luisa an SOS text message after her non-confrontation with Tom that morning, asking if anyone would be free to meet for lunch and to talk some sense into her. Some measure of grace must be working in her favor, because Andie had the early afternoon free in between clients, and Luisa already had a lunch date scheduled in the same part of the city.

"I'll be done with my lunch by then. Why don't you two save me a seat, and I can come join you for a coffee before I head back to the office?" Luisa had written.

You have to admire her work ethic, Maya thought. *Otherwise, you have to wonder if it's time to hold an intervention* because *of her work ethic.*

The restaurant was a couple of blocks away from Andersen Consulting, and Maya appreciated the chance to stretch her legs as she made her way there.

"Hi hi hi!" a voice called over her shoulder. Maya turned to greet Andie, but before she could complete the turn, she was engulfed in her friend's bear hug.

Andie held Maya's shoulders in place as she kissed—not air-kissed, but full lip-kissed—her on both cheeks. Then she took a step back, with her hands still firmly planted on Maya's shoulders, and peered directly into her soul.

Maya blinked and looked away. That was strange. She wasn't normally one to shy away from eye contact, but something about Andie's gaze felt like it was seeing a little *too* much. She shook her head to clear her mind and smiled before returning Andie's cheek kisses.

"Thanks for meeting me," Maya greeted her friends with a smile. "It's such a perfectly wonderful surprise to get us all together on a weekday for lunch. We never even try to make a plan like this, and here we are by dumb chance making it happen!"

There was a sadness in Andie's eyes as her lips raised into a smile. "I wish it happened more often, too. But don't call it dumb chance, please. You put out a call for help, and *of course* your two best gals came through for you. So let's sit and you can tell me what's got you so twisted up today. Luisa will only have time (ahem, and attention span) for the quick and dirty version of the story, anyway."

Maya stepped to the front of the line, and she and Andie placed their lunchtime orders—a hearty salad for Andie, and a cup of tomato soup and half a grilled cheese sandwich for Maya. Maya knew Andie well enough to know what her lunch order meant (that she was craving raw veggies and—TMI?—might be needing a little fiber for her digestion), and she knew Andie was interpreting the tomato soup and grilled cheese as well.

"Comfort meal?" Andie asked, raising her eyebrows towards Maya's tray as they walked to the table. "It's not a rainy day, and we aren't curled up on the couch in your dorm reading romantic comedies, but..."

"Yep, the principle still applies." Maya smiled as they sat down at a corner table. "When something feels off in the outside world, whether it's the weather or work drama, nothing beats grilled cheese dipped in tomato soup."

"Amen to that!" Before Maya could react, Andie reached across the table, picked up her sandwich, dipped it in the soup, and bit off the corner. With a mischievous look on her face and a mouth full of heaven, she deposited the cornerless sandwich back on the plate.

"I can't even be mad," said Maya. "I couldn't have resisted the pull of this perfect meal if I were you, either. I thought you were vegan this week, though."

Andie shook her head as she dug into her salad. "Nope, I found a better word for it in something I read the other day. Freegan! As in, sure, when it's up to me to cook or choose something off the menu, I'll probably pick a plant-based meal. But if it's coming from someone else and it's free, then all bets are off. At least that's how I'm choosing to define it."

Maya laughed. "I like that. And it does sound more like you in all your 'go with the flow' vibes."

"That's me." Andie smiled. "*And* that's also enough about me. Let's talk about you. What's going on today? Why the emergency friend bat signal?"

"Ugh," Maya groaned. "Honestly, I think I'm losing my mind. I'm fixating on the impression I made on this Tom character, I'm obsessing over the nature of his relationship with Catherine, and it's been so hard to focus on the actual project. I've got a status update meeting with Tom this afternoon—yay for me for actually scheduling it—but I can't help but be afraid that I'm just going to blow it again. What's happening? Why am I fixating on this guy? Is it a sign? Any wisdom from the ancestors?"

"I know you're asking that as a joke, but it could actually be a legitimate question. I have a friend who connects with and channels ancestral wisdom, if you're ever interested."

"I'll remember that. But seriously. Why am I doing this?"

Andie grimaced. "You might not like this, but I've got an idea. I know you're looking for meaning about Tom's role in all this—is there something significant or special about him? But I think you've got to look at yourself before you look at anyone else. You were just given this massive extra responsibility at work. How are you feeling about that?"

"I'm barely feeling anything about it." Maya shrugged as she let out a deep exhale. "The human factor has just been so messy, so complicated..."

"But what if that's not what it is at all? What if the extra responsibility is messing with your head, challenging your ego's comfortable position? It's a classic problem, and it happens to a lot of people. Something starts to go well in one area of your life, so you get really uncomfortable and start self-sabotaging."

Maya blinked. "Self sabotaging? This isn't about me. I mean, it's about me making a horrendous first impression on Tom and then letting Catherine down, sure, but it's also largely about them, too. Why can't Tom be the kind of person who gives people the benefit of the doubt? And why can't Catherine be the kind of boss who sets reasonable expectations for her employees so she isn't let down by them?"

"And what about Maya? How would you finish that phrase about her? 'Why can't Maya be...?'"

Maya sighed. "'...better at her job. More professional. Less nosy about other people's business?' Any of those sound good?"

"They all sound just fine, and they also all sound like they're accepting defeat. Like it's not possible that you're going to succeed in this new role. Like, 'if only I were different I could do this, but I can't, so that's that.' Is that really how you feel?"

"No," Maya admitted. "I want to grow in this role. I want to prove to Catherine, to *myself*, that I'm ready for more responsibility. I want to handle this project so well that she won't even consider giving the next one like it to someone else. I want to be an invaluable member of the team."

"Hmm." Andie paused. "It sounds like there are two distinct voices talking here. There's the one that's defeatist, ready to give up. And there's the one that's dreaming of more, that's ready to take it on. Personally, I'd call the first one your ego and the second one your higher self, but that's just me. The question is, which one are you going to listen to?"

"Wait, how is that my ego talking? Honestly, it's been way too long since I took Psych 101 and I'm almost embarrassed to admit I can't actually remember what an ego is..." Maya cringed as she waited for Andie's response.

Andie chuckled. "I'm not using the word ego like Freud would. I'm speaking more from a spiritual perspective, where ego is your individual identity, separate from the larger whole. So, in this instance, your ego has become identified with your profession. And the leap to more responsibility and autonomy is scary for your ego. Because sure, you might succeed. But you might fail, too. And either way, you're going to find yourself in a different place, in different circumstances than you've been in before. And the ego likes the status quo. It likes to be comfy, just like you and me."

Maya dropped the rest of her sandwich on her plate and stared at it. "Are you telling me I'm eating grilled cheese and tomato soup because my *ego made me do it*? Because my ego is uncomfy and it's making me uncomfy too?"

"Kind of." Andie smiled, "But not exactly. Spirituality isn't exactly science, you know. This is just what makes sense to me. If it's helpful to you, take it to heart. If it's not, let it go. I promise I won't be offended either way."

"That's a lot to think about," Maya said. "Thanks, Andie."

"What are you thanking Andie for? What did I miss?" Luisa's voice broke through the pensive calm, bringing a smile to both Maya's and Andie's faces.

"Oh, I'm just giving her a spiritual perspective on this whole work mess, what else?" Andie teased. "We solved the whole thing without you, I think, so you're free to go if you've got another meeting lined up?"

Luisa rolled her eyes and reached over to snag the last bite of Maya's sandwich. "Yeah, right. I know you all were just waiting for your project manager to show up to get to work. So...I'm here now. Let's knock this thing out in, oh, say, five minutes?"

Andie laughed. "By all means, I'm sure another perspective is very welcome. Maya?" She gestured for Maya to take over.

Maya sipped her coffee and cleared her throat. "It's just that this whole promotion—not that I can even call it that because there isn't a raise or even a new job title to go along with it—this whole thing at work is really messing with my head. I'm excited about the extra responsibility, the opportunity to make an impression and *actually* make a promotion happen, maybe, one day. I just wish I weren't stuck dealing with people like *Tom* to make it happen. That guy is the worst. On his own, this morning...he seemed fine, friendly enough. But I can't shake the bad vibes from our first meeting the other day. And then there's the whole thing with Catherine, too..."

"Maya, honey." Luisa was shaking her head. "You're talking about two different things here. There's the career opportunity, and there's the personal drama. Which one do you want in your life? Which one do you see keeping you warm five or ten years from now? Do you want the corner office, or do you want to be invited to Catherine and Tom's wedding?"

Maya wrinkled her nose. "Wedding, huh? I didn't imagine *that* in my five-year plan. No, you're right. I get it. I'm missing the point again. Of *course* I'd rather have the promotion, the raise, the corner office. The job security, the prestige that comes along with the whole thing...yeah. That. I want that."

"Good." Luisa said. Then, to Andie, she continued. "What? Is that not what you told her?"

"You know it isn't," Andie was laughing. "But if the two of you would rather update your LinkedIn profiles than transcend this busted reality, that's one hundred percent your decision to make."

"Damn right it is," said Luisa. "Though I think we can do a little better than LinkedIn. Maya needs her own website, but that's a problem for another day."

Maya's eyes widened. "I do? But I'm happy at Andersen. I'm not trying to strike out on my own or anything."

"Maybe not now, maybe not ever. But you can't go wrong with personal branding."

"Huh." Maya opened the notes app on her phone and wrote a reminder to her future self to learn how to build a website. "Anyway, what do I have to do today? Now? What's the game plan?"

"Glad you asked." Luisa smiled. "This is the fun part."

Five

It had been 36 hours since Maya, Andie, and Luisa met for lunch. And right now, at midnight, Maya was feeling every single one of them all the way down to her bones.

In the last day and a half, Maya had been working her tail off, thanks to Luisa's input. She had left the lunch with a notes app full of to-do items, and she had steadily been working her way through them. They covered the gamut, from double and triple checking her meeting agendas prior to distributing them to anyone else, to anticipating client needs before the client even knew what they wanted. She had been reading everything she could find about Conley Corp, both on the company website and every single bit of press they had received in the last five years. She had been brushing up her PowerPoint skills outside of office hours, showing up for meetings with carafes of coffee and boxes of pastries, and shopping for new pantsuits on her lunch break.

In short, Maya had been eating, sleeping, and breathing work. Over her morning toast and orange juice, she scrolled through social media apps—or "kept her pulse on current marketing trends", as she called it. While walking to the office, she listened to business podcasts, rotating through a range of topics from marketing to non-profit management to career development for women in the workforce.

And it was helping. She felt more confident with every meeting that she walked into. She was in control, far more than she'd ever been at work. And control felt good and safe, and Maya liked both of those things. She was tired, sure, but preparation would feel better tomorrow than an extra hour or two of sleep would.

Maya was in bed, sitting up against her headboard with the night table lamp on beside her while she pored through all of Conley Corp's past press releases. Eyes blurring with tiredness, she rubbed her thumb and forefinger at the bridge of her nose. Coffee would probably help, if she drank it. Maybe just one cup of tea, and then she'd go to sleep.

As Maya swung her feet out of bed, her phone, carefully positioned on the nightstand, buzzed with an incoming call. Immediately, she felt her heart race, panic setting in more swiftly than a Chicago snowstorm in January. Who would call at midnight just to chat? It had to be an emergency.

Her vision was unclear as she picked up the phone, struggling to focus on the name on the screen over the pounding of her heart and the racing thoughts in her mind.

Mom was the name displayed on the screen. Had something happened to Maya's dad? Was her mom calling from the hospital? Or could it even be something worse than that? What if...?

Her hand moved on autopilot, her finger sliding across the screen to accept the call. "H-h-hello?" she asked with a trembling voice. "Mom? Is everything okay?"

"Oh baby, I'm so sorry. I didn't mean to worry you." Maya's mom's voice was calm and soothing as it reached Maya's ear. "Everything's fine, nothing's wrong. I just missed you, hadn't heard from you in the last couple days, and...well, I saw you were online on Instagram, so I figured I could call you without waking you up. That's all."

Her words jabbed Maya right under her ribs. "...a couple of days..." The last time Maya's mom had reached out to her, it had been on Nina's birthday. She had promised herself she'd check in with her mom after that, and then she never had. There was a gnawing feeling growing in Maya's stomach now, and it was telling her that she had not only been cold and unappreciative to her mom, but she had let Nina down, too. She had practically ignored her, acted like she'd forgotten her, and on her birthday of all days.

"Mom, I'm so sorry." A wave of emotion crashed over Maya, her fear and anxiety replaced with grief and despair. "You texted me on Nina's birthday and I never even wrote back. I'm such a terrible friend. I barely thought of her all day. It hurt too much, and then I couldn't even send you a text back. I'm so sorry, Mom..." Maya sniffled as the tears in her eyes threatened to spill over.

"Maya, don't you dare apologize," Janice Jefferson said, her voice gentle and kind. "I did not call you in the middle of the night to give you a guilt trip or to weasel an apology out of you. I called you because I love you and because I want to make sure you're doing alright. You know, eating and sleeping, which you clearly aren't, since you're talking to me at midnight."

"You caught me." A laugh croaked out of Maya, tripping over the lump in her throat on the way out. "I really am sorry, though. I've just been so busy with work, and I don't always do a very good job of keeping up with my personal relationships when I'm busy. I keep meaning to get better at that—"

"Again, that's not the point of this call," her mom interjected. "Are you alright, honey? How was Nina's birthday? How was it *really*, I mean? Are you feeling alright? Do you need to talk?"

"It was so weird, Mom. And I'm feeling guilty about it, I think. I barely thought about her that day. I think of her every day, I mean. Why wouldn't I on her birthday, of all days? But...it was too much. Too sad. It didn't feel right not to be with her on her birthday, and it didn't feel right to celebrate it in her honor, either. I just worked. I didn't even tell my friends about it."

"Your friends care about you so much, Maya. They'll be there for you, you know. You can let them in on things like this, on days like that. That's what friends are in our lives for, anyway. They help cheer us up when we're down, and if they can't do that, then they at least sit with us and let us get their shoulders all snotty with our tears."

"I know, Mom. It's just hard. It's a little scary to think about letting anyone in too much these days. Because apparently—" The sob wasn't staying down anymore "—it really hurts when you lose them." Maya was crying now.

Harder than she would have expected, but she couldn't stop it.

"Oh my sweet, sweet Maya. I wish I could be there with you right now. It's going to be okay, as okay as it can be. It's not always going to hurt like this, and you're going to continue to be the strongest and bravest and most amazing gal I know."

Maya struggled to speak through the tears. "When it...stops hurting...this much....is that because...I've forgotten her?"

There was a sharp intake of air from her mom. "No honey, no. We never forget the people we love. I think of your grandpa every day. Now, though, I think of him and I smile. It doesn't hurt like it used to. That first year after he died, every time I thought of him, I either cried or forced the memory away because it hurt too much and I didn't want to cry again. Now, I love to remember him, to laugh at his jokes, to tell people about him. It comes with time, honey. Believe me."

"I'd like to...and maybe someday I will. That's pretty hard to imagine right now. It's not that I don't miss Grandpa too. This is just different."

"Of course it is, honey. It's normal and natural to lose people like we lost your grandpa. He had lived a good long life, and it was just his time to go. That's all any of us can hope for, you know? But Nina, that was different. A tragedy. Death came when we least expected it, and it stole someone from us way before we ever imagined it was her time to go. It was a shock, and that made it even harder. People your age are supposed to believe they're invincible, you know? But that tragedy wouldn't let you. And that was really hard…it still is, isn't it?"

"Yeah," was all Maya could manage to say through the emotion lodged in her throat. Once again—and this really shouldn't surprise her anymore—her mom had managed to nail the exact emotions she was feeling right on the head. It felt good to be understood, even if it didn't take the pain away.

"Is there anything I can do for you, honey?" Janice asked. "Anything I can take off your plate that might help you get some rest tonight?"

"You're the best, Mom," said Maya. "And no, the call was enough. I'm glad I got to hear your voice, and I do feel a little better now. I think maybe I just needed a good cry…or a bath. Or both."

"Let it out, okay? Holding emotions in isn't good for you. If you didn't get enough of it out with me, then by all means, go cry in your bathtub. The water will wash it right away, and you'll wake up tomorrow feeling like it's a new day. Which it will be, by definition."

"Or else I'll wake up all puffy eyed right before I have to go in and wow a client at a meeting. No, I'm not sure that's going to work…"

Janice made a sound of soft disapproval. "That's kind of a weak excuse. You know that, right? Holding in your tears just so no one realizes you're a human…that's why they invented concealer, baby! Cry all you want tonight, then dab that magic goo on with your ring finger tomorrow morning. Nobody's going to know, I promise."

Maya laughed despite herself. "Alright, alright. You win. I love you, Mom. Good night."

"I love you, too, baby. Call me anytime, okay? Sleep tight."

As always, Maya's mom was the wisest of them all. A bit of concealer dabbed right under her eyes had removed all evidence of her late night cry fest, and by the time she was ready to leave for the office, she had managed to fool even herself about the nature of the previous night's activities.

"Dang, girl," she said to her reflection. "It looks like you got a full eight hours of sleep and have been up since five o'clock this morning drinking lemon water and meditating. Knock 'em dead today, alright?"

Her reflection said nothing back, of course, but Maya still left her apartment that morning with a little extra bounce in her step. The previous day's sadness was a distant memory—not that distant, as her fingers touched the necklace that reminded her of Nina, but distant enough that she felt confident today was going to be okay.

As if on cue, her phone pinged with a new text message alert from her mom.

"Feeling better today?"

"Actually, I am! Way better than I expected to. Thanks again for the chat last night."

"Anytime, love. Will we see you this weekend?"

Maya groaned. She had almost let herself forget that this weekend she had promised to join her parents and Nina's parents for a cookout. She felt obligated to check in on Nina's parents, and doing so made her feel like she was still connected to her friend, even if at times it made her unbearably sad to be with them.

"I hope so. This new project at work has been keeping me BUSY lately. I'll try to get everything done on Friday so I can come."

"If you can make it, we'd love to have you. Just let us know if you can't, so we don't worry, okay?"

"Of course, Mom. Love you."

"Love you, too!"

Catherine Andersen summoned Maya into her office at ten o'clock. For once, the *summoning* didn't leave Maya with a pit of dread in her stomach. She was prepared on all possible fronts for this meeting, and she couldn't fathom a forthcoming scenario or status update question she hadn't already thought of. It was like preparing for a debate—know every point the opposition could make, and then address it before they could.

But when she walked into Catherine's office, ready to launch into her update about Conley Corp's project, she was surprised to find Tom already there. He was sitting across from Catherine's desk, coffee in hand, and from his expression when he looked up at her, Maya had the distinct feeling that she had interrupted something. She startled a bit, sputtering. "Oh! S-sorry. Do you want me to come back in a few, Catherine? I didn't realize you were in a meeting."

"Nonsense!" cried Catherine. She gestured to the chair next to Tom, motioning for Maya to take a seat. "Tom was just filling me in on the latest at Conley, so you're right on time to join in on the conversation. What have you got for us?"

"Alright..." Maya hesitated as she began. She had been working on some marketing ideas, of course, but she wanted to pose them to Catherine before she introduced them to Tom...or vice versa. At this point, she wasn't sure which one of their approval she was striving to win more. No, that wasn't true. It was Catherine, definitely Catherine. Catherine held the keys to Maya's future career success in the palm of her hand. But...in a way, so did Tom. His report back to Catherine, whether positive or negative, was sure to be the deciding factor in determining whether Maya was offered a partnership or a severance package. *Crap crap crap*, she thought. *I don't even know who I'm trying to impress right now. And I'm definitely pausing longer than I should to think all these thoughts. I'd better say something soon or else I'll be impressing exactly zero of the people in this room. I've already lost my approval, that's for sure.*

"Maya?" Catherine prompted. "Would you care to begin?"

"Absolutely." Maya smiled at each of them in turn. "I've been kicking around a few different marketing ideas, looking to see what's really hot in the non-profit sector right now. I know you've talked about your device being functional both for people on a camping trip and for communities without access to reliable sources of clean water. And I think we really need to lean into that second function. Focus on the good that this product does, and then show people they can support your mission by getting one of their own. There's a major overlap between folks who enjoy outdoor adventure activities and folks who like to support good causes."

"That's a good start," Catherine encouraged. "Right, Tom? Are you liking what you're hearing so far?"

"I am, actually," Tom said. He sounded surprised. "I do want to be sure we keep this all above board. You know the way a lot of companies claim to do so much good in the world, and then they actually give 0.2 percent to charity or some shit like that? We need to focus group test all of this with a wide range of people. If we come across as goody two-shoes or looking like we want to be clapped on the back for being such selfless saints, that won't work. So we'll have to tread carefully."

"By all means, yes," Maya agreed. "The days of applauding people for traveling abroad and then 'saving' the people there are gone...I hope. I mean, I'm sure there are still charities doing that, and I'm sure it still works for some of them to get donations...but we aren't going to do that. And it's going to stop working, too. The younger generations, the ones who are going to be buying this product and supporting your mission, that kind of messaging isn't going to work with them."

"Grand," Tom said. "What messaging do you propose, then?"

"I don't have the exact wording yet, or anything like that. But I think we need footage of people using this in the kinds of communities we'd like to target. Not footage of wealthy foreigners bringing it in and being celebrated for it, but footage of locals doing it for themselves and being happy with the result. Maybe cut that in with people on camping trips around the world using the same thing at the same time. Something about how water connects us all. We'll have to focus test different phrases, different messages, but that's what I'm thinking right now."

Catherine's tight-lipped expression was difficult to read, and Tom's brow was furrowed in thought. The seconds Maya waited for them to speak stretched, feeling like minutes, until finally the silence broke.

Catherine spoke first. "I think you're definitely on the right track, Maya. Well done. What do you say, Tom?"

He nodded. "I agree. I see the vision you're proposing, and I think it makes sense for our little device. I'd love to see it more fleshed out, though."

"I agree," said Catherine. "I think it's time to get the creative part going. And the focus group to test the different messaging. Maya, can you handle that? Start mocking up the print campaign, storyboarding the larger video campaign that will tie in to it. And put out a call for focus testers. It's a few different areas to focus on, so it might seem like a lot. That's the nature of this project, remember? I need you at the head of all of it, not outsourcing or involving others."

Tom looked concerned. "Can she handle that? That's an awful lot to ask of one person, Cath..."

Catherine darted her eyes in his direction at the use of the nickname. "Of course she can handle it. And don't talk about her like *she* isn't in the room, Tom."

Yikes. It just got cold in here. And it feels like they don't need me for this conversation. Maybe I can just...fall through the floorboards and disappear. Maya stared at the floor, willing herself to be invisible. Wishing and hoping that neither of them would remember she was in the room until they stopped shooting daggers at each other with their eyes and talking about her in the third person.

"Alright, well, that's me sorted then." Tom stood up. "Maya, I'll be looking forward to your updates. Catherine..." He gave Maya a close-lipped smile and nodded in Catherine's direction as he briskly left the room.

Catherine sighed. "Sorry about that. Things get a little weird with me and Tom sometimes, but I don't mean to involve you in any drama."

I hadn't noticed, Maya wanted to say. *You both did such a good job of hiding it.* "That's not a problem for me, Catherine. I don't need to know—"

"I was engaged." Catherine blurted.

"To Tom?" Maya fought to keep her eyes from widening into saucers on her face. She hadn't been being polite, she *really* didn't want to know the history between Catherine and Tom. Especially not if it was some soap opera-worthy stuff like this. What was next, an evil twin?

Catherine shook her head and continued. "Not to Tom, no. He and I met when I was in college. I spent a semester at Trinity College in Dublin, and I met him at a pub, of all places."

"Oh?" Maya said, because what else was there to say? Clearly there was more to the story, and from the far-off look in Catherine's eyes, it was going to be a minute or two before she continued to speak, unless Maya continued to encourage her.

"We became friends. Our groups of friends became a bigger group of friends. It was a great time of life, really. Tom introduced me to Declan."

"Sorry...who's Declan?" Maya asked.

There was another meaningful pause before Catherine spoke again. "Declan is my ex-fiancé. And he's Tom's older brother."

Six

Maya blinked twice, unsure of what to say to Catherine. The two of them had never talked about their personal lives before, and this seemed like an awkward time to start.

"I…didn't realize you'd lived in Ireland. What was that like?" she asked tentatively.

Catherine looked surprised. "It was…it was a great experience. I loved it there. I go back as often as I can," she admitted. "But I think we both know that isn't the most interesting thing I just told you. It's okay, we can talk about this."

"Okay then," Maya nodded. "What…uh…how is it that you and Tom can work together? I mean…*can* you work together? Is this a problem? Are you on good terms with him? And his family?" *What happened with Declan?* But there were some questions you couldn't just come right out and ask.

"I'll admit I was surprised to hear from Tom. I haven't seen or communicated with anyone in his family since Declan and I broke up. We were kids, honestly. I was twenty-four, he was twenty-six, and neither one of us was mature enough to commit to a lifelong relationship, never mind an international one that comes along with big decisions about which continent to live on, immigration, different cultures, and all that jazz. It's been ten years, and I'm sure we've both moved on and made choices that make a lot more sense for our lives."

"Have you and Tom talked about what happened at all?"

Catherine sighed. "No, and I doubt we will. He came to me for professional support, and that's what I intend to give him. If I get too comfortable and start asking personal questions, like what Declan's up to these days, it could easily turn into a rehashing of the old days. And if anyone should be having that conversation, it would be me and Declan. Tom and I were always friends. He and I were friends before I even met Dec. It's not strange to think that we could be friends again, is it?"

"I honestly don't know," Maya admitted. "I've never been in this situation—I haven't even gone through a significant breakup, let alone one where the was an ocean of distance, or families getting involved, or an engagement coming into play. I wish I could help, I just...I don't know what to do."

"It wasn't realistic to think that you—or anyone—would be able to solve this for me." Catherine said. "Thanks for listening, though. It's good to clear the air, at least."

"It is," Maya agreed. "I had gotten the sense there was some history with you and Tom, and it's really helpful to know what it is, actually."

"I'm glad. And I hope this helps you understand why I've been so demanding about this professional relationship going well. And why I wanted you to manage it rather than keeping it for myself."

Maya nodded. "Absolutely. It's all making a lot more sense now. So, if you don't mind—" She stood as she continued to speak. "—I've got quite a bit of work to do now." She and Catherine said their goodbyes, and Maya left for her own workspace to begin tackling the next steps of her project.

Being let in on Catherine's relationship history felt major, like the level of trust the two of them shared had just increased exponentially. Maya felt pleased to be trusted, at the same time that she felt her discomfort twisting in her solar plexus as she empathized with the mess of emotions Catherine must be feeling right now. Underneath all of that, there was the vaguest hint of another emotion—was it relief?—over the fact that there wasn't a romantic past or present between Catherine and Tom. That feeling was by far the most puzzling one, and it wasn't something she had time to worry herself about now. If it was still there later, she could think about it then.

For now, she had graphics to design, a focus group to create and prepare for, and no clue which priority to tackle first. The only thing to do was to braindump it all onto a piece of paper and then begin putting it in order.

Maya began writing, jotting down everything she could think of that she needed to accomplish.

Get brand fonts and colors from Tom.
Search through licensed images to find appro-
priate ones for print campaign.
Post a call for focus group members on the fo-
rum.
Storyboard the commercial idea—how did I
get put in charge of this? I don't know anything
about video? What a nightmare. [That was
the great thing about braindump lists. They
could be as honest as they needed to be, like
a journal entry.]
Check in with Tom - suggest he go through me
rather than Catherine?

Maya felt herself lingering on that last item on the list.
She shouldn't be so concerned about Tom's feelings, she
told herself. It's not like he was the one who had broken
off an engagement, and she didn't even know his brother.
Come to think of it, she didn't know if Declan or Catherine had been the one to end the relationship, a detail which
suddenly felt like it was very important to the story. After
all, did Tom have a right to be angry with Catherine, or
did he owe her some measure of sympathy? One way or
another, at some time or other, Maya would get to the
bottom of this. If only to know whose side she was on, who
had been scorned, who she'd rather be friends with.

Not that she and Catherine were friends now. One personal detail shared did not a bosom buddies friendship
make. And it's not like she and Tom were friends, either.
Their meetings had been more cordial— even bordering

on pleasant—since that initial negative first impression, but Maya was still wary around him. That first meeting hung over her head, reminding her regularly that jokes and harmless comments could always be misinterpreted, and that kept her from speaking up more often than she cared to admit.

After the braindump list was complete, Maya logged onto her work computer to check her email. There might be something in there to add to the list, and if not, at least it would be a nice distraction before she began to actually tackle said list.

At the top of her inbox, there was a new message from Tom, a response to her last email confirming their upcoming information-gathering session. She had been preparing a list of questions for him, and the message had been sent to confirm the date and time that they'd be devoting their undivided attention to tackling that list.

From: tom@conleycorp.com
To: maya@andersenconsulting.com
Subject: Re: Confirmation

Dear Maya,

Tomorrow at 10am is grand for our Q&A session. The conference room as usual? Or shall we make this a walk and talk type of meeting? I find sometimes that taking a stroll is helpful to get the creative ideas flowing. Additionally, I'm

a bit embarrassed to admit it, but taking a break from the Andersen office might not be such a bad idea. I don't know how much Catherine has told you, but I'm sure you know enough to understand our personal history. I apologize for any inconvenience our awkwardness caused you. It's hard to let go of the past sometimes, you know? Even if it's in our best interest to do so.

Please let me know about the meeting. We could walk around the neighborhood or even go grab a coffee in a cafe. If you've got any ideas for neutral locations, feel free to share.

Warmly,
Tom

Between the apology and the "warmly," Maya was befuddled after reading Tom's email. Seeing a crack in his armor, in the somewhat icy exterior he'd been displaying on and off since their first meeting, was disconcerting. They'd never interacted anywhere but the Andersen offices, and now he was suggesting what...a stroll along the beach? Why not make it at sunset just to send an even more confusing message?

The whole thing left Maya feeling strange and in need of backup. She was glad to have the standing weekly happy hour and painting date with Luisa and Andie to look forward to. She had juicy updates to give them, along with the advice she needed to ask for, too.

∙❤∙❤∙❤∙❤∙❤∙

By five thirty, the bar was filling up with happy hour partakers, and Maya, Luisa, and Andie were lucky to claim a spot on the rooftop patio. The view of Lake Michigan was a definite perk of being up there, even if it took a little longer to get refills and service. They ordered their ginger ales, iced teas, and a few appetizers to share, then positioned their chairs so that they'd all have a view of the water, leaving one side of the table open like they were a panel of judges waiting for a contestant to come wow them. If Lake Michigan was that contestant, she was doing a stellar job. The blue water stretched as far as their eyes could see, though Luisa swore she could see Michigan across the water.

Maya took Lake Michigan for granted at times—she'd grown up spending her summers on its beaches, and the idea that a lake was a small, dirt-bottomed body of water that you had to check yourself for leeches after swimming in was completely foreign to her. Her summer days had been spent walking the beach, body surfing in the waves, and even when she had been in college in Chicago, she'd still spent as many weekends as she could grounding herself in the water. Nothing made her feel more connected to nature than standing on the shore of the lake, feeling the water rush over her feet and then pull her lower each time it receded. But as much as she took it for granted, at moments like this, she remembered how special this massive expanse of water was.

Andie leaned over and nudged Maya with her elbow. "Hey. Where are you?" she asked.

Maya shook her head and turned to face her friends. "Wow, I got lost for a minute there. I forget how fortunate we are to have the lake, you know? It's massive, it's beautiful, it's right here...and yet it just blends into the background like anything else."

"Guilty," said Luisa, shaking her head. "I remember the first time I saw Lake Michigan and how I forgot for a minute that it wasn't the ocean. And now...I paid too much for that great lake view from my condo, and yet I close the blinds as soon as the sun shines through a moment too long."

"I suppose this is a friendly reminder from the universe for all of us to do a bit more appreciating of what we already have," Andie offered wisely. "And yes, I need the reminder, too. So before you give me some crap for being more spiritual or grateful or whatever...know that I'm in the same spot you both are right now."

"We've all got some growing to do, I suppose," Maya agreed. "What would life be if we didn't? How have the two of you been, anyway? How's your work going, Luisa? Andie?"

Luisa and Andie started to speak at the same time. Luisa's words about "market share" and "return on investment" overlapped with Andie's soft-spoken yet powerful, "Let's not do that."

They both turned to Andie. "Do what?" Luisa asked.

"Do the regular newsy updates. I mean, I've got stories to tell, don't get me wrong. But sometimes it just feels like we're performing for each other, bragging about how busy we are or how important we are, and I just don't want to do it. Let's dig a little deeper. In honor of this view—" She gestured back to the lake. "—and in honor of this friendship. Let's not do the surface-level thing."

Andie turned to Maya and took her hand. "I know there's probably something going on at work that you need our advice about. But...can you sit with it a bit longer? Have you asked *yourself* what you're supposed to do? Or are you waiting for us to tell you?"

"Ouch," Maya said. "No, no...you're not wrong, Andie. It's just...damn. Yeah, you hit on some truth there. I think I've outsourced my intuition to you two. I don't even give myself a chance to wonder what I think about something, I just save it all to crowdsource with you."

Luisa chimed in. "I don't see what the big deal is, honestly. We all have different strengths, and we help each other by sharing them. Goodness knows I'm not going to become some spiritual earth mother like Andie anytime soon, but we all need a bit of her influence in our lives."

"You're right, too," Maya agreed. "I don't think she's suggesting that we keep everything to ourselves, just that we dig a little deeper. Spend a little time in silence from time to time."

"Exactly." Andie was nodding. "Save the surface level stuff for the situations that call for it, but not here, not with each other. Be surface level with your dentist, bring your hopes and dreams to your best friends."

·❤·❤·❤·❤·❤·

After happy hour had turned into pizza and messy canvases on Luisa's balcony while watching the sunset, the friends went their separate ways. It had been the kind of evening Maya hadn't even realized she'd needed, full of deep belly laughs, heartfelt connection, and even a few tears—the good kind, not the sad kind.

Maya returned home feeling refreshed and fulfilled, grateful for the friends in her life and the opportunity that had brought her here. But when she closed the door of her apartment behind her, a familiar gnawing returned to her stomach. It was as if the evening had been a pause, a break from real life, but being alone again in her own space had abruptly returned her to it.

She flopped onto the couch as the sequence of worries played on repeat in her mind. There was the ever-expanding to-do list of projects and responsibilities at work. There was the weirdness between Catherine and Tom, and—*oh crap, she hadn't responded to him yet*—that bizarre email Tom had sent her. There was the weekend gathering with her parents and Nina's family that she had almost forgotten about, too. That last one pulled a groan out of her from deep in her belly.

And then, at the memory of Nina, the worries that had been flitting from one corner of her mind took on a new gravity, like a weighted blanket had settled over Maya's entire brain. It wasn't the good kind of weighted blanket, though, the kind that you used when you felt anxious and it made you feel like you were being hugged in a cocoon of warmth and love and care. It was a weighted blanket of sadness and impending doom, like her heart had put on ankle weights that were tugging her under the riptide of grief and depression.

Things to do with Nina often had this effect on her, and it didn't help matters that Maya had had such a fun evening with her friends tonight. Too much lightness in her life often meant an overcorrection of darkness was impending.

Maya began talking out loud to herself, repeating the things she'd heard from therapists over the years and from her mom, who'd been the one constant since the beginning of her grief. "It's okay to have fun. It's okay to laugh. It's not a betrayal. Nina would want you to be happy. It's okay to have fun. It's good that you laughed. It's wonderful that you have friends. Nothing bad is going to happen tonight. You're safe. Your friends are safe. It's safe to have fun. It's safe to laugh. It's good to care about people."

That last sentence hurt the most. There was definitely a part of Maya's head and heart that was feeling scared because the closer she got to Andie and Luisa, the more she was scared to lose them. Not that she wanted to be the kind of friend who kept people at arm's length and didn't really care about them...she just didn't want to get hurt like that again.

"Gee, it sure is a mystery why you're perpetually single, huh?" She laughed cruelly at herself. Maya knew her resistance to being hurt and left behind had *a lot* to do with her perennially empty dance card, but she didn't see herself tackling that particular problem anytime soon. Who was she supposed to be dating, anyway? She hadn't exactly been overwhelmed by an onslaught of eligible bachelors in recent history.

Anyway, the problem at hand—apart from the obvious grief and fear of future loss—was the fact that an entire evening had passed without any progress being made on her current work drama. And Maya had a meeting with Tom tomorrow that, whether it took place in a café, on the beach, or at the zoo, was probably going to be pretty darn weird.

Seven

"Thanks for agreeing to meet me here," Tom said, standing up from his table at Beans Café as Maya approached. "I hope it wasn't too strange for you, stepping out of the office like this."

"Not at all," Maya smiled, placing her to-go cup of tea on the table. "It's nice to have a change of scenery, and I spend entirely too much time at the office, anyway." She looked around as she took her seat, admiring the cafe's cute décor and the quiet hum of people working at nearby tables, fingers typing away on the keyboards and hushed conversations on their cell phones. "If anything, it's a good reminder that work can happen in all sorts of spaces. I should come here more."

Tom smiled, his eyes creasing at the edges. "That's kind of you to say. It…I hope you don't think I'm avoiding Catherine or the office or anything like that. It's just…it's all a bit complicated and messy. Again, I don't know how much you know, and I didn't invite you here to gossip. Shall we…?" Tom gestured to the notebook on the table in front of Maya, the same one she'd been jotting down notes in since their first meeting.

"By all means," Maya agreed, picking up her pen and uncapping it. "Only...I just wanted to say that I don't know *that* much about the...er...situation with Catherine. But...well, I know you're alone here, and if you ever want to talk or anything, I'm a pretty good listener."

Where had that *come from?* Maya had not come to this meeting looking to become friends with Tom, so what was she doing offering to be a listening ear?

Tom looked just as surprised as she felt. "Erm, thanks Maya. I'll keep that in mind. Now then..."

As Maya returned to Andersen Consulting after her meeting, she could sense something was up before she even walked in the front door. Through the glass, she saw more movement than normal, people running from the printers on one side of the room in every other direction, it seemed. What was so urgent?

"Oh, good. You're here! Finally, I might add." Catherine's assistant, Chris, ran to Maya's side and hooked his arm through hers. "Come with me. It's total chaos in here." He ushered Maya into Catherine's empty office and closed the door.

"What's going on?" Maya asked.

"You didn't hear?" Chris asked. "Catherine's disappeared! She didn't come in this morning, no one can get a hold of her, and the last contact any of us had with her was *this* cryptic message she left on my voicemail last night."

Chris thrust his phone in Maya's direction and pressed play on the message. In it, Catherine's voice sounded far away, almost tinny.

"Chris, I've got to leave town. I think. I'm not...really sure, honestly. Tell anyone who needs me that I'm away. Better yet, tell anyone who needs me not to need me right now. I'll...be back when I'm back. Maya can handle whatever lands on my desk, she's more than capable."

"I'm sorry...what?" Maya screeched. "Can you play that again, please? I can't have heard what I thought I heard."

But less than a minute later, it was confirmed. Catherine was gone, leaving no clues behind as to where she had vanished, and she had left Maya in charge like a substitute teacher. The only difference was, Maya couldn't just put on a movie to pass the regularly scheduled class time. This was the real world, apparently, where responsibilities didn't wait for the person in charge and there were no snow days. *Crap crap crap crap crap,* thought Maya. *I've already got my hands full with Tom's project. What was she thinking?*

Maya spent the rest of the work day playing at being the boss. Just when one fire was put out, something else landed on her desk. She had a newfound respect for just how much work Catherine actually did—it turned out, she wasn't just sitting in her office filing her nails and polishing her business card holder. She had final approval on client proposals, contracts, and the vast majority of the creative decisions the company made, and her phone extension and email were regularly lighting up.

Whenever there was a lull, which was rare, it took Maya minutes to remember what she had been doing before the most recent urgent thing had landed in front of her. She had just gotten off the phone with one of Andersen's oldest clients, retaining their business for another year after almost losing it due to a contract misunderstanding...when she remembered she had been in the middle of responding to Tom's most recent email. There were at least twenty tabs open in her internet browser, and that number was only increasing. Every time she managed to close one, she opened two more in the worst possible version of the hydra myth she could imagine.

Maya's desk phone rang, and she steeled herself, expecting Chris to tell her it was yet another one of Catherine's calls that had been redirected to her. "Hello?" she asked through gritted teeth.

"Er...Maya? Is everything alright?" It was Tom, and he must have heard the harried tone in her voice.

"Tom, hello! Um...not really, actually. I was just emailing you back. I'm sorry, it's been an absolute zoo here, I've been filling in for Catherine and it's got me absolutely swamped—"

"That's actually why I called...wait. Did you say Catherine is gone?"

"...I did. I'll explain in a minute. Sorry, *why* exactly did you call?"

"Well, you *did* actually email me. Only I don't think you meant to. It just says 'Dear Tom, Thanks for the information you shared. The meeting minutes are attached.' Except there's nothing attached, and I don't remember you or anyone taking any minutes at our meeting this morning. Was there a secretary there, and I didn't realize it?" There was laughter in Tom's voice, and the pink was rising on Maya's cheeks to meet it, even though he couldn't see her.

"Oh my goodness. See, this is what happens when you try to do too many things at once!" Maya cried. "I remember it now...at the same time I was emailing you, Catherine's assistant called me with an urgent request to forward some meeting minutes to another client. And suddenly I'm having flashbacks to all the times my mom told me multi-tasking was a myth as a student. It turns out, you can't type one thing and say another, actually. Thanks for the reminder to slow down, though I don't really see how that's possible right now."

"You're welcome, of course. But about that...why are you covering for Catherine? Is she out sick?"

Maya didn't know how much she could say. She'd been keeping it vague with the other clients she'd spoken to today—whatever was going on with Catherine, she didn't need to return home to gossip in her honor. But then again, she and Tom had a personal connection. Maybe he'd know where she was, or want to reach out. That seemed unlikely, considering it had been a decade since they'd seen each other outside of work.

Maya decided to give a vague response, but slightly less vague than what she'd been telling everyone else. "Cathe rine's....out indefinitely. I'm not entirely sure when she'll be back, but I'm confident that she will be. And I'm also confident that everything is going to be just fine in her absence."

Tom laughed. "Say that last part with a little more conviction, Maya. You're perfectly capable, and don't forget that you can ask for help. There's a team there at Andersen; you don't have to do any of this on your own."

"Except your project, of course," Maya said, before she could stop herself. "Sorry. I'm not complaining. It's just...you're right. It *is* easier when you're working with a team and not trying to do everything by yourself."

"Is that why you've been so hands-on with our project? Maya, I don't understand. I never said you had to do everything yourself. I specifically came to Andersen because you've got such a wide talent pool to pull from. And perhaps also because of the personal connection, but still. What's this about?"

Tom hadn't requested one person to manage every single aspect of the project? That was news to her. If he hadn't requested it, then Catherine must have. And she must have had her reasons for doing so. Reasons she probably didn't want to share with Tom. So...Maya probably shouldn't be about to spill it all to Tom. But it was too late to backpedal now. She'd already come this far.

"Well, that's totally new information. When Catherine assigned me this project, she told me you had specifically requested one person who could handle every aspect of it. It was about creative control, keeping your intellectual property under wraps. I didn't think anything of it. I welcomed the chance to stretch my creative wings. But it's a bit strange—and confusing, I'll admit—to learn that you didn't actually request that. I wonder what she was thinking."

"I think I might know," Tom said. "Catherine's always been a private person. That's what made our friendship weird when she was with Dec and even weirder once she wasn't anymore. She's the master of boundaries, but sometimes she's a little too good at setting them, if you know what I mean. I suppose in this instance, she didn't want more people than absolutely necessary to be interacting with me. Probably afraid of what I might say about her. She had good reason to be, I'm sorry to say. I haven't always been particularly kind to her, though it's been years since all of that..." He trailed off, as if he was remembering something painful.

"Thanks for telling me, Tom. I don't have time to talk about this much more right now—" The light on the phone was blinking again with incoming calls to her extension. "—but considering that I'm the acting boss at the moment, it seems like we can make some changes and get your project rolling forward quicker than ever. Do you have time tomorrow morning to meet and talk it over?"

"Erm...tomorrow?"

"...yes? Is that a problem?"

"It's not a problem per se, but you know it's Saturday, right?"

"It's not a problem for me if it's not a problem for you," said Maya. Here it was, official. She was working on Saturday. Her personal life had ceased to exist, and now she was giving up her weekends for the foreseeable future just to get ahead of the mountain of work waiting for her on Monday morning. *Darn you, Catherine,* she thought. *Not really, I mean...I hope you're okay. But come back soon, okay?*

"Grand then. Would it be strange if I brought coffee and pastries to your apartment? I don't mean to intrude, I just think if we're doing work on a Saturday we should make it bear the least resemblance to work as actually possible. And I don't exactly think inviting you to my hotel room would be appropriate. I mean—"

"It's okay, I know what you meant," Maya interjected. She could feel the heat in her face as she contemplated what *else* it could mean to be invited to Tom's hotel room. Obviously, he wasn't saying it in that context now, but it was...strangely interesting. Some part of her liked the idea of being invited to his room, maybe after an evening meal. She'd have to explore that later; now wasn't the time to wonder if she was developing a crush on Tom. *Later* probably wasn't the time to think about it either—only *much* later, once they were no longer working together and he was safely back in Ireland where he belonged. Yes, that was much, much safer.

Maya brought herself back to the conversation in time to give Tom her address and decide on a time for their meeting tomorrow. At his insistence, she made her pastry request—cake donuts, not yeast donuts. Chocolate or vanilla, with sprinkles. Nothing filled with anything. He'd sounded like he was writing it all down, and that made Maya's insides feel dangerously warm.

"See you tomorrow, Tom." Maya smiled. She hung up and was immediately thrust back into damage control mode, putting out fire after fire and wondering the whole time why there were so many work emergencies happening on a Friday, of all days.

•♥•♥•♥•♥•♥•

By the time Maya dragged herself through her front door, she was worn down to nubs. There wasn't energy left in her body to prepare a meal, to change her clothes, or even to form a coherent sentence. Because of that last one, she ignored the incoming call on her phone when it started buzzing. It was her mom, and Maya promised she'd call her back once she had a little more pep in her step.

Still in her work clothes, all the way down to her shoes, Maya slouched onto the couch and finally let all the air out of her lungs. Playing the boss was hard work. It was fun, in a way—or rather, it had the potential to be fun because being busy was the same as having fun in Maya's mind—but it was a heck of a lot of work.

Maya's stomach rumbled, disrupting her thoughts. She groaned, unwilling to acknowledge the gnawing feel of her empty belly. The couch was so comfortable, and it had been such a long time since she had just sat and breathed for a moment without being pulled in a million different directions.. Well, it had been since she left her apartment that morning, but the last twelve hours had been *very* long.

With as little movement as possible, Maya fished her phone out of her purse and opened her food delivery app. Now to find the place with the shortest delivery time, because staying awake until her dinner arrived was going to be a real accomplishment if she managed to make it happen. It was a battle of wills—would her empty stomach or her exhausted body win?

Scrolling through the restaurants in the app, Maya settled on a Thai restaurant. The food was good, the restaurant was close, and there was nothing more soothing to the soul than noodles in any form. Well, a bath could compete with noodles. Or a nice hug. But in terms of things that Maya could request with a few finger taps on her phone screen, noodles were definitely the soul balm she was seeking.

Once the order was placed, Maya shuffled into her bedroom to change into her sweats. A matching sweatsuit—matching in its coziness, not in its cuteness—just needed a spot on the couch and a romantic comedy on the TV, and she'd be all set for her noodle heaven evening. Which was bound to be an early evening, so she'd better make it a short movie.

"Oh crap! Are you kidding me?" Maya groaned as she took in her apartment's living room with fresh eyes. Tom was coming here in the morning. In about ten hours, actually, if she was getting technical. And while Maya's apartment was perfect for a Friday night noodle cocoon and rom-com, it was definitely not appropriate for hosting a coworker for a semi-professional working brunch. Discarded outfits had found their way to the back of her couch, the dishes were piled high in the sink, and if there was a coffee table under the books and papers scattered all over the living room, Maya hadn't seen it in at least a week.

"Crap crap crap," Maya mumbled under her breath as she surveyed the mess. She had to do something about it now...if she waited until after she ate, she'd end up going to bed without cleaning a thing. And if she deluded herself into thinking she'd do it in the morning, she'd be greeting Tom with a messy apartment for sure.

But maybe this time…maybe this time I could just set an early alarm and get it done. I'm so tired now, and I just don't have the energy to do it. But after a good night's rest, I'm sure I'll feel great at 6 am. I can put on some good music and just dive in. By the time he arrives, I'll be feeling so alert and the place will be looking great. Yeah, that's it. I'll do that. Satisfied by the lies she was telling herself, Maya reached for the remote again and opened up her streaming apps to scroll through the new releases.

When the phone rang and it was her mom calling *again*, she had to answer. She already felt guilty for ignoring her mom's first call, but doing it twice in once night was unheard of. Plus, it had to be something important if Janice was calling again already. Maya felt the briefest flash of pride in herself for not freaking out and assuming the worst before she remembered she had probably been too exhausted to do that the first time she saw her mom's name on the phone screen.

"Hi Mom," Maya said, as she flipped the phone to speaker and set it on the coffee table—or on the mess of papers that covered the invisible coffee table. "What's up?"

"Hi honey!" Janice chirped, sounding far too cheery. "Just calling to see how you're doing. Is everything okay? I figured you weren't coming tonight, and I tried not to call…but I got worried. I'm sorry. I just had to check—"

"Oh my gosh, I completely forgot!" Maya cried. It was Friday. She was supposed to be on her way home—she checked her watch—no, she was supposed to have been at her parents' home *hours* ago. She was *supposed* to be getting ready to go to sleep in her childhood bed now. No wonder her mom had called. It was only surprising she hadn't done so sooner. "I'm so sorry, Mom. It's been the craziest day, and I honestly didn't even remember it was Friday. It doesn't feel like it's Friday. I mean, I'm working tomorrow..."

"Oh." Her mom said the syllable with such disappointment that Maya flinched. "Wow. Working on a Saturday? That's unusual, isn't it?" She was trying to sound peppy, Maya could tell, but she wasn't quite succeeding.

"My boss just...disappeared today. It was the weirdest thing, Mom. And I've been in charge of everything. I mean, not just my projects...everything. One phone call after another, putting out all the fires...I don't know how Catherine does it," she admitted.

"She had more time to get used to it. It sounds like you just got thrown right into the deep end."

"Yeah, pretty much. I hope she comes back soon. I don't even know where she is, I have no way to reach her..." Maya heard the panic in her own voice. This was unsustainable. Today had been harder than hard; she couldn't keep this up for long, could she?

"Well, I was hoping we might still see you this weekend, but it sounds like that's not going to happen."

Maya hated the brokenness in her mom's voice, and she rushed to make it go away. "Maybe I can—"

"No." Janice interjected, her tone firm. "I'm not having you rush here after your meeting finishes. That's just asking for trouble, and you know it. Rushing in the car, trying to get here faster than your GPS tells you is possible...no. You need to rest. You're doing too much lately."

She was right, and Maya knew it. A day off—not a full day, but at least several consecutive hours—would be good for her. "You're right, Mom. I'm sorry again, I really am."

"I know you are, honey. But it's okay. Really. Just...don't forget about next weekend, okay? It's the anniversary event, and I know Nina's parents would really like to see you there. It would mean a lot to them if you could come."

"Of course," Maya choked out. How was it already the anniversary of Nina's death? Every year, the community put on an event in her honor, raising money for the various causes she had supported in her young life. This year it was going to be a five kilometer run/walk, and the turnout was looking good. "Give my love to everyone, okay? I really wish I could be with you all this weekend. Next weekend, though. I'm writing it in big letters on the calendar right now, so even if Catherine takes over my whole brain this week, I won't possibly be able to miss it."

"Sounds good, honey. Now tell me, what's keeping you busy on a Saturday, anyway?"

Maya felt herself blush as she explained the work she was doing with Tom.

Janice was quiet while Maya spoke, and when the opportunity presented, she asked her first question gently. "Is something going on with this Tom fellow? I've heard you mention him before, and it's not like you to work on a Saturday morning...or invite a man to your apartment, as far as I know."

Maya flubbed her response. "Well...actually...it was kind of his idea. I wouldn't say I invited him, I'd say he suggested it, and the idea didn't seem strange to me, so I accepted."

"Interesting," her mom murmured. "Well, I'm sure you've got some tidying up to do before tomorrow, then. I'll leave you to it, and I'll expect a full report after the *meeting* ends."

Maya groaned, partly at the eyebrows she could practically see her mom wiggling in her direction, and partly at the reminder that her apartment was the single twenty-something professional's equivalent of a frat house. "Don't remind me, Mom. I'll talk to you tomorrow."

Eight

Maya bolted out of bed when her alarm clock went off the next morning. It's not like she'd been sleeping deeply, anyway. There was something about going to sleep with an early alarm set—early for Saturday, at least—that had her tossing and turning and sitting bolt upright to check the time in a dead panic that she had overslept and missed her alarm. It turned out that she hadn't missed her alarm at 3am, 4:30am, or 5am. Now that it was going off at 7am and she was wide awake, she cursed her nighttime self's inability to rest and trust that even *she* couldn't sleep through the combination of a shrieking alarm clock and the sunrise creeping through her uncovered windows.

That had been another failsafe strategy—leaving the blinds open all night. Maya's bedroom window faced east, and the sun streaming in as it rose did wonders for the reformed over sleeper.

While she brushed her teeth and picked clothes from her closet, a nervous feeling crept into Maya's gut. It hadn't seemed strange yesterday when she and Tom had made these plans, but now that his arrival was just a couple hours away, it suddenly felt...intimate. There was so much of *her* in her apartment. So much of her personality scattered all over the place, from the books on the shelf to the art on the walls to all the little touches in between. There was so much of her humanity here, too. It was the place she slept, fed herself, took a shower, used the bathroom, brushed her teeth...Maya felt a surge of panic coming on. She had always worked so hard to keep her professional boundaries in place. She only brought as much of her personality and humanity to work as was necessary to connect with clients and make small talk with her coworkers. And now one of her clients was about to descend on her home, the place where she shuffled around in her pajamas, blew her nose, and let her guard down. What had she been thinking?

This was definitely the kind of situation that warranted reaching out to the group text. Maya hadn't been keeping Andie and Luisa quite as updated since their last chat. She'd been trying her hardest to lean in to the advice she'd received from each of them—to focus on her career in a way that would make Luisa proud while also embracing the spiritual lessons of her journey in the way she knew Andie would. Clearly, it had been a hot mess since then, with her major increase in responsibility at work suggesting that Luisa's dreams were coming true in Maya's life, while the way she was handling it might leave something to the imagination. Regardless, this was a situation that called for best friends to weigh in.

"Help! Tom is coming to my apartment for a 'working breakfast.' What even is that? Good morning, btw!" she texted.

Three dots appeared next to Luisa's name. Of course Luisa was at the ready to respond; Andie was probably doing an extra long meditation since it was Saturday and all.

"Why is 'working breakfast' in quotes? Is that a euphemism? Are y'all eating breakfast and working or...like...'eating breakfast' and 'working?' Inquiring minds need to know! ...And my advice depends on your answer."

Maya shook her head, and then her stomach dropped. What if it *was* a euphemism? What if this was somehow a date? People had brunch dates all the time, and people dated their coworkers all the time. Did that just *happen*, or did those people talk about it? She didn't want to end up accidentally dating Tom. If she was going to date Tom, she wanted to be darn well aware that she was doing it.

Wait. What? Did she want to date Tom? No, that was definitely just a slip up.

"Oh, it's definitely not a euphemism. I got so swamped at work yesterday after Catherine disappeared that I actually forgot today was Saturday when I scheduled the meeting. Brain fart! Anyway, for some reason he agreed to it, and now I've just spent the last twelve hours freaking out about having a judgey, critical Irishman in my apartment. Where I LIVE."

"So many responses. Um...what happened to Catherine? Spill! Also, you need a calendar, that's embarrassing. And finally, has the Irishman been judgey and critical since your first meeting, or are you mayyyybe overreacting there?"

"Catherine is AWOL. It's a whole story, and I don't have time right now since TOM IS GOING TO BE HERE IN 20 MINUTES. And how should I know if he's been being judgey and critical? He only did it out loud the one time, but I'm not a freaking mind reader! He's probably judging me every second of every moment that we spend together."

"Wow, I got here just in time. Maya, give Tom the benefit of the doubt. He behaved badly once...leave it in the past. Or else you'll behave badly 'in response' one too many times and then you'll just be the one being a jerk." That was Andie, swooping in with the voice of wisdom, patience, and compassion as always.

Maya groaned. "I'll try! Any last advice from either of you?"

"Make sure you're wearing nice underwear...just in case!" Leave it to Luisa to make a joke when Maya was in the pits of anxiety. Wait...was that a joke?

"...that was a joke. Assume this is all 100% professional unless you're given a VERY CLEAR reason to believe it isn't." There was Luisa's follow-up, answering the question she must have known Maya had been asking herself.

And one final message from Andie: "Let's not forget the most important question: do you have any interest in things getting a little friendly between the two of you? Because if not, this isn't even a concern. In fact, it would just be harassment if he tried to take things there. So ask yourself what you want, love. Then go get it." The winking emoji at the end of Andie's text supplied the playfulness missing from the seriousness of what she'd had to say. The fact that

Maya was even having this conversation suggested she had at least some level of interest in Tom...right? Otherwise, she'd be worrying about having a strange man in her home for her safety, but that wasn't it. She trusted Tom, and she had no reason to think he was remotely interested in something non-professional developing between them. That thought hadn't even crossed her mind, though now that she entertained it, she was glad she had at least told her friends and her mom that he was coming over. If she'd learned anything from being the designated point person every time one of her friends went on a date with someone they met online, it was the importance of people knowing where you were and who you were with. Better safe than sorry, always.

She spelled it out one last time for her friends: "I'm not worried about my safety, though I am freaking out slightly about the possibility that I might have a non-zero level of interest in Tom. Just know that there is going to be a man in my home soon, and that is not cause for concern...but if I've misjudged him and it becomes cause for concern, I'll be SOS texting the two of you. Duh."

"Duh," wrote Luisa.

"Also duh," wrote Andie. "I've got a good feeling about this one. But I'm still glad you've got a 'just in case' plan."

Maya put her phone in her back pocket as she stood up. It was almost time, and she needed to do one final check to make sure all embarrassing things were stowed and only her most professional face was about to be displayed to her client. While she was walking through the kitchen, stuffing the box of animal crackers she'd been munching on for breakfast back into the cupboard, she heard a knock on the door. She glanced at her phone to confirm it was five minutes before Tom was due to arrive—there was no one else she was expecting now, so it had to be him.

Here goes nothing, she thought, as she tucked her hair behind her ear and put a smile on her face before opening the door. "Good morning, Tom!" she called.

Tom was dressed more casually than Maya had seen him yet. He was in jeans—she hadn't realized he owned those—and a forest green henley shirt with the sleeves pushed up his forearms. Maya balked at his casual - and attractive - appearance before catching herself and picking her jaw back up off the floor.

"Good morning, Maya." Tom smiled. There was a playfulness to that smile she hadn't seen before at the office, and the combination of factors caused her to forget—for just a moment—how normal human social interaction was supposed to work.

Tom held out a paper bag to her with one hand while lifting his other hand to show a cup carrier with two to-go coffee cups in it. "May I come in?" he asked.

She stepped aside to let him in as she took the bag he offered her, growing increasingly aware that she had said far fewer words than a polite host should.

"How are you, Tom? Did you find the place okay? Come on in and have a seat. That's okay, you don't need to take your shoes off. Here—is the couch okay? We could sit at the kitchen table, too. We've got both options, so just have a look and see what looks best to you." *Wow. Dial it down, weirdo.* In her mind, she was chastising herself so thoroughly that she almost didn't hear Tom speak up.

"I'm sure the couch is just fine. Come on and join me. You can check my work on the donut front—I hope I haven't let you down." His eyes were twinkling as he said it, and Maya felt her stomach drop a little lower in her body. What was *happening* right now?

She sat down as far from him as she could while still being on the same couch, placing the bag on the table between them. She unfolded the top of the bag to open it, then realized she needed a plate or a tray to put the pastries on and jolted off the couch and into the kitchen in search of one.

Once in the kitchen, her thoughts came out as muttered words. "Get yourself together, Maya. It's not like this is the first time you've had a man in your apartment. I mean...well, okay, sure. If you don't count relatives and your friends' boyfriends...then yes, maybe it is the first time. Holy *crap*! What was I thinking?"

"You all right, Maya?" Tom's voice was coming closer, suggesting he was walking towards the kitchen and not staying put safely out of ear range on the couch.

"Fine!" she called. "Just getting a plate to put the donuts on. Do you need anything else from the kitchen?"

"Not a thing. Come join me before your tea gets cold. I'm sure we can manage with what we've already got here. Look, there are napkins in the bag."

Maya pulled herself together and went back to the living room, plate in hand. She smiled nervously at Tom before putting the plate on the coffee table and filling it with the donuts. As she touched each one—was she supposed to use one of those wax paper napkin thingies?—she made a mental note that Tom had done an impeccable job of choosing the donut assortment. There wasn't a yeast donut or anything filled—with jelly, custard, or otherwise—in sight.

"How did I do?" Tom asked, beaming up at her where she stood.

"I'm not going to lie. I'm quite impressed. You followed my specifications to the letter! There's not a single thing in here that I'll pretend to like and then toss in the trash as soon as you leave."

Tom laughed. "Well, I must confess I'm relieved. I remembered a few of your preferences, but there were a few details that were a bit hazy. I mean, we don't have the same pastry selection in Ireland, so I just went with what looked tasty to me. I'm glad to hear that you're happy."

"In that case, it sounds like we are donut soulmates, Tom. It's not every day you find someone who has the exact same taste in sweet treats." As soon as she used the word 'soulmates,' a strange feeling came over Maya. It was a combination of embarrassment, thrill, and foreboding. It was fun to tease Tom like this—it felt natural, even if at the same time it felt dangerous and unfamiliar. This wasn't how she normally talked with men, especially single, attractive ones. But maybe, rather than thinking of how scary it could be to embark down a path with all sorts of potentially terrifying twists and turns ahead, it might be an interesting experience to...just see what happened? The thought of doing that made her feel ever so slightly nauseous, though...

"Agreed." Tom interrupted her thoughts with an enthusiastic grin. "If we'd known this sooner, we could have been enjoying our donut soulmate status the whole time. That might have made our meetings a bit more enjoyable, but at least now we're aware of it. Better late than never, eh?"

"That's right." She smiled back at him. And before she could stop it from coming out of her mouth, she continued speaking. "If it's not overstepping, actually...I have to ask. It seems like we didn't get off on the right foot back at the beginning. Do you remember? Our first meeting...it didn't go well. And I never had the nerve to say anything about it, but I've just felt so weird ever since."

Tom shook his head, looking chagrined. "I know just what you mean. I've tried to play it off too, but I admit I get embarrassed about that first meeting whenever I think of it. You handled it like an absolute champ, though, so I thank you for that. I've wanted to apologize to you many times, but I kept hoping that maybe you hadn't actually noticed how strange and rude I was. Of course, now that you've admitted to noticing exactly that, I need to tell you how sorry I am."

"No, no...that's not why I brought it up. You don't owe me an apology or an explanation. I just wanted to clear the air, I guess. Make sure that we are, in fact, on the same team and that there's no lingering weirdness."

"There's no lingering weirdness on my end, I promise. And despite what you think, I *do* owe you an apology and an explanation. I was feeling uncomfortable, having recently arrived in the States and not having my usual support network here. Plus, I had been bracing myself that morning for seeing Catherine again, so the last minute news that she wasn't actually going to be working with me took me a bit off guard—"

"Sorry, what? I don't mean to interrupt, but....seriously? Did you just learn that morning that we were going to be working together?" Tom nodded in confirmation, and she continued. "Well, that makes two of us. I think we did *very* well, considering how late we got the information."

Tom was shaking his head again. "I don't know what she was thinking. I shouldn't be too hard on her, though, I'm sure it's been unbearably strange having me back in her life. But yeah...there was all of that, plus walking in to find you with a bottle of whiskey in your hand. I didn't know if it was a joke or something Catherine had put you up to. Back when she and I knew each other, I was no slouch when it came to drinking. We met in a bar, of all places."

Maya laughed. "She mentioned that, yeah. But she's changed since then and I'm sure you have to. And the Catherine Andersen I work for would never make a joke at the expense of a potential client, even if that person were her ex-future brother-in-law. I swear the whiskey really was under the table from a retirement party. I was trying to get rid of it before you arrived, and we both know how well that worked out."

Tom was holding up his hands, gesturing for Maya to stop. "Really, I believe you. I knew, on some level at least, that it wasn't a terrible joke at the expense of my being Irish. If that's even a thing. No, and how Irish would I be if I couldn't take a joke, anyway? My ancestors would be spinning in their graves at the thought. It was just me being on edge about Catherine. I had told Declan about it just that morning, and as you might guess, he hadn't taken it particularly well. Drink is a bit of a sore subject for me—how untrue to my Irish roots, I know—but I'm not sensitive about it if others want to partake. So by all means, if you'd like to pour a little bourbon in your tea, don't let me stop you."

Maya chuckled. "I promise I don't want to do that, so no need to worry about it. I'm not really a drinker either, for what it's worth. Another thing we have in common, huh? One of these days, we'll have to go through all the categories of food and beverage, now that donuts and alcohol are covered, and see if it's all compatible or if this was just a lucky coincidence today."

"I'd like that." Tom smiled. "Though if we're going to be talking about food, it would only make sense to do so while we're actually eating it. You're not going to tease me with the idea of fish and chips or a nice roast and then send me home—if you can even call a hotel room 'home'—to listen to my stomach rumble."

"I certainly wouldn't want that. No, we can share a meal when we're talking about our favorite foods. That could be a nice way to finish out this project, don't you think?"

Tom paused, hesitation in his eyes. "Actually, I've been wanting to talk to you about that. You're doing a great job on the project, you really are. Especially knowing what I know now about how abruptly Catherine thrust you into it. I'd had this idea I wanted to run by you and was hemming and hawing over it, but now...I'm sure of it. Have you ever thought about striking out on your own?"

"I'm sorry, what?" Maya sputtered, choking on a sip of tea. "Leaving Andersen? I can't even imagine it. There must be something in my contract that forbids me from being co-opted by clients. Catherine doesn't even let our clients talk directly to our creative team. Can you imagine? She'd have me served a lawsuit before I was even out the door."

"Are we talking about the same Catherine who vanished yesterday without a trace? And more importantly than that...are you content working at Andersen? Before we talk about any of the rest of it, if you tell me you're living the dream working there, I'll drop the subject right now. But if you're not...well, then we can talk."

"I...uh..." Maya struggled to find the words. Of course she was dissatisfied working for Catherine Andersen after the last 24 hours. Not only that, but of course she had been feeling like something was missing for quite a while now. But people like her didn't just strike out on their own. People like her didn't start their own businesses or become their own bosses—how would she ever be able to feel secure in her career if she were working for herself? Was that even what Tom was suggesting, or did he just want her to come work for him? And had she been awkwardly silent for far too long while she asked herself all these questions? What was she going to say to him?

"I didn't mean to stress you out, Maya." He ran a hand through his hair, a touch of pink coloring his cheeks. "Actually, there's a little event I'd love to invite you to, if you're at all interested in what I'm talking about. It's next weekend, and it's an opportunity to meet some business owners, make some connections. It's here in the city, so we could drive there together. There's no pressure at all for it to mean anything about your career. If you go, it'll just be an opportunity to practice your small talk skills. What do you say?" His eyes were bright with hope as he waited for her response.

"Well, when you put it like that," Maya smiled. "I mean, I could definitely use the practice. And I'll be sure to leave all my whiskey bottles at home this time."

Nine

"**W**hoa there, you've got to rewind. I'm missing something. Am I missing something?" Luisa turned her inquisitive gaze from Maya to stare at Andie in that *are you seeing what I'm seeing* way she had.

"You're not missing anything," Andie was shaking her head, "Or if you are, then I am, too. But I think what Maya's trying to tell us is that things went so well with Tom that now she's thinking of starting her own business."

"That's what I *thought* she was saying, too. But surely…I mean *surely* if she was entertaining an entrepreneurial day-dream, she would have mentioned it to us before today, right? *Right?*" At that, she turned back to Maya, eyes boring holes through her skull and out the other side.

Maya laughed. "I can assure you, it's not like I was sitting at home with secret Pinterest boards about the dream business I wanted to start. And I don't think Tom put the idea in my head, exactly…I think he just said some words at just the right time and it sort of clicked. It made me aware of something that's probably been there for a while, and I just didn't realize it."

Andie and Luisa exchanged meaningful glances, and Maya reacted immediately. "What? *What?* Don't do that! What?"

Her friends were silent, each waiting for the other to speak up and clue Maya in on what they were eye-talking about.

"Ugh." She groaned. "This is definitely the worst thing about being a three-person friend group. It's fun to be the one who's in on the inside joke or the meaningful gaze, but holy cow does it *suck* to be the one who's left out. Throw me a bone here, ladies! I'm drowning!"

"Pretty sure a bone isn't going to do you much good when you're drowning," Luisa moved her straw up and down in her smoothie, mixing the melted parts with the icier parts. "You're either mixing metaphors because you're frustrated, or you just have boning on the brain."

Maya was blushing now, and any minute her friends were going to notice. "Enough!" she cried. "Tell me what the hell is going on or I'm going to hide *your* crystals—" She looked at Andie. "—and change the password of *your* cell phone." The intense gaze she directed at Luisa with those last words persisted until her friends relented.

"Okay okay okay," Andie reassured through her laughter. "It was just something you said, something about becoming aware of something that's been there for a while. And I think Luisa and I were both thinking that while that might be true about entrepreneurship, it might also apply to your love life a little bit. Or at least to the potential for you to actually have a love life. Or, like, at least a crush."

Luisa jumped in. "Or a solid banging. Maybe you don't have time to fall in love with someone—I know I sure don't—but that's no reason your vagina has to suffer in solidarity along with you. Give her what she wants."

"Can we not talk about my vagina right now? Or maybe ever? Because if I'm going to give her what she wants, let's be honest—first and foremost, she'd probably want some privacy and not to be the topic of conversation in a public place where we're surrounded by plenty of respectable looking people, none of whom are probably talking about their private parts in the third person."

"If we promise not to talk about your vagina, do you promise to try talking *to* her later?" Andie asked. "I'm not making a joke, I swear. Have either of you actually asked your lady parts what they want? Or do you just drag them along for the ride wherever your head takes you? Seriously, get a hand mirror and then get the conversation started. Who knows what she might have to say? She may surprise you." Andie leaned forward, placing her chin in her hand and blinking at Maya expectantly.

"Andie, you are taking this from romantic intervention territory into a very weird woo-woo vaginas and hand mirrors space now, and I'd like to go back to where we were, please." Luisa chimed in. "I still had some things to say about Maya's future plans to be successful and perhaps also get laid."

"By all means, go ahead," Maya gave in. "I'm all ears. Happy to listen to the two of you now and my vagina later, apparently. Just let me know if you need my input about any of this."

"Thanks." Luisa smiled. "So it sounds like you dug up a hidden desire. Let's just talk about the entrepreneurship thing for now. Do you really want that? What is it that got stirred up there, do you think? Is it about the freedom of working for yourself, the potential to make money, getting out from under Catherine's thumb...?"

"There's definitely a part of me that wanted to escape after all the overwhelm of Catherine disappearing," Maya admitted. "But I don't think it's just that. I think it's more about the freedom...the excitement of having to take ownership of it all, having to solve problems when they arise because they're *my* problems. *My* challenges. *My* rewards, too. At a big company like Andersen, it feels like I'm never holding on to any one project long enough to feel like it's really mine. My part of the job ends, and someone else takes over. Whatever problems I had get passed on to them, if they haven't already been solved. Maybe if I was at the top, in management, I'd feel more satisfied with the project cycle. This project with Tom has been super rewarding, and I think it's because I've been involved in every part of it. I really feel like it's *mine*, you know?"

The more Maya shared her feelings out loud, the more she discovered them for herself. That was the beauty of friendship—of real, close female friends. She'd had good guy friends before, of course, but this kind of meandering conversation full of self-discovery was a rarity with them. Or perhaps that wasn't so much about their gender as it was about Maya's comfort level with them.

"A penny for your thoughts?" Andie interrupted Maya's silent reverie. "Are you writing your letter of resignation in your head, or are you having second thoughts about all of this? Or something else entirely?"

"Something else entirely, I think," Maya admitted. "I was just thinking how grateful I am for the two of you and how much close friendships with other women lend themselves to all sorts of growth and self-discovery. And then I started wondering what's wrong with myself that I'm not actually that good at being friends with dudes." That last part came out in a rush, embarrassed as Maya was to admit to her friends that she had boys on the brain.

Andie exchanged a look with Luisa before she spoke again. "You can't be too hard on yourself, Maya. It's not like you've gotten the chance to hit all the major milestones of relating to the opposite sex. Heck, you were just a child yourself when you lost Nina. That was bound to put some extra barriers between you and any sort of real intimacy. What feels like a natural next step to you on that front?"

"Definitely not anything Luisa has ever suggested." Maya glared at her friend. "So thanks for asking like that. No, I won't be pursuing a one-night stand anytime soon. But I don't know...maybe something like today, spending time with Tom...maybe I could do something like that again? He seems like a good choice for easing myself into relating to dudes a little more."

There was that meaningful look between Andie and Luisa again, and then it was Luisa's turn to speak. "I'm not trying to freak you out, I promise. Ahem, that's why I'm not suggesting having a no pants party with Tom, but I digress. Just...can you be open to the possibility of something more there? I'm not telling you to go for it. I'm not claiming to know something you don't about the future for the two of you, just...don't assume Tom is destined to be your friend and nothing more. He sounds like a good guy who likes to spend time with you, and I think that's pretty neat. That's all."

"And remember," Andie chimed in before Maya could speak up again. "There's no reason at all why you don't deserve to have the attention of a caring, sexy man with a delightful accent. I know you...I know you're probably already talking yourself out of why he'd ever be interested. But this isn't high school, there are no rankings of who's cool and who isn't...and even if there were, you'd be right at the top of the list as the coolest, most wonderful and sexy and smart and compassionate person I know."

Maya was quiet for a beat. "You know, there was something you just tapped into there that was definitely way deeper than I was looking at any of this stuff." She reached for a fry and groaned. "Why does it always have to come back to some shit from your childhood?"

"Because that's usually where whatever you're trying to undo began. You picked up a belief or something traumatic happened to you, and then you carried it around for years and years just treating it like it was normal. Like it was part of the furniture that was nailed down to the floor. It's only when you're older that you realize you can move it, rearrange it, reupholster it, or throw it out altogether. It just helps to figure out how it got there in the first place, so maybe it doesn't happen again."

"That makes sense," Luisa chimed in, "And I'm going to have to remember that for some shit of my own the next time it comes up. Maya, don't you have to head back to Kalamazoo soon, though? I don't want to hijack your weekend plans with girl talk."

"No, I'm not going this weekend. Next weekend is the event in honor of Nina, and I'll need to be there for that, of course. You both are welcome to come. I know my parents would be happy to see you again."

"I'll keep it in mind," Andie smiled. "I can't make any promises because a week can change everything in the land of the dying. Who knows what reality my clients will be in seven days from now?" She reached over and squeezed Maya's knee. "I'll be there in spirit, and if I can make it work, I'll be there in the flesh, too."

"It's a no from me, I'm sorry to say," said Luisa. "It's just been too busy at work lately, and I can't give up a whole weekend even for you. But I'm just a text away if you need me."

"Me, too," said Andie, smiling. Maya reached out a hand for each of her friends, and they took them in their own. They supported her and held onto her always, and she would remember that if and when she was alone with the memory of losing Nina.

After the longest week of her career, Maya was home with her parents outside Kalamazoo, in the house where she had grown up. It seemed like she had barely blinked since her afternoon with Andie and Luisa, and yet here she was, preparing for Nina's memorial walk already. Time was flying with Catherine gone, and not in the good way. Maya had barely slept in the last week, and when she did drift off into unconsciousness, she had stress dreams about unopened emails and a phone that never stopped ringing. She had arrived at her parents' house late Friday evening, grateful both that they still left a key in the secret spot under the porch and that her mom had actually heeded her pleading that she go to sleep and not stay up until 2am to be the welcome committee.

Now it was Saturday morning, and Maya was sitting at the kitchen island, sipping a homemade turmeric latte while her mom bustled around the stove and her dad read the paper. Bill and Janice Jefferson had been together for over three decades now, and the comfortable air between them was something Maya had always taken for granted as an only child. Her parents were a well-oiled machine, filling in the gaps for each other. Their classic evening routine had been to take turns cooking, cleaning up, and setting the table. Maya was almost always assigned to table setting duty, and she had taken a lot of comfort from the intermittent laughter, easy silence, and playful teasing that were the soundtrack of her childhood.

It wasn't quiet that morning, though. When her parents had seen the new dark circles under Maya's tired eyes, they had had questions about work, about Catherine, and about how Maya was (or wasn't) managing it all.

"It's fine, really," Maya promised. "She'll be back, and I won't have this workload forever. I'm sure it's got to be soon." She wished she believed the words she was saying, but even with the extra emphasis she was putting into convincing her parents not to worry about her, she hadn't managed to reassure herself.

"It's ridiculous," said Bill. "Completely unprofessional! There should have at least been a raise, a title change, something to make it worth your while to take on all this extra work."

Janice gave him a look that Maya couldn't quite read. "I think what your father means to say, honey, is that we're worried about you. It can't be healthy taking on this much work with no definite end in sight. I know you probably don't want to hear it, but...have you thought about looking for another job? One where you're actually treated the way you deserve?"

Maya picked up her mug to sip and hid a smile behind it. "That's funny, actually. You're not the first person to suggest it. You haven't been talking to Tom, have you?"

"Tom?" Bill asked. "Who's Tom? Do I know him? Should I?" Janice simply raised an eyebrow and waited for Maya's response.

"He's the client I've been working with. The Irish entrepreneur with the water filtration system. Last weekend he put the idea into my head to think...maybe...about working for myself. And I don't know...it's been on my mind a lot since then. I'm not saying I'll do it. Just...I'm thinking about it. I...actually, I need to leave pretty early tomorrow morning to get back to the city because of it. He invited me to an event with some other entrepreneurs, and I'll need some time to get ready."

Bill and Janice exchanged another unreadable look, and Maya felt a wave of frustration wash over her. It was strangely nostalgic of her teenage years, and she didn't like the thought that merely sitting in her parents' kitchen, watching them communicate telepathically, could turn her into an eye-rolling, scoffing, attitude-laden teenager. For that reason alone, she bit back her gut reaction and forced a smile to her face. "What?" she asked. "What's that look about? Care to let me in on the secret?"

"Well—" Bill began, as Janice held up her hand and shook her head at him. Bill gestured to his wife to go ahead with a smile and a twinkle in his eyes.

"There's no secret, Maya," said Janice. "Your father and I have just been worried about you...about the stress, about the job, about the loneliness of living in the city. I know you have Andie and Luisa, but still, you're living alone and that makes your parents, living hours away, worry about you. So from my standpoint, seeing the excitement in your eyes when you talk about this career prospect makes me feel a little giddy."

"It's not just about the *job*," muttered Bill under his breath.

"Your father is right, even if he's grumbling to himself," Janice continued. "It sounds like Tom has become a good friend to you." Maya nodded, and Janice kept talking. "Just a friend? I don't mean to put you on the spot. I just can't help but wonder if there's some potential there for more."

"And that's my cue to go get ready for the day," Maya stood up from her chair. "Nothing personal to the two of you, but I'm not ready for another conversation about my love life."

"Maya, please," Bill said. His tone was gentle and his eyes were kind as he reached out and put a hand on her forearm. "We're not trying to embarrass you or poke fun or anything like that. We just want you to be happy."

"We want to see you take a chance on a relationship, honey. I know you've always said you're happy to be single. I just want to be sure that you're really *choosing* it and not just defaulting to it because you're afraid of getting hurt."

"Jeez, Mom, isn't it a little early to be going quite that deep?" Maya choked on her tea. Noting the expression on her mom's face, she continued more gently. "I mean...what exactly are you talking about? Fire away, I can take it...really. Really!"

"It's just that...well, I've seen this happen before, especially with people who are grieving. They close themselves off, or they keep themselves so busy with a million projects that they just never have time for a relationship. They don't even know they're doing it, not until it comes out in some other way. They have physical pain, or a problem in a family relationship, increased anxiety...something that makes them reach out to me as a friend or come to me as a client. And it's only when they start to pull on that thread that they get to the root of it."

"And what's the root of it?" Maya was thinking of all the stress in her own life, all of which she had blamed on Catherine and her vanishing act. That it could have a different cause was a tough idea to swallow, but she always humored her mom on the rare occasions she shared her expertise like this. Janice was a physical therapist, a deeply spiritual person, and the go-to source of wisdom and comfort for no small number of Maya's peers' parents.

"There's a hole. A wound. Something they're so afraid to look at because it still hurts them so, *so* much. And it's the effort to avoid looking at that wound that causes everything else—the relationship tensions, the overwork...the isolation."

Maya was silent. Bill moved to her side, as if sensing that her emotions were about to bubble over and she was going to need to prop herself up against him to stay standing.

Janice continued. "There's hope, though. Really, I promise. The wound is never as scary or as nasty as they think it is. It hurts, of course, but once they look at it, they can start to treat it. And it can start to shrink. Or rather, their heart can start to grow bigger around it."

"Does it ever go away?" Maya asked.

Janice shook her head. "I don't think so, honey. When that hole is caused by the grief of losing someone...it's the reminder of the love that we had for that person. In order for it to go away completely, all evidence of them would have to be gone from our lives and our hearts. And we never want to forget them. We never want to let that love go. But we can find expansiveness within ourselves. We can find the space to love the ones we've lost and still have room in our hearts for new people to love."

Bill sniffed loudly and wiped his eyes as Maya blinked rapidly. "Wow." She was stunned. "How did you...?"

"How did I know?" Janice asked, smiling. "Because I care about you. I see you. And your dad and I, we lost Nina, too. I know it's not the same as how it feels for you, but we loved her, too. I struggled a lot with my own fear of losing you after that. The nights you came home late or didn't return a call for hours—"

"I'm so sorry, Mom. I had no idea." Maya held back a sob. "I never meant to make you worry. I wish I had known..."

Janice held up her hand. "I didn't tell you that to guilt trip you. There's a reason you didn't know about it when it was happening. That was my own grief, my own journey that I had to go on. Your dad, my sister, my therapist...those were the people who held me up when I was anxious and fearful of losing you. And they did that so that I could be a better support to you. It wouldn't have been fair to you if I'd told you those things then."

"Wow, I'm...." Maya was speechless. She stood from her chair and walked around the kitchen island and right into her mom's waiting arms. The two women hugged for a solid minute and a half, and when they pulled back and smiled at each other, both of their eyes were glossy and their cheeks were stained with the tracks of the tears they had shed. Bill had rubbed both of their backs as he made his way out of the kitchen, leaving them to their mother-daughter moment.

"Thank you, Mom," said Maya. "For the support when I was buried under a mountain of grief. I don't know how you did it. And thank you too for everything you said today. I feel like you broke something open...a wall I didn't even know I'd put up. I'm...I don't know what I'm going to do about it, but I'm going to have to do *something* about it, that's for sure. I think I'm going to sit with this for a while, really think on it...get to the bottom of it and figure out what to do next."

Janice's eyes crinkled with a love-filled smile. "My sweet, sweet brainy daughter. You're a type 5 on the enneagram for sure, if we didn't already know that." She tapped Maya gently on the side of her head before resting her palm over Maya's right collarbone. "It's such a gift to have a beautiful, capable brain like yours. But don't let your capacity to solve problems by thinking your way through them lead you to forget to feel. Sometimes you'll find the most profound wisdom right here." Her hand was still resting on Maya's chest. "You can't strategize your way through grief.

And the progress of that particular journey is never linear. But you *can* ask yourself what feels like the next right thing to do. What scares you, but you want it anyway?"

"First thing that comes to mind?" Maya asked. Janice nodded. "What Tom said about exploring entrepreneurship scared the crap out of me because it felt like something I needed to do. Like I was being led towards it or something, though I know that sounds a little wacky."

"Not at all. Anything else?" Janice raised her eyebrow with a question.

Maya sighed. "Tom. I don't know, I just...I like having him in my life, I like his input, the way we work together. It's been...awhile since I felt that way with any men that had actual romantic potential."

"Awhile? Or...?" Now both of Janice's eyebrows were climbing towards her hairline.

Maya laughed and playfully pushed her mom away. "Okay, fine. Never! I guess unrequited childhood crushes don't really count, do they?"

"Not at all and you know it," said Janice. "Now you know what you need to do, what you need to *pursue* when you get back to the city tomorrow."

Ten

Saturday had been a beautiful day. After a morning rain shower, the sun had come out and shined on the entire memorial walk event. The rainbow that was intermittently visible in the sky had contributed to a lot of teary eyes and choked up words, all of which had been cathartic for the walkers.

The turnout had been far better than Maya had expected. There were classmates she hadn't seen since their high school graduation, friends of Nina's from the summer camps she had attended without Maya, and, of course, Nina's entire extended family. They had shared memories of her with laughter and tears, exchanged far more hugs than Maya normally got in a year, and raised a few thousand dollars to donate to Nina's favorite causes. All in all, the day had been a success.

As the event was winding down, Maya stood aside with her parents and Nina's parents. She felt the gaping hole at her side where her best friend should be, where she always *had* been when the two families had enjoyed a meal or taken a vacation together.

"We're so glad you could be here today." Nina's mom squeezed Maya's hands in her own. "It wouldn't have been the same without you. Now I know you need to head back to Chicago soon, and I'm all cried out for the day, so why don't you tell me about your work? The more technical, the better...I mean, please just absolutely bore me. Otherwise, I'm going to be thinking about your life in the big city and how it should have been you two girls being roommates together, and...oh dear. No, this won't do. Tell me about your job please, and quick!"

Maya squeezed the woman's hands back. After the conversation with Janice this morning, she had a new appreciation for the need to find the balance between looking at the grief wound in your heart too darn much and avoiding it entirely. She had a feeling Nina's mom had done enough looking at that wound today for at least the next month, and she was more than happy to fulfill her request. "Anytime, Mrs. Stern." Despite the insistence that Maya call her by her first name, especially after all the extreme emotions they had shared in the last few years, Maya couldn't do it. Claudia Stern was going to be Mrs. Stern for the rest of Maya's natural life. "I work for a marketing company in the city. I've got a client right now who's been keeping me busy with market research, focus groups, split testing, content marketing...let's see, what other buzz words can I throw at you? Would you like a copy of my latest meeting minutes to put you to sleep tonight?"

Bill interjected before Maya could continue or Janice could respond. "My brilliant daughter is underselling herself, so don't believe a word she says. Maya is single-handedly running the firm she works for while her boss is on an indefinite leave of absence. And she's thinking of going into business for herself soon, actually."

Mrs. Stern raised her eyebrows to match Maya's own. "Wow, Maya, that's very exciting news!" she said, at the same time Maya was remarking to herself that apparently her dad had been paying attention to the conversation this morning even after he left the room. Or else her mom had shared the details with him. Nothing that one of her parents knew was ever kept from the other one for long, and Maya was grateful for the reminder that they shared their pride in her with each other as readily as they shared their worries and fears.

"Thanks, Mrs. Stern. And thanks, Dad, for sharing that. It feels a little strange to say it, especially since it isn't even real yet. But it's encouraging to me that you seem to think I can do it."

"Of course I do!" her dad exclaimed. "I've always believed you are capable of whatever you set your mind to. I'm just trying not to be one of those overbearing parents who tells you that so many times that you develop some sort of complex. And before..." He looked at Mrs. Stern with compassion. "Things have been hard for you these last few years, and the last thing you needed was me telling you to go take on a majorly stressful professional challenge. If you're ready for it, I'll support you all the way."

Janice chimed in. "And if you're not quite ready yet, that's okay, too."

It was Mrs. Stern's turn to impart her own wisdom. "None of this is linear, hon. Do what you're ready for today and let tomorrow worry about itself. If tomorrow you wake up engulfed in grief again and can't get out of bed all day, I'll be the last person to judge you on that." She smiled as she blinked rapidly. "I'm very happy to hear that you're doing so well, and I'm grateful that you shared your joys with me, too. I want to hear them, I really do. I miss Nina…I always do. But that doesn't mean I want to sit and grieve every time I see you. I want to experience life through you—it doesn't make me miss her less, but it makes me happy to see you going on…living. And it's definitely what she would have wanted."

Maya knew the words were true on some level, but it was hard not to feel a fresh wave of despair wash over her. Nina wasn't having work stress or wondering about pursuing a relationship with an attractive Irish man, and she never would. The reminder that her best friend in the world wasn't going to experience life beyond the age of 18 put everything into harsh perspective. Maya was growing older and facing the new challenges that came along with it, while Nina was frozen in her mind as a child. It was so unfair, and it felt so wrong. The more years that had passed since the car crash, the more distance Maya felt from herself as the teenager she was when it happened. Did that mean that same distance also had to exist between her and Nina?

Maya's head hurt with the incomprehensible nature of grief combined with all the emotional output of the day. She hugged Mrs. Stern, promised to come by for tea the next time she was in town, then followed her parents to their car for the short drive back to their house. The ride was quiet—a comfortable silence settled between her parents while Maya stared out the window, taking in the view while her mind swirled with a strange combination of stress and sadness. She knew there was a mountain of work—and the possibility of exploring a romantic relationship for the first time *ever*, no big deal—waiting for her back in the city, causing a pit of anxiety to form in her stomach. But at the same time, the guilt she felt over focusing on that stress when Nina wasn't even alive to have a job or a date or any of the experiences Maya was currently being blessed with...it was enough to make her want to crawl under the covers and refuse to face the day.

"What are you so quiet about back there?" Bill asked, glancing at Maya in the rearview mirror. "Anything you want to talk about?"

"I'm okay, Dad. Just tired," said Maya. It was better to keep it simple than to get into all of this again. The last thing she needed now was to hear her dad talk about how proud he was of her—it would just be another reminder that she wasn't being grateful for all the blessings in her life and was stressing out and taking them for granted like the spoiled brat she was.

"What time do you need to leave in the morning?" Janice asked. "I'd like to have breakfast together before you get on the road. Make sure you're nice and awake and alert before you take off."

"It'd be so much easier if she drank coffee, wouldn't it?" Bill asked his wife. "I know I'd worry less about her driving across the state if she had a cup of hot caffeine in her hand and a rapidly filling bladder to keep her awake."

"I'm a good driver, guys. You two have nothing to worry about. Maybe we can have breakfast together at...9? I'll get on the road after that...try to be back by lunch time. The event tomorrow is in the evening, and that way I'll have time to rest, shower, get ready..."

"Sounds great, hon," Janice said. "Now let's get home, put on our comfy clothes, and spend the rest of the evening chilled out on the couch."

On Sunday morning, after a nice breakfast together, Maya's parents walked her out to her car to say goodbye. The three of them had spent the prior evening eating a pizza delivered from their favorite local place and watched a movie until two of them fell asleep on the couch. The pizza was Detroit-style—Maya had a soft spot for it still, though she was a quick convert to preferring Chicago-style pizza above all others after moving to the city. Even with her willingness to defend deep dish Chicago pies and the less famous thin crust delicacies, last night's pie, covered in all of her favorite toppings, had hit the spot at the end of that long and emotional day.

The movie they had watched...well, Maya couldn't help but suspect her parents were trying to send subliminal messages to her about Tom. The male lead in the romantic comedy they'd settled on—a movie she couldn't remember the name of the next morning though she was sure she had already seen a few different versions of it in her lifetime of rom-com consumption—was Irish, naturally. It was hard to convince herself that it was a coincidence, especially after her father (who *always* preferred an action movie) had agreed to the romance without a single word in disagreement.

"Bye, Mom and Dad. Thanks for everything." Maya hugged her parents in the driveway. "I love you both."

"We love you too, honey." Janice said. "Drive safely, and let us know when you get there, okay?"

"I will," Maya promised. "I hope you two have a fun day planned today."

"Oh, definitely!" said Bill. "We've got yard work to do—my favorite."

Maya laughed. Her mom was known for her ambitious landscaping plans that changed every year, and her dad was known for going along with them all with only minimal grumbling.

"You have fun today, too," said Janice. She winked. "I want to hear all about it. Oh! And send me a picture of your dress this evening."

"Just the dress? Or do you want to see me in it?" asked Maya.

"Obviously, I want the whole package. You're going to be absolutely beautiful, and even more importantly than that, you're going to knock the socks off of everyone with your skill, your intelligence, your confidence..."

Bill was nodding. "You might even come away from this event with your first few clients. No pressure or anything, though. I'm just thinking out loud."

Maya chuckled to herself. "No pressure at all. Okay, I've got to go...for real this time." She kissed her parents on the cheeks and drove away as they stood arm in arm in the driveway, waving after her until she was out of sight.

•❤•❤•❤•❤•❤•

"This is a complete and total disaster, and *no*, I am *not* exaggerating!" Maya was video chatting with Andie and Luisa, propping her phone up on her bookshelf and stepping back to give them the full body view they had requested.

"A total disaster, indeed," Luisa deadpanned, rolling her eyes. "You look like the actual troll under the bridge. That's appropriate for a Michigander from under the bridge, I suppose, but what will the fancy entrepreneur types think?"

"Lu!" Andie interjected. "That's a great joke—very Upper Peninsula specific, which is strange considering you've been there once in your life—but probably not what Maya needs to hear right now. Maya love, what's the problem? You look beautiful!"

Maya looked down at the emerald green gown she was wearing, the off-the-shoulder neckline and curve-hugging fit. "It's too...*something*! I feel uncomfortable...over dressed, I think? Too much skin? Too sexy? Is this even appropriate?"

"Tom said it was a formal event, right? Black tie?" Luisa asked. Maya nodded. "Then, it's perfect. I know it feels fancy, considering you wouldn't wear it to work or to your weekend yoga class, but it's just the right level of fancy for a formal event. What's the premise tonight, anyway? Why are all these people gathering and dressing up all fancy?"

"I think it's some kind of entrepreneur award ceremony," said Maya. She hated that she didn't know more about the event Tom had invited her to. She had meant to do some research of her own, but between the work week from hell and the weekend chock full of emotions, she hadn't gotten around to it.

"Dang," said Andie. "So you're like his date?"

Maya was silent for a beat. "Well, I hadn't thought of it that way. He invited me like it was an entrepreneur meeting where I could do some networking, but then the actual invite turned up and it's like some kind of formal ceremony and celebration. Oh shoot oh shoot! Am I supposed to treat it like a date? I'm not ready for this."

"I'm sorry I even asked," said Andie. "I didn't mean to psych you out. Don't think of it like a date...even better, don't think of it at all. Just go out there dressed like the absolute hotness, beauty, and poise that you are and have so much fun. Really. No expectations, no plans....just enjoy it. It looks like a great lineup this evening from what I can see on the website."

"You're looking it up right now?" asked Maya. "Anything I need to know?"

"Er..." Andie hesitated, and Maya saw her eyes scan as she scrolled through the page. "Nope, I think you're good!" The corners of her mouth were tight, and she wasn't quite looking at the camera. Maya knew Andie well enough to know she was hiding something, and for the first time in the history of their friendship, she decided not to ask. As long as it wasn't slime being dumped on the attendees to raise money for charity, she didn't need to know. And Andie would definitely tell her if there was slime coming her way...she hoped.

"Do I really look okay?" Maya asked, twirling in front of the camera. "Too much boob? I should have tried this dress on again. My proportions have apparently changed a little bit since prom."

"Shut. Up," said Luisa. "Is that your prom dress?" Maya nodded. "Okay, let's not even get into the fact that your prom dress still fits you, because that would be approximately the most boring comment I could make. What I'm gobsmacked by is the fact that you had such good taste when you were a senior in high school. What in the world? Did your mom pick it out? I've never seen a prom dress that wasn't covered in sequins or glitter or cut out to show as much skin as possible. Yours looks like something an Oscar nominee would turn up in."

Maya shrugged. "Maybe a perk of being an only child is developing a more mature sense of style. And actually, my grandma made this dress. She was a really talented seamstress. All the dresses at the department stores were expensive or tacky or just not quite right...so she made this. No one else wore anything like it, I can tell you that. And yeah, I was getting weird looks from all the other girls. *Most* of the other girls, I should say. I felt like a little bit of a freak, but Nina had a dress her grandma made, too. And when the two of us were together, we didn't really care what anyone else thought."

Luisa smiled gently. "I like it when you talk about her. She sounds like she was such a special person."

"She really was," Maya agreed. "And thanks for saying that. I always feel a little strange talking about her with people that didn't know her. I mean, I don't want to bum you guys out..."

"Don't ever worry about that," said Andie. "We're your friends, we love you, and we want to share with you. We want you to share with us, too. The good, the bad, the memories that make you sad...all of it."

"Thanks, guys," said Maya.

She felt the emotion of the weekend bubbling up in her again and was about to change the subject when a notification popped up at the top of her phone screen. It was from Tom, and he'd written, "I'm on my way upstairs. Just wanted to warn you since I'm a little early. I promise I don't mind waiting."

"Shoot!" cried Maya. "Ladies, I've got to go. Tom is on his way up, and I've still got hair and makeup to finish. Any final words? If you've got something to share that will magically impart confidence and courage, now's the time to share them."

"Knock him dead, love," said Luisa. "In that dress, with that body, you just might do that the second you open the door. And have fun. Don't take any of this too seriously. You're not going there tonight to bag your first million dollar contract *or* snag a husband. Just enjoy it."

"Yeah," agreed Andie. "And be proud of yourself for every step that you're taking on this path. No matter what happens tonight, you're taking a chance. Taking the next step for yourself. And even if the road ahead is a little twisty and turny, you're on the path now. And that's not nothing."

"No, that's not nothing at all," said Maya, nodding. "Thanks. That's a good way to look at all of this. I love you both. And I'll tell you all about it tomorrow."

"We'll hold you to it," said Luisa. "Don't you even dare think you can hold out on us. We're going to hear it *all*."

"I promise," said Maya. There was a knock on the door, and her eyes widened despite the fact that she'd known it was coming. "Gotta go, that's Tom!"

She ended the call as she walked to the living room, pulling the door open just as she finally switched off the screen of her phone. It wasn't until she was standing face to face with Tom that she realized slowing down and taking a breath before flinging the door open might have been a good idea. As it was, she was flustered, out of breath, and unprepared for the sight of Tom in a tuxedo. The man looked good whatever he was wearing, she'd noticed of course, but seeing him in a tuxedo took it to a new level. Like it was New Year's Eve, and he was showing up to spirit her away to an exclusive, romantic ball. Not that she'd ever attended such a thing, but the image came into her mind unbidden, regardless.

Of course, she had been silent and wide eyed as those thoughts swirled through her mind. There was an unreadable expression on Tom's face —shock mixed with something else—as he was the first to break the silence.

"Maya, you look absolutely stunning," he said. "That's a beautiful gown." He was pointedly not looking at the gown when he said it, though apparently his peripheral vision was excellent if he could register its beauty while his eyes were locked on her own.

"Thank you, Tom," Maya said. "You look very handsome yourself. Come on in." She stepped aside to let him in. "I'll just need a few more minutes to get ready. I hadn't quite finished up my face and hair when I got your text..."

"By all means," said Tom, gesturing to her to return to her task while he entertained himself in the kitchen. "I know I'm early, and I'm sorry for that. I'll make myself comfortable here while you do whatever you need." His eyes searched her face, flicking up to her hair. "Though I can't imagine there's anything you actually *need* to do. You're welcome to try to improve on perfection, though they say it can't be done."

Maya blushed at the compliment. "I'll just be a moment," she said, hurrying out of the room and back to the bathroom where her makeup bag and curling iron waited. Things felt different between them, and she was grateful for the escape to delay whatever was about to happen just a little longer.

Eleven

"That's as good as it's going to get," Maya said to her reflection. She had curled her hair with her straightening iron—a concept that still sounded ridiculous in her head, despite how flawless the end result always looked—and pinned up the top half. Now she was checking to make sure there was no lipstick on her teeth. Her makeup was subtle, apart from the pop of a bold red lip. She hoped it wasn't too much. Glancing at the time on her phone, she knew she couldn't stall any longer. It was time to face Tom, and time to head out to the event after that.

"Wow." Tom whistled. "I am definitely going to be the luckiest man at this party with you on my arm."

Maya blushed. So it *was* a date, or at least the kind of event two people went to arm in arm. "Thanks, Tom. Could you actually tell me a little more about the event? I meant to do some more research of my own about it, but between Catherine being AWOL and heading home this weekend—"

"Not at all. I'll tell you about it in the car on our way over. Shall we?" He offered her his arm, a gesture Maya appreciated more than she should. She wanted to let her grin spread across her face freely, but something stopped her. Don't let anyone see how happy you are—or, perhaps, don't let life/the Universe/whoever's up there in the sky see how happy you are. Because if you do, you might jinx it. You might lose it. The higher you go, the further you can fall. Better to stay at a happyish medium than reach for the stars.

Carefully managing her face, Maya took the arm Tom offered and let him walk her out the door of her apartment and down the stairs to the car waiting below. He had hired a driver for the evening—unless he regularly got around with a chauffeur. That was something Maya had never considered and should probably know about her client...friend...date.

Tom began to speak once the doors were closed on either side of them. "The event tonight is a gathering and celebration for entrepreneurs in the non-profit sector. There are a few awards being given out for innovation and impact, but apart from that, it's really just a nice time to socialize with other founders. I've made quite a few valuable connections at these events in the past, and perhaps the same might be true for you tonight."

"What kind of awards are being given out tonight? Is it like the Oscars of non-profit entrepreneurs?" Maya asked.

Tom chuckled. "Something like that, though it doesn't have any of that hoopla to it. No red carpet, no best and worst dressed lists...though there will be a photographer or two, and there will definitely be free flowing champagne."

"Food?" Maya asked. "I was in the car for hours today and could definitely eat." Her stomach rumbled in agreement.

"There will be food." Tom smiled. "And if it's not to your liking, I'll take care of it. I can't have you fainting of hunger on my watch. I would have brought you a donut if I'd known you were driving all day. Where were you going? You mentioned something about going home this weekend? Where's home?"

"Kalamazoo, Michigan." Maya answered. "And the drive wasn't bad, just a couple of hours. I was visiting my parents there, and I came back this morning." That was all Tom needed to know. Diving into the sob story of losing her best friend to a drunk driver wasn't exactly the kind of thing you talked about on a maybe-first date.

"I've heard good things about Michigan," said Tom. "I'm a fan of Lake Michigan, of course, but that's about all I've seen of it."

"I may be biased, but I definitely think it's worth a visit," said Maya. "I can give you some recommendations when you decide to go. And if I ever make it to Ireland, maybe you can do the same for me?"

Tom's eyes brightened with excitement. "Of course! You've never been?"

Maya shook her head. "I'm one of the many Americans who claim Irish ancestry, even think of it as the motherland to some extent...and yet I've never set foot on the Emerald Isle. Everything I know about Ireland is a cliché, I'm afraid."

Tom laughed. "Like what? Leprechauns and potatoes and saying 'top of the morning to you' as a regular greeting?"

It was Maya's turn to laugh. "Well, I knew leprechauns weren't real, but....I may have *just* this moment learned that's not actually how you greet each other. You really don't?"

"Afraid not, love," said Tom. "Though I'm sure you'd make some Irish folks very amused if you said it to them."

"Duly noted," said Maya. "Do you miss it? Ireland, I mean?"

"I miss my family, naturally. But I talk to them regularly, and I'll be going back soon."

"Back?" Maya asked. She felt her heart drop as she said it. "Your time in America is almost up already?"

Tom smiled at her. "I didn't say I'm going back forever. The nature of my work is that I need to be here sometimes and there sometimes, so I rack up a lot of frequent flier miles. Don't think you can get rid of me that easily." He winked.

Maya blushed for the umpteenth time of the day. "Am I that obvious?" she asked.

"I might be projecting," Tom replied. "Because I know if our roles were reversed, and you'd just mentioned that you might be moving to the other side of the ocean...well, I'd definitely be concerned about that."

His admission emboldened Maya to probe further. "And why exactly is that?" she asked.

"I like to be around you," said Tom. "I've enjoyed working with you, that's true. But I might enjoy your friendship even more. Especially when it includes perks like tonight and that dress. Have I mentioned how beautiful you look?"

"You have," Maya said. "Though the compliment doesn't get old. I'm glad this old dress still has its charm."

"Old dress?" Tom asked. "I'd assumed you went out and bought it in preparation for this event. Though admittedly, I don't really know how these kinds of things work for women. Me, I just rent a tux, nothing to it."

"Have you never had a date for an event like this before?" Maya asked. "Surely you could have asked her."

"I've never actually been to one quite this fancy," Tom admitted. "And considering that Conley Corp is up for an award tonight, it seemed right to pull out all the stops."

"Is that why you wanted me to join you? So you know you've got someone in your corner, or on your arm, rather? In case you don't win?"

"It's not like that—I'm not waiting to see if I'll be recognized. I know I will be, and that I'll be asked to make a speech. I just want someone to sit with me, to laugh with me and enjoy the evening with me, and to keep my ego in check if too many people start telling me I'm doing such great and meaningful work."

"You are, though. You know that, right?"

"I definitely believe in the work that Conley Corp is doing," said Tom. "But I'm under no illusions that our work couldn't exist without me. I might be the boss who keeps it all moving forward, but my employees are some of the best people I've ever met. They always say you should hire people who are smarter and better than you, and my hiring decisions are some of the best decisions I've made as a business owner."

"What about the idea for your filtration device? If you hadn't come up with that, those talented people wouldn't have anything to do in the first place," Maya offered.

"Anyone who takes sole credit for an idea doesn't understand how inspiration works," said Tom. "It comes from somewhere, that's for sure. But if you've ever seen a movie or an invention that you swear you thought of once upon a time, you know the truth. It's in the ether. Floating around in the air, invisible to all of us, are the ideas and inspiration that keep our society moving forward. Sometimes one of us is lucky enough to have one sneak into our consciousness. But that doesn't mean we thought of it on our own." He chuckled softly. "I didn't even think of that explanation there, but I *did* hear a great speech about it once."

Tom was humble, and Maya was impressed. In the years she'd worked at Andersen, she'd met a lot of innovative thinkers. Tom was the first one who wasn't full of himself and in awe of his own potential. And there was definitely something magnetic—sexy, even—about the way he cared for his employees and acknowledged his own humanity.

"Here we are," Tom said, as the car pulled to a stop in front of one of the fancy downtown hotels. Maya wasn't sure which one it was, as she'd never actually had a reason to visit any of them. Tom stepped out of the car and then held out his hand to assist her.

Even the street view of the hotel was impressive—the lights in the lobby, the uniformed doorman...it was all a far cry from the roadside motels she was accustomed to from her childhood family travels. Nevertheless, she worked to keep the "country mouse" expression off of her face and smiled up at Tom. "Thanks for inviting me," she said. "Have I said that already?"

He smiled back at her. "You may have mentioned it. And it's my pleasure, really. Thank you for accompanying me."

Arm in arm, they walked into the hotel lobby, where they were directed to a ballroom on the top floor of the hotel. As they rode the elevator to the top of the building, Maya felt her ears pop once. The view from the ballroom was bound to be stunning, as high as they were ascending. Her hand was still nestled in the crook of Tom's arm, and he reached his other hand across to place it over hers. "Are you nervous? I promise this is supposed to be a fun evening, not something to stress you out."

Maya laughed quietly. "I thought I was hiding my nerves better than that. But yeah...I am a little bit. It's not every day I go out dressed like this, and I've never actually been to this hotel before."

"Let me let you in on a little secret." Tom leaned in conspiratorially. "The people here are just people. They might be dressed up a little fancier than most—though you fit right in on that account, so nothing to worry about there—but they're just like the rest of us, with all our needs, emotions, and bodily functions."

"Well, that's one way to look at it." Maya smiled. "You really just took the whole 'imagine them all in their underwear' trick to the next level, didn't you? If anyone looks too fancy and I start to feel nervous, I can just imagine them using the bathroom like the rest of us mere mortals and feel one hundred percent at ease."

"Precisely." Tom smiled at her. "Don't let anyone—and especially not yourself—make you feel like you don't belong here. Hell, one of the honorees invited you. It's not like you snuck in to crash the party. Relax, it's going to be just fine."

"I promise I will...*try*...to do just that," said Maya. Looking back at Tom, she felt something unfamiliar. There was a mixture of comfort and exhilaration in being with him, a playing off each other that felt natural and normal, while at the same time she was continually uncovering facets of his personality, of his being that she hadn't realized existed before. It was making her very aware of the lack of close relationships with males who weren't related to her, and while it was exciting and enticing on one hand, there was also a part of her that was ready to pull a Cinderella and fly towards the door, shoes be damned.

And somehow Tom seemed to sense just that. As the elevator doors opened to the ballroom, he took her hand in his and tugged her gently forward. "Come on, then. Let's go have some fun." His smile and his touch created a stir of flutters in her lower belly, and Maya let herself be pulled forward. She could be Cinderella another time; tonight there was no pumpkin to think about, just the part of the story where she got to dance at a ball with a prince.

Wait a minute. Was there going to be dancing? The thought of being pulled close to Tom's chest to sway in rhythm with the music flipped a switch Maya wasn't sure she'd had prior to that moment. But the possibility of being in that position while also visible to a room full of strangers was flipping a different switch—one that made her want to vomit with nerves.

Tom looked down at her with a question in his eyes, and it was only then Maya realized she had come to a halt. "What's wrong, Maya?" he asked.

"I...just..." she sputtered. She didn't want to lose any of her allure by revealing her fears to him...but she also knew she wouldn't feel settled until she knew for certain what was awaiting her. And if there was something anxiety inducing like dancing in front of this entire crowd of fancy people, well, then she could hide in the bathroom until it was over. "Is there going to be dancing at this thing?"

Tom chuckled. "Well, when you ask it with that tone, it's hard not to be offended. But no, darling, you won't be expected to dance with me this evening. And in fact, you'd get quite a few strange looks if you did since that's not exactly the kind of party this is. Would it be so bad to dance with me to a song or two, though?"

"Of course not!" Maya answered more quickly—and more honestly—than she had intended to. "I mean, I'm sure it would be nice."

Tom was smiling. "I can promise you it would be. And maybe one day you'll find that out for yourself."

The evening was a delight. From the moment they arrived, Tom made Maya feel at ease. He stayed by her side, introducing her to his peers and raving about the work she was doing for him. Maya noticed he never referenced her working for a firm or named Andersen Consulting, and she appreciated his efforts to help her make a name for herself in her field.

At one point, Tom had been pulled aside by an old colleague who wanted a word with him. Before he stepped away, he leaned in to check with Maya that she would be okay on her own. She smiled and nodded, encouraging him to take all the time he needed while she continued to chat with the circle of entrepreneurs she'd found her way into. Even though Tom was on the other side of the room, she was keenly aware of his presence, and more than once she glanced in his direction to check to see where he was and what he was doing, only to find that he was already looking in her direction.

Through the dinner and awards ceremony, Tom and Maya were seated at a table with the other honorees and their plus ones. Maya got to know the founder of a groundbreaking educational program supporting children in remote areas, as well as another entrepreneur who was directing her resources and brainpower towards creating economic opportunities for women where they historically didn't exist. She was inspired whether she turned to the left or to the right, though even through all of those good feelings, a bit of doubt managed to creep in.

What was she doing here? She didn't belong at this table, not with the amazing work these people were doing. Who was she to sit with them and act like they had anything in common?

"Penny for your thoughts?" Tom leaned in and spoke quietly into her ear. "What's going on in that head of yours?"

She shook her head and forced a smile as she turned to him. "Nothing. It's just really inspiring, what everyone is doing."

He peered into her eyes. "Hey. I see you in there. Come out of your head and play with us. And if there's anything telling you that you don't belong here, you tell that voice to shut up right now. You belong here because I invited you to be here...but even if I hadn't done that, you'd still belong in the same room as any of these people. You're intelligent, talented, and you can problem solve with the absolute best of them. Half of the people in this room are just full of ideas, but they never actually act on them. That would never be said about you." He raised her hand to his mouth and lightly kissed her knuckles before replacing her hand on the table with a squeeze.

Maya's smile back at Tom was genuine now. "Thank you, Tom. Really. For the kind words, for this evening... it's been absolutely wonderful."

"For me, too." Tom said. His eyes pierced her own with an intensity she couldn't quite read...or wasn't willing to let herself understand. Not quite yet. Not when what they were saying might be scary enough to make her run in the other direction.

By the time the plates were cleared away, Maya was feeling at ease, comfortable by Tom's side. As the emcee came up on the stage at the front of the room, they all turned their chairs to face in her direction. She took her place on the stage and smiled at the group gathered as she leaned into the microphone.

"Thank you all for being here tonight," she began. "As you know, we gather every year to honor the innovation and empathy that drive our community of non-profit entrepreneurs. And tonight is no exception. Tonight we are celebrating the leaps and bounds being made towards ending gender inequality and violence against women, towards creating equal opportunities for access to education in the areas where it is most needed, and, of course, towards providing access to clean drinking water around the globe. Between our three honorees tonight, we have seen technology and new ways of thinking that could mean real change for the generations to come. Without further ado, I'd like to invite our honorees on stage to share their visions with us. As always, we encourage and promote collaboration and cooperation, and we can't wait to see what you all will do next."

While the room erupted in applause and cheers, Tom climbed on stage with the two other honorees who'd been seated at their table. Maya's smile was wide as she joined in the cheers and as she listened to the speeches each of them made.

When it was Tom's turn, he made an inspiring speech relating stories from his travels and the things he had learned from local engineers in India and Sierra Leone when he'd been a bright-eyed, naïve volunteer. Maya was enraptured—his deference and humility in the way he talked about his partners, many of whom were now working with him at Conley Corp, revealed another level of depth of his being that had been unexpected.

"None of us got here on our own," Tom continued. "And it's the nature of the work we do and the problems we solve to cooperate with each other. I'm grateful to every single one of you in this room for the inspiration you've provided, the support you've given, and the ways we've challenged each other. And I'd especially like to thank the newest invaluable member of my team, Maya Jefferson, for being here with me to share this moment. Your support has meant more than you know, and I have the feeling this is just the start of something beautiful." And then he *winked* at her, of all the ridiculous things he could do with his face.

Maya's reaction was instantaneous. She froze, eyes wide and mouth slack. She hadn't expected to be shouted out at all, let alone to be singled out by name with the implication that something of significance was brewing between the two of them. Realizing that the rest of her table was looking at her while they gave Tom a standing ovation, she pasted on a smile and joined them in their applause. Why did it feel like everyone was looking at her? And when had the room gotten so hot?

The smile was still in place when Tom rejoined them, leaning in to kiss her on the cheek. "Something wrong?" he asked.

"Just feeling a bit stressed about all that's waiting for me at work tomorrow," she said, pulling out her phone to look at the time. "I hadn't realized this was going to go so late, and I should probably be getting home if I'm going to be any use to anyone at work tomorrow."

Tom took her elbow and made to walk towards the exit. "Come on then, let me get you home."

Maya stopped him, lifting his hand off her arm and being sure to smile as calmly as possible. "No, Tom. This is your party, and you should stay and celebrate some more. Don't let me tear you away from it."

"I really don't mind," he said, concern creeping across his face. "In fact, I'd almost certainly rather be with you than anyone else in this room. Can I at least offer you a ride? I won't even invite you out for a cup of coffee, or tea, rather. Just take you straight home like a gentleman and leave you there."

"Really, I insist," said Maya. On the screen of her phone, she was already pulling up the ride share app and requesting a driver. "Look." She held out her phone to show him. "Andres will be here in three minutes to pick me up, and I'll be home and in my bed fifteen minutes after that, at most. It would take you at least seven minutes to say all your goodbyes and get your driver to bring the car around."

"You've got me there." Tom lifted a hand to rub the back of his neck. "This just seems so...sudden. Did something happen when I was up there? Was it something I said? I didn't mean to make you uncomfortable, it just felt wrong not to acknowledge you. I hope you didn't think I was trying to pressure you into something..."

"No, it's not that." Maya reassured him. "All the speeches were lovely. I just lost track of time and didn't realize until you were coming back to the table how late it was getting. I appreciated the acknowledgement, even if it felt undeserved."

"You really have been a partner to me through this whole project," said Tom. "Especially when I'm here in the States without my entire team. I realized it before, but it really crystallized for me when I was up there talking about the people I've had the privilege of working with over the course of my career...and I realized you belong right up there with the rest of them."

"Thanks, Tom." Maya smiled. She glanced at her phone. "My ride is going to be here really soon. I'll talk to you tomorrow, okay?"

"Okay." Tom's expression was pained. "I wish it didn't feel like this was all ending so abruptly, but I honor your wishes. Can you please text and let me know you got home safe?"

"I will," Maya said. "Bye, Tom." She walked quickly out of the room, breaking into a jog once she was out of sight of everyone in the room. The storm of emotions, the same thing driving her feet away from Tom as quickly as she could move, were threatening to come out all over her face, and she needed to be alone if and when that happened.

Twelve

Maya's ride home was uneventful—or at least, she assumed it was because she didn't remember any of it. She had stared out the window, taking in the skyline of the city she loved while repeating everything that had happened that evening over in her mind. It was like she was a detective combing over the evidence for clues. Clues of what, exactly, she wasn't sure. And it didn't matter. This wasn't something she was going to get to the bottom of, but it *was* something she was going to think about until she passed out from exhaustion.

Any mystery about Tom's feelings for her was gone. This invitation clearly hadn't been just an offer to boost her career—from the way he looked at her to the sweet things he said to her to the electricity that zapped between them at every touch, it was clear something more was at stake. And that thought made Maya want to run. In fact, it was that thought that had led her to run. Of course she didn't need to get eight hours of sleep before the big day at work tomorrow—she just needed not to be in such close proximity to Tom, feeling so comfortable perched in her chair with his arm across the back of it. Or letting him lean in to speak quietly into her ear. Or flirting, if that's what all that playful banter had been. Maybe it was just him being himself, for all she knew.

She texted Andie and Luisa. The notifications from the two of them had been popping up at regular intervals throughout the evening, but she hadn't had the chance to even read their messages until now. They brought a smile to her face now, despite the stress that was wearing on her nerves.

"Hi my loves. I'm on my way home now. It was a really nice evening, and I'll tell you more soon."

It didn't take long for the text bubbles to pop up in response.

" "

…

"…really? That's IT?!"

"Yep, what she said!" That message contained an arrow emoji pointing to the message above.

"Spill it, friend! Unless you're not headed home alone, in which case use protection and tell us everything tomorrow."

That got a response from Maya. "I am 100% alone right now. Apart from the driver of this car, but I'm alone in the way you're talking about. I left Tom there so I could get a reasonable night's sleep and he didn't have to leave the celebration."

"Look at this wacky friend of ours, talking about getting a reasonable night's sleep when she could be dressed like an actual queen, on the arm of a very attractive man, out on the town like the young person she is." That was Luisa.

"What happened, Maya? You don't sound like yourself." That was Andie, perceptive as always. Maya should have known better than to think she could hide her true emotions, even via text message.

"Just...nothing. I don't know. I think I got a little freaked out by the situation, the attention...it was all kind of a lot."

"Of course it was!" responded Andie. "Honestly, I'd be concerned if you weren't freaked out right now. It's totally normal to feel uncomfortable about a big change like this, whatever 'this' is."

That made Maya feel a bit better. "Really? It's normal to not be totally on board with having a hot guy—one I actually *like*, even—lavish attention on you and hint about wanting to spend more time with you?"

"Ahh, did he really?" Luisa was texting now. "I love it when they don't play hard to get. How adorable!"

"It's definitely normal." Andie wrote. "Considering that you weren't doing any dating at all, tonight took you from zero to sixty really, REALLY fast. Don't focus too much on what freaked you out, okay? When you get home, relax, drink some tea, and think back on all the highlights of the evening. Better yet, write them down in your journal. Those are the moments you want to remember, I promise. And you can write about what's scaring you too...it might help!"

"Do you want us to call you when you're home?" Luisa asked.

"No, that's okay. I'm a little tired and wired to do the whole debrief thing right now. Let's talk tomorrow though, okay?"

"You got it!" Luisa again.

"Sounds great. We're so proud of you, love!" That was Andie.

Maya smiled to herself. There was something about just knowing that her feelings were normal that took away some of the intensity. Maybe there wasn't something wrong with her...maybe she was just human.

But maybe not, too. No one else in that ballroom had looked the least bit freaked out or out of place. She hadn't belonged there *or* on Tom's arm this evening. She sighed. This roller coaster of emotions didn't seem like it was going to stop anytime soon.

In front of her apartment, she thanked her driver and wished him a good night. She fired off a simple "I'm home, stop worrying, and I love you" text to Andie and Luisa, and then sent the same message to her mom and dad. She sent a message to Tom too, thanking him again for the lovely evening and letting him know she had made it home safely.

She made her way up the stairs to her apartment, and once inside, she left her purse, keys, and phone on the kitchen counter closest to the door. As she walked towards her bedroom, she kicked off her shoes and did the awkward dance of unzipping her own dress. Putting it on had been hard enough, but she'd had the motivation of avoiding the embarrassment of having to ask Tom for help. Embarrassment or something else, she wasn't quite sure now.

Once the green dress was flung across Maya's bed where it belonged, she flounced into the bathroom to remove her makeup and take a nice, hot shower. Seeing her reflection in the mirror, just before she swiped over her eyelids with the makeup remover-soaked cotton ball, she could admit that she looked good. She didn't magically believe that she belonged in the ballroom, but for a moment of clarity, she didn't believe that Tom was joking with her when he'd called her beautiful.

"Good makeup works wonders, I guess." Maya looked down at her body, clad only in her bra and panties. "And not a bad body, if I do say so myself. Heck, I look...kinda hot, actually."

Maybe these were all things she should have experienced for the first time years ago. Maybe she should have realized she was an attractive woman and looked at her body with these eyes when she was in high school, or college at the latest. But she'd spent those years grieving, and it had felt like her body only existed to carry her emotions around. As she finished wiping the remains of the night's makeup off her face, Maya willed herself to see herself like this more often...like a woman. No longer like a sad, awkward teenager. But a grown woman, with the face and the curves and maybe even someday the confidence to go along with it. That seemed a long way off tonight, but the revelation was significant, regardless.

After she was showered and cozied up in her robe, Maya took Andie's advice and poured out her thoughts and feelings into her journal. They already felt less intense, like the shower had helped at least as much as talking with her friends had.

"It was uncomfortable," she wrote, *"but I can't help but wonder if that was just because it was unfamiliar. It wasn't wrong to be there, and it's not like I couldn't belong on Tom's arm someday...I'm just not sure if I'm ready for it yet. I don't want things to move too fast and fall apart because of it. But if he wants that, then maybe I need to put a stop to this...turn our relationship back into strictly a professional one..."*

Writing in her journal didn't feel like it was taking Maya directly to a logical conclusion to her problems, and in fact it seemed to continue to bring up new problems and additional worries that she hadn't thought about yet. But by the end of a couple of pages, she still felt better. Even if she didn't know what her next plan of action was, she felt more grounded, more comfortable in her own skin, and more ready to see what her next interaction with Tom would bring.

She heard her phone ding in the kitchen then and went to find it where she had left it. Speaking of Tom, he had sent a couple of texts while she had been showering and journaling. There was one wishing her a good night, thanking her for coming, and saying he looked forward to seeing her again very soon. The other message was a photo, a selfie she had almost forgotten taking with him just before they had gotten into his car.

Opening up the image, Maya zoomed in on their faces and was surprised by the genuine smiles they had both flashed. Tom looked more comfortable, perhaps, but there was still a level of nerves bouncing off of both of them that warmed Maya's heart. They looked like two teenagers headed to prom, flashing a relieved, excited, and nervous smile for the camera after the plastic ones they'd pasted on for the photos their parents took. Was it possible he was as unsure of himself as she was with regard to whatever was blooming between them?

Andie and Luisa would want to see this picture, to say nothing of Maya's mom. And they would...eventually. For tonight, it was just for Maya. And she took full advantage of that, reopening the image every few minutes to smile down at Tom's handsome face.

Maya woke up the next morning feeling rested, but it only lasted for a second before the panic set in. The sky was too bright, and she felt too good, like she'd actually gotten a proper night's sleep. She fumbled for the phone on her nightstand and sat bolt upright when she saw the time. It was eight o'clock, and her work day started in an hour.

There was no time for her regular morning routine. There was barely time for getting dressed and brushing her teeth when she considered just how long the commute was bound to take.

She flew out of bed, grabbing a button-down shirt and a pair of pants from the wardrobe on her way to the bathroom. While she did the bare minimum of prep, she dressed herself. One hand was brushing her teeth while the other was fumbling with the buttons on her shirt. It was possible it was all taking longer because she wasn't letting herself use both of her hands to do any of it, but she didn't have time to debate that with herself right then.

Breakfast—and tea—would have to wait. Maya grabbed her briefcase from where it had been sitting since Friday, trusting that everything she needed for the day would be inside. Then she ran out the door and down the stairs of her apartment.

Thirty minutes later, she was panting inside the doors of Andersen Consulting. She had run from her apartment to the bus stop, where she had anxiously waited for the standing room only bus that dropped her off a few blocks away from the office. She had run from there, too, and she was paying for her exertions now by gasping for air and (hopefully not) pitting out the shirt she was wearing.

"I made it!" she exclaimed to Chris. "My alarm didn't go off this morning, but I still made it in time. I've been on the run since I jumped out of bed this morning." This was more personal information than she would normally share with Catherine's assistant, but the frantic start to her day had stripped her of all workplace propriety.

Chris looked confused. "Why didn't you just work from home? Or ask me to redirect calls to your cell phone while you were on your way?"

"Why would I do that?" Maya asked. "I'm here now."

"No, I mean you didn't have to rush, you know? You're, like, the boss now. I forwarded calls to Catherine's phone all the time. She was pretty much only ever here at nine if she had an early meeting."

Huh. Maya hadn't considered that there might be some perks along with the stress of her new-but-hopefully-temporary role. She had noticed Chris's use of the past tense while talking about Catherine, and she hoped that wasn't an omen that she wasn't coming back.

"Thank you for that reminder, Chris," said Maya. "Actually, I will step out for just a few minutes if you don't mind redirecting my calls or taking a message." Skipping breakfast wasn't going to make the morning any easier, and the café across the street made a carrot cake muffin that was to die for. It wasn't a donut, but it would definitely do.

"Sounds good, boss. See you in a few."

Maya stepped back outside, making her way to Beans Café at a more reasonable pace than she had so far traveled all morning. While waiting for the streetlight to change, she took a minute to breathe deeply, closing her eyes with gratitude that she'd made it to work on time and that her nightmare morning hadn't been such a big deal at all.

While her eyes were still closed, she heard the sound of a masculine throat clearing next to her. She opened her eyes and startled to see Tom standing there, looking a bit sheepish. "I didn't mean to disturb you," he said. "But I was afraid if you opened your eyes and saw me standing here without any warning, you might take off into the street and get smushed by a car."

Maya laughed, louder than she anticipated. "Is that really what I made you think last night? Tom, I promise I had a lovely time. I'm not going to choose getting hit by a taxi over standing next to you on the street. Really. Want to join me for breakfast at the café? What are you doing here, anyway?"

"Wow, dinner *and* breakfast? That's not quite the way it usually happens on a first date, but I'll take it." Tom smiled at her, seeming more at ease now. "I was actually coming to see you this morning—a business call, I swear—but I couldn't turn up empty-handed. I was going to the café for carbs and sugar for you."

"For me?" Maya asked. "So thoughtful! Well, come and sit with me then. We can talk about your project over breakfast." She fidgeted with the strap of her purse. "Is it really just the project you're wanting to talk about or...?"

Tom's eyes looked sad as he smiled. "I don't want to push myself on you, Maya. I can tell you're not totally comfortable with whatever this is between us. I can back off if that makes you feel better."

"No!" Maya started, surprising herself. "I mean...you're right. I'm not totally comfortable, but that's nothing to do with you. I just...I haven't done this before, not really. So I'm having a hard time with, like...being a grown up, I guess."

Tom laughed. "You? Having a hard time being a grown up? Maya, do you have any idea how capable you are?"

"That's not what I meant," said Maya. "I'm not talking about being responsible or being good at my job. I guess I'm talking about emotional things...relationship things...dating things...'whatever this is' things..."

Tom put his hand on her arm. "Hey. I understand." His eyes were kind. "I think maybe this is all moving a little too fast for you, eh? Why don't we slow it down a little, then?"

"I'm not saying I don't want to see where things could go." Maya's voice was rising higher with the strain of communicating her feelings. "Don't be upset, I don't mean it like that..."

"I'm not upset, Maya. When I say we can slow things down a little, that's exactly what I mean. I'm not suggesting we shouldn't even bother dating each other just because you don't want to move in together this week. Why don't we just enjoy each other's company and see what happens?"

"What...what would that look like?" Maya asked. "I'm not joking when I say I've never really done this before."

"Really? Because you seem like such a natural." Tom elbowed her lightly in the ribs. "Only joking. And it can look like whatever we want it to look like. Why don't we start with coffee and a muffin for now?"

"Replace the coffee with tea and you've got yourself a date, mister." Maya smiled. She felt lighter now, knowing that whatever this was between them was up to her. It would take some adjustment to start communicating her needs and wants and feelings to Tom, but he seemed willing to take it slow, at least for now. If that changed, though....

"Hey." Tom raised her chin so their eyes met each other. "I saw you disappear somewhere again. Come back to me, please. It's just tea and/or coffee and a muffin. Come on." He dropped his hand from her chin and picked up her hand, tugging her to follow him into the coffee shop.

After a green tea latte—yes, even Maya Jefferson could enjoy a small amount of caffeine from time to time, as long as it didn't become a habit—and half an hour of easy conversation and laughter, Maya was feeling better. The carrot cake muffin and its cream cheese frosting had definitely helped, too.

As she and Tom stood and cleared their dishes away from the table, they fell into a companionable silence.

"Walk you back to the office?" Tom asked. "I've got some work to do anyway, and if your conference room is available, I could set myself up in there. I'd suggest using Catherine's office again, but—"

"No, that's fine. You can use her office."

"You haven't moved into it?"

Maya shook her head. "I don't want to believe that this change is permanent. I'm keeping it free for her so she can show up again at a moment's notice and find everything just the way she left it."

"Still no word from her?" Tom looked concerned at the lack of communication from his ex-future-sister-in-law.

"Not a peep." Maya's mouth cut a straight line across her face as she pushed the door open of the café, letting the two of them out into the bustling street. "I haven't made much of an attempt to communicate with her lately. After the total radio silence those first few days, I just can't be bothered. I hope she's alright, wherever she is, and I hope she lets the rest of us know what her plans are one of these days."

"I hope so, too," said Tom. The two of them jogged to make it across the street before the light changed to red. "It's not like her to disappear like this, not unless..." His voice trailed off as he looked up from the sidewalk towards a figure in front of them, leaning up against the building containing the Andersen offices. "Declan? What the hell are you doing here?"

Thirteen

T he man pushed off from the wall with one foot and a grin broke across his face as he walked towards Tom with open arms. "Baby bro! Surprise!"

Tom didn't look pleased, but he still put up his arms to return his brother's hug. Pulling back, he asked again. "Seriously, though. What are you doing here?"

"Can't I check up on an old friend?" Declan asked. "Speaking of friends, who is this beauty?" He turned to Maya, smiling a charming smile and wiggling his eyebrows mischievously.

Tom bristled. "This is Maya. We're working together on a project. Maya, this is Declan. My brother."

"Nice to meet you, Declan," Maya said, offering her hand.

"You too, beautiful." Declan clasped her hand in both of his. "What kind of 'project' does my baby brother have you working on, anyway? From the looks of it, it must be some sort of top secret coffee and pastry retrieval mission." He looked meaningfully at the cups in their hands and the paper bag Maya was clutching.

"Dec, cut the crap." Tom's face was flushing redder with every moment he spent near his brother. "Catherine has been missing for over a week now. She disappeared and left Maya in charge of everything and has been unreachable ever since. I don't suppose you know anything about that?"

The impish gleam was back in Declan's eye. "Now now now. What would make you think I'd have a thing to do with Catherine's mysterious vanishing act? Don't you know she and I are ancient history, Tom?"

"Yeah, I would have believed that two weeks ago, but not anymore. The coincidence is way too strong to be real. She disappears and now you're here? All the way from Ireland, you find yourself, what...'in the neighborhood?' And you just had to pop in and say hello? I'm not buying it."

The front door opened then, and a familiar silhouette popped out. After her sudden disappearance and the total lack of communication, here she was—Catherine Andersen. Only something about her seemed...different. Off. Maya couldn't put her finger on it before Catherine turned in her direction and crowed, "Tom! Maya! Oh good, you're both here. Come on in!"

Catherine ushered all three of them in the door, giggling when Declan whispered something in her ear and one of his hands disappeared behind her back, where Maya couldn't see it.

"Tom, what in the world?" she whispered through gritted teeth. "Are the two of them always like this?"

Tom looked chagrined. "It's been a long time since I saw them together, but...yes. It would seem that nothing has changed since they parted ways a decade ago. He brings out this side of her, for better or worse. If you ask me, it's definitely for the worse."

Once all four of them were in Catherine's office—where she had apparently been shepherding them all along—Maya turned to her boss. "Catherine, I'm...glad to see you back. Are you really back, if I may ask? And would you mind telling me where you've been? It's been quite an ordeal to fill in for you, especially without any warning, and..."

"Don't I look like I'm back, darling Maya?" Catherine was giggling again, and there was a distinct lack of focus in her eyes when she tried to meet Maya's gaze. "Thank you, of course, for all your help and hard work while I was gone. I just needed a vacation, you know? 'All work and no play makes Catherine a dull girl' and all that."

"Where did you go on your, ahem, *vacation*?" Tom asked, a bite to his tone that Maya hadn't heard before.

"Oh, here and there. Back to Ireland, actually!" crowed Catherine, grinning at Declan.

"And I suppose you two reconnected there and have been inseparable ever since?" asked Tom.

Declan and Catherine were holding hands now and smiling at each other with the doe eyes that answered Tom's questions without any words.

"Shite." He pinched the bridge of his nose with his thumb and forefinger. "You two were never exactly the best influence on each other. I suppose that's why you both smell like you're soaked in liquor and have the general demeanor of a teenager who's been out partying all night."

Maya worked to keep the shock off of her face. It was two fold - for one, she couldn't believe that *Catherine Andersen* of all people would show up to work drunk. But she also couldn't believe that she, Maya, was inexperienced enough about all things alcohol that she hadn't even recognized what was going on here. She turned her wide-eyed gaze to Catherine and Declan, who were giggling in confirmation of Tom's accusations.

"Right," Tom began. "Dec, you need to get the hell out of here. Back to your hotel, or wherever it is that you're staying. And Catherine, you need to get out of here, too. If any clients encounter you like this, your reputation is going to be in the toilet. Hell, if too many of your employees see you like this, you're going to lose all respect as the boss and spend the next ten years fighting to get back everything you've lost."

"But—" Catherine interrupted, though Tom silenced her with a raised hand and a gentle but stern expression.

"No buts, Cath. You can try again tomorrow. For today, leave Maya in charge. She can handle it, you know. No thanks to you and your total lack of preparation, she's done an excellent job in your absence. But we can talk about that more when you're sobered up. Is that alright with you, Maya?"

"Of course," she answered. "I can handle today. You go home and get some rest, Catherine."

After a few more moments insisting that they really were feeling totally fine and not tipsy at all, Tom escorted Catherine and Declan out the door and out of the building. Maya stayed behind, waiting for him to return and processing all that had just happened.

She sat down in Catherine's chair, looking around her with fresh eyes. Something felt different today, less like she was stealing the position from her boss and more like she was providing an anchor in her absence—one she would readily relinquish when Catherine was up to it again.

"I'm sorry about that." Tom had returned. "I get a bit bossy when Dec's in one of his states, and I think I directed that at Catherine, too. And you too—are you okay?"

"You didn't give me any responsibilities I hadn't already expected to have today. Don't worry about it." She smiled at him. "I was really glad you were here—I wouldn't have known what to do with the two of them on my own. I didn't even realize they were drunk. I could tell something was off about Catherine, but I didn't know what it was."

"Well, I have a lot of experience with my dear brother. He's had a bit of a problem with the drink for a while. It's part of what drove him and Catherine apart in the first place. I'm afraid he's become a bad influence on her this time around, though."

"It wasn't like that before?"

"Not at all. She ended their engagement because he couldn't keep himself sober long enough to make a single wedding plan. I think she took it personally, like he was so uncomfortable with the idea of committing to her that he couldn't bear to face it sober."

"Wow," Maya breathed. "That's really harsh."

"Who knows if that played a part in it," said Tom. "But what I know for absolute certain is that alcoholism is a disease. And it's a disease that's been afflicting Declan since long before he met Catherine. So it's not fair to blame any of this on her or on their relationship, even though I'm sure he tried to do that. I just can't believe that she's back in this mess with him again."

"I'm really sorry to hear that," said Maya. "It must have been hard on you, too, going through this with your brother."

"It is. I care about him a lot, and I support him the best I can, but...between the alcohol and whatever other trouble he gets himself into....well, it's hard. I've had to set some boundaries there, and the rest of the family doesn't always understand. They think I'm being cold with him or that I should lighten up, but I just..."

"You don't know how to do anything halfway, do you?" Maya asked with a gentle smile. "I mean that in a good way. I mean...whether it's your work or wooing me or your personal boundaries, you don't half ass any of it."

Tom returned her smile. "*Wooing* you? What is this, a Jane Austen novel?"

She smiled back, feeling her cheeks turn pink. "I didn't know a better way to say that."

"You said it just fine." He put his arm around her shoulders. "And I think you're right. I do tend to go all in when I want to do something. I've had to rein myself in at times from the idea of cutting Declan off completely. He's not dangerous, he's not even a bad guy...it's just that being around him hurts the people who love him sometimes. We get our hopes invested in his growth and his health, the promises he makes us that he cares about those things. But then it all just turns out to be empty promises, and that really hurts."

"I can't imagine," Maya said, looking up into Tom's eyes. "I'm sorry your family is going through that. And I hope Declan does what he needs to do to get help or healing or whatever it is..."

"I hope so too," said Tom. "And thanks. I appreciate your understanding and your support." He squeezed her shoulder before he dropped his arm to his side.

"Is there anything we can do for Catherine? To help keep her from getting swept up in all this?" Maya asked.

"Catherine's a smart cookie," said Tom. "And I don't think this party girl lifestyle is going to be sustainable for her. In fact, I'd guess that when she has a moment away from Declan, she'll look at herself, at the last week, with different eyes. She might feel ashamed and embarrassed about it, but she'll do the right thing. I really hope so, anyway."

Maya put her arm around Tom's waist and gave him a side hug. It was awkward, sure, but it felt right in the moment. "I'm sorry you're going through this with your brother, too. It can't be easy. Do you want to talk about it some more, or...?"

"You're kind to ask. But I think getting to work is probably the best thing to do for both of us. Did you want to stay in here? You looked pretty comfortable in that desk." He smiled at her, though it didn't quite reach his eyes.

"No, I'm perfectly happy in my cubicle. I'll leave you to it, then. Let me know if you need anything, okay?"

"Absolutely. Thank you for everything, Maya. I'll see you later on, maybe for lunch?"

"Sounds good." Maya stepped out of the room and closed the door lightly behind her. What a day it had been so far, and it was only—she pulled out her phone to check the time—a little after ten in the morning. She hoped this wasn't a sign of what the week ahead was going to be like.

·♥·♥·♥·♥·♥·

It turned out that being away from work all weekend when she was "sort of" in charge of the company had not been the right move. Or at least, not the right move if she didn't want to be buried under a mountain of emails and voice messages come Monday morning. By the time Maya was ready to take a break for lunch, she had only managed to work her way through half of her new emails. How did Catherine do it?

Oh, right, she thought to herself. *Maybe it was the stress of all of this that drove her to reunite with her ex-fiancé and take up a drinking habit of her own. There's got to be a better way...*

But if there was a better way, Maya wasn't going to discover it today. No, that was a luxury that could wait until after she'd dug herself out from under the mountain of urgent tasks that demanded attention from her and *only* her. Why did everyone *need* her so much? As she opened yet another email that seemed as unnecessary as it was almost predatory in its passive aggressive requests for action NOW, she had to stifle a groan.

Her phone chose that moment to buzz with a new text message from Tom. "I'm ordering Chinese for lunch. You want anything?"

Before she could reply, her stomach rumbled in response. Apparently, her answer was going to be a resounding, "YES AND THANK YOU VERY MUCH."

She dialed it down a bit. "Yes, I'm starving! Got so bogged down in emails I almost forgot I need to feed myself. Could you order me some chicken lo mein, please?"

"You got it. I'll let you know when it's here. I can bring it to you, or we can eat together in Catherine's office."

"Why don't we step away from our desks and have a picnic outside? A few minutes away from my inbox would be very good for me right about now."

"Sounds like a great idea. I'll see you in 20 minutes or so. xx"

Maya stared at those two x's at the end of his message for a solid minute. She'd signed a card with x's and o's before, but now she was having a hard time remembering which one was hugs and which one was kisses. If Tom had just kissed her for the first time with a mere slip of his finger on the keyboard of his phone, well....she didn't know what she thought about that. *Maybe it was a normal thing for Irish people to do*, she told herself. *Best not to read into it too much.*

Another message pinged then. "Sorry about the xx, force of habit. I think that's more common on the other side of the pond, but I'm realizing now it might not really be a thing here. In case you were overthinking it, stop. Please."

A chuckle snuck out of Maya's lips. Even when they weren't in the same physical space, Tom knew when she was overthinking and he could bring her out of it so easily. Like he was snapping his fingers. She liked that about him. Or rather, she could add that to the list of things she liked about him. That list seemed to be growing every day. It had certainly added a few new items this morning when she had seen the unique combination of firmness and compassion he had used to handle Catherine and Declan. He was capable, but he wasn't domineering. He really was a good man.

Twenty minutes later on the dot, Tom was standing in front of Maya, raising a plastic bag stuffed to the gills with steaming Chinese takeout. He raised his eyebrows and tilted his head towards the door, and without even a word passing between them, Maya smiled and stood up to follow him out of the building. On her way, she called to Chris to take messages for her if anyone called. Knowing that she had the option of having calls redirected to her phone was great...but it didn't mean she didn't want to have fifteen minutes without having to worry about the phone ringing while her mouth was full of tasty noodles.

Once they were out of the office, Maya led Tom to a small courtyard behind a neighboring building. They were away from the noise of the street there, and there was a vacant picnic table just waiting for them to make themselves comfortable.

"What did you order?" Maya asked, as Tom unpacked the bag and handed her a set of chopsticks.

"Beef and broccoli," he responded. "It's always been my favorite. Though your selection smells very tasty, too."

"We can share," Maya offered. "If you don't mind sharing germs."

Tom smiled at her. "First of all, I think sharing with chopsticks is fairly hygienic. But more importantly than that, let me assure you I am not in the least bit afraid of your germs."

Maya felt her face color as blood rushed to her cheeks. "That's good to know," she said.

"Aw shite, I swear I'm not trying to embarrass you, love. That may have come out wrong. I'm not saying I want to make out with your toothbrush or anything like that. I just...well, I'm not a germaphobe, and even if I were, I'd make an exception for you. It's hard to be attracted to someone and repelled by their germs at the same time."

"I'm sure it's hard, but not impossible," suggested Maya. "In fact, it's probably a major obstacle for germaphobes who are trying to start new relationships. We mustn't belittle their plight."

She continued to tease Tom, anything to distract from the fact that he had just come right out and said that he was attracted to her. Who *did* that anyway, just spelled out their feelings for all the world to see? As far as Maya understood from all the movies and TV shows she'd consumed in her lifetime, as well as the friends who had always loved to vent their dating woes to her, game playing was a major component of most modern relationships. In fact, she was pretty sure someone behaving like Tom was right now was practically unheard of. Men these days were much more likely to act like they didn't even like the women they were interested in, a practice called "negging" that had made Maya want to roll her eyes until she could see her brain inside her skull. What was wrong with the world that revealing your feelings for someone was a sign of weakness, while treating them like they were scum was supposed to be the way to get them to pay attention to you?

"Have you heard from Declan since this morning?" Maya asked. She held out her takeout container to Tom, and he reached in with his chopsticks to scoop up some noodles before holding his own container out to her.

Between bites, he responded. "Just a text or two. It seems he's staying with Catherine, which can't possibly be a good idea. But at least the two of them are safe and sound there, not out on the road or causing any trouble."

"I hope it stays that way," said Maya. "Drunk driving...it's, well, it's probably the thing I hate the most in the world. It's so dangerous, so selfish, and so easily avoided. Take a cab, for Pete's sake. Or just stay home. But when people get on the road, putting their own lives on the line and the lives of everyone else who's on the road with them...it's unforgiveable. It's so stupid, and...yeah. It's unforgiveable."

Tom's facial expression tightened to the point of being unreadable. "It's definitely stupid, and it's definitely selfish. It sounds like you've got personal experience...? I've never heard someone speak quite that strongly about drink driving."

"Yeah, I do. But before things get really heavy, I just have to ask...do you really call it 'drink driving' in Ireland?"

Tom's chuckle was stilted at best. "We do, I'm afraid. I realize a lot of our expressions are considered cute and quaint here, but it's still a very serious thing."

"Absolutely." Whatever trace of humor had been in Maya's voice and expression was gone now. "To answer your question, my vehement opposition to drunk driving comes from the fact that a drunk driver killed my best friend when I was in high school." She poked at her takeout container, her appetite gone. "I've never gotten over it, not really, and every time I hear about someone doing something like that, it brings back all the anger I felt then and still have access to now." She blew out a sigh. "I mean...accidents happen. We all know that when we get behind the wheel of the car. But adding alcohol into the mix just makes everything so much more dangerous. The driver who killed her, he wasn't even injured. I'm not saying I wish he had been hurt or died or anything like that. It's just...it's *so* unfair..."

Tom reached across the table to take Maya's hand. His eyes were soft and sad. "I'm so sorry, Maya. That's just terrible. It must have been awful losing your friend, and I understand your anger. That driver did something really foolish and selfish, and he probably didn't think twice about his decision. And because of that, you lost your friend. You had your whole world rocked, and it'll never be the same. What was your friend's name?"

"Nina." Maya sniffed, batting a hand across her face to wipe away a stray tear before it made its presence known. "We'd been friends since we were little girls. We were in-separable...except for that day. She had an errand to run, and she didn't even invite me to join her. I've thought about that the most over the years. Every time one of us had to go somewhere after school, we almost always went together. Or at least we invited each other. I'd picked up prescriptions with her at the pharmacy, and she had come with me to the pet store to buy cat food. But that one time...I'll never know why, but she didn't invite me to join her. I don't think it even struck me as being strange at the time...I don't know, maybe it did. It definitely seems strange to me now, and I can't remember how I really felt then. Every time I look back, it's colored by the way I perceive it now, you know?"

"I know what you mean," said Tom. "After something becomes significant to us, every memory we look back on makes it seem like it was obviously significant then, too. But we can't possibly know what we really felt, what we really experienced before we knew that thing had significance. Memory is strange like that...it works backwards and forwards, coloring everything it touches."

"That it does." Maya was quiet, thoughtful, as she remembered her friend and remembered losing her. It was always like this, thinking about Nina. The good times they shared were there, in her memories, but they were hard to access underneath all the sad memories created by her untimely death.

"Do you wish she had invited you to come along with her that day?" Tom asked gently.

Maya shook her head as she sniffled. "No...I don't think so. I'm grateful to be alive, and I know it would have been so much worse for my family, for my community, if both of us had been in the car that day. But I think I feel bad that she's gone and I'm not sometimes. I feel guilty. We should both be alive, you know? Or maybe...maybe if I had gone with her that day, things would have been different. I could have warned her that the other car didn't seem like it was going to stop. Or maybe just because she had to drive to my house to pick me up, she'd be on the road fifteen minutes later and she wouldn't have even been in the same place as that car at the same time."

"That's a lot of maybes." Tom stroked the back of Maya's hand with his thumb. "And they can eat you alive if you let them. Playing around with hypotheticals is a very effective way to torture yourself."

"I know," Maya agreed. "I know I can't change anything, and it's pointless to wonder what could have been different. Because it isn't. The crash happened, and she's gone. And I'm still here. And maybe it's my job now to figure out *why* I'm still here. If that's even how this works." She lifted her gaze to meet his. "Do you think it is? Like, I have some kind of mission and I have to uncover what it is?"

Tom shook his head and looked down. "You don't have to earn your value as a living human being, Maya. You're here and Nina isn't, and no one....no one on this earthly plane, anyway...can tell you why that is. If you want to have a mission in life, you can look for one. But if you just want to live a good life, enjoy yourself, and take the opportunities that come your way, there's nothing wrong with that either."

Maya let herself give him a small smile. "Thanks, Tom. I get so wrapped up in this sometimes, in philosophizing about the meaning of it all. Thanks for the reminder. I'm here, and I may as well enjoy being here rather than spending all my time wondering why I still exist."

"It's easier said than done, though, isn't it?" Tom asked. "Don't be too hard on yourself. Just take it one day at a time."

"One day at a time." Maya nodded. "I think that's how they talk about, like, staying sober in a 12-step program, isn't it? Don't think of it like something you have to do forever...just do it today. Maybe that's a good way to look at my apparent addiction to overanalyzing and feeling guilty."

"Maybe it's not a bad approach to life in general," agreed Tom. "Every day is a new start, but we forget that sometimes. We get so caught up in the yesterdays and tomorrows that we overlook today."

They finished eating in comfortable silence, then walked back to the office slowly. They kept the conversation light, in an unspoken agreement that the intensity of their lunchtime discussion needed to be tempered with something easy. Maya teased Tom for his taste in eighties action-adventure movies, and Tom warned her against becoming addicted to houseplants after she revealed she'd brought another snake plant *and* a pothos back from her parents' house.

As they made the final approach to Andersen Consulting, the air around them changed. There was a frantic energy about the building, with people running back and forth from the door around the side of the building to the street. Maya saw Chris on the phone, pacing in front of the building and shouting into the phone.

Maya rushed to Chris's side in time to hear him say, "Yes, send an ambulance right now! There's been a car accident just in front of Andersen Consulting. Two people are injured. We need an ambulance!"

Maya blanched, feeling as if the sidewalk had dropped out from underneath her. As she turned to Tom with a question in her eyes, he bolted past her and around the side of the building towards the gathered crowd. "Wha—?" she began.

Over his shoulder, he called back to her. "It's Declan. I just know it."

Fourteen

Maya was in shock. She was frozen in her spot on the sidewalk, unable to turn towards the building and enter and unable to follow Tom to the accident. She couldn't go back to her desk, not when she didn't even know what had happened to Declan. And Catherine. Catherine must be with him. If it was even them in the car…Tom's gut feeling wasn't the absolute truth, was it?

But she couldn't bring herself to walk towards the crash site either. She didn't know what she would see there, and she was terrified at the thought. Would there be stomach-turning injuries…or…worse? That old expression about not being able to look away from a car accident didn't make any sense to Maya right now. She didn't want to see what had happened, and she wished she didn't even know about it. She wished she was back home in her bed, snuggled deep under the blanket where the outside world couldn't reach her. Where there were no cars, no streets, nothing that could go wrong. Just an isolated, safe cocoon. She wished more than anything she was in her cocoon.

Something jolted Maya from her waking nightmare, and her eyes refocused on the scene in front of her. Her feet started carrying her towards the gathered crowd, deciding for her that it was better to be involved and help if possible than retreat. Her mental state didn't matter as much right now as the health and safety of the people involved in the car crash.

As she pushed through the crowd, she saw Tom. He was crouched next to the open driver side door, where Declan was sprawled, his eyes half closed. Tom was speaking softly to Declan—Maya couldn't hear what he was saying, but his tone and his expression were reassuring. Declan was awake, at least. Tom was noticeably not touching him, which Maya assumed he was doing in case Dec had a spinal injury. Better to leave him where he was until the paramedics could safely move him.

It was only then that Maya noticed the front of the car. Not only was the car on the wrong side of the street, but the front of it was wrapped around a sturdy streetlight. The hood was severely indented from the post of the light, and Maya wondered how fast Declan had been driving to make that happen. As far as she could tell, despite the crowd around the scene, there were no other cars involved. There were vehicles stopped, the ones that had slammed on their brakes to avoid being involved in the accident, but from the looks of it, they had all been successful. That was a miracle, in Maya's eyes—in a split second, things could have been very different for the other drivers who were standing around their cars now, peering in the direction of Declan's car.

After reassuring herself that no one else had been hurt, Maya turned backto Tom and Declan. Looking at the car head on, it dawned on her that Dec had not been alone. There was someone sitting in the passenger's seat, though Maya couldn't see the person's face. The airbag had deployed, and it was still obscuring her view. She walked around to the passenger side window, and was simultaneously shocked and not surprised at all to see Catherine Andersen sitting there, eyes closed. For a terrifying moment, Maya worried she was unconscious or worse, but she heard a feminine groan at the same time she saw a slight stirring from the passenger seat.

Catherine's eyes opened, and they slowly focused on Maya. Maya watched them shift from confusion to horror and alarm as she took in her surroundings—the airbag, the streetlight, the crowd around them, Declan in the driver's seat, and, finally...Maya. Maya approached the car, hesitating in front of the door. She didn't know if she should try to open the door or wait for paramedics to arrive. She was terrified that anything she did might somehow make the scene worse than it already was. Her eyes were locked on Catherine's, though, and they seemed to be pulling her closer even if she wanted to resist.

Once she was next to the door, she looked at Catherine with a question in her eyes. *Are you okay?* Catherine gave the slightest nod, and Maya tried to open the door. The impact had pushed the door in somewhat, making it impossible to open without wrenching on it. Maya pulled harder, afraid the movement might hurt Catherine or trigger another airbag on the side.

Finally, the door gave way and opened with a creak of the hinges. Catherine made as if to lean forward, pulling against her seatbelt, and Maya lifted a hand to gesture to her to stop. "Don't move, Catherine. You've got to wait for the paramedics to get here. You don't know how badly you're injured, and you don't want to make it worse."

Catherine sat back and gulped, her eyes turning glassy. "Will you stay here with me, Maya? Will you stay here and talk to me? I don't know what happened. I...I think I fell asleep, and when I woke up, you were standing there. What happened? Is Dec okay? Is anyone else hurt?"

Maya crouched down near Catherine, positioning herself at eye level. "I'll stay here with you, Catherine. You're going to be alright, okay? I don't know what happened, but it looks like Declan lost control or something. He crossed to the other side of the street and hit that post. I think he's okay...Tom is with him, talking to him now. And it doesn't look like anyone else was hurt, thank God."

"Thank God." Catherine seemed to shrink into her chair as she sighed. "I can't believe this. It's just... it's so terrible. I don't know what I was thinking, even getting in the car with him. I know better than this. I'm so ashamed. I'm so grateful that we're alive, that we're okay, but I'm so so ashamed. If this was a wake-up call, then message received." Her eyes closed as her lips formed a tight line.

"Catherine, I have to ask. Was Declan drinking? Had he had more to drink since we saw you this morning?"

Catherine gave a tiny, almost imperceptible nod. Maya fell back on her heels. Following her conversation with Tom mere minutes ago, this was all too real, all happening too fast for her to comprehend. Even in her confusion, she felt her rage bubbling up, and it came out before she could stop it.

"What the hell were you thinking?" she demanded. "Catherine, he could have killed someone. I don't even care that the two of you could have been killed...your terrible choices could have *killed* an innocent person. A child walking down the sidewalk. A minivan full of a family on their way to the aquarium. An elderly man carrying home groceries for his sick partner. Seriously! What the *hell* were you thinking?"

"You have every right to be mad at me," Catherine said, shock all over her features. "It was stupid. It was irresponsible. I made a huge, huge mistake."

Maya stopped herself from saying anything further, as she got to her feet, numb. She felt the blood rushing to her head, the light-headedness that came before fainting, just as the sound of the ambulance arriving coincided with the feeling of two strong arms coming around her body.

Tom held her as the paramedics attended to Catherine and Declan. As sobs began to wrack through Maya's body, he pulled her head into his chest, encircling her in the safety of his arms and rubbing his right hand slowly up and down her back. He slowly and gently guided her to take a seat on the curb, continuing to soothe her with his soft, reassuring touch on her back.

"It's okay. It's okay." He repeated that phrase softly while they watched the paramedics take Declan and Catherine out of the car on stretchers towards the back of the ambulance. They were both checked over on site, and when it was determined that they were both fine—physically, at least—they were released.

In the time it took for that to happen, Tom was by Maya's side, patient and comforting. By the time Catherine and Declan were released, Maya had found the ability to speak again, and she was raging. "How could they be so stupid? Don't they know what was at stake? I...I don't know if I can even look at her the same after this..."

"I'm sure that's true, Maya," said Tom. "But right now might not be the time to march over there and give her your two weeks' notice. You see it, don't you? The processing that she's already doing, the remorse she's already feeling. This might be just the catalyst she needs to get my brother out of her system and come back to herself."

"Catalyst?" demanded Maya. "Is that what this is? Just a divinely appointed happening intended to wake her up? People could have died!"

"I won't argue with you about that," said Tom. "The fact that they didn't...well, that feels like divine providence to me, whatever that means, though I imagine to you it feels like dumb luck. Maybe those are the same thing...I'm not a philosopher or theologian. But I'd suggest we let Catherine think and feel what she needs to think and feel today. Let's be there for her, see where she gets on her own. You're welcome to give her your letter of resignation tomorrow. Plus, I'm pretty sure if you gave it to her today, it'd be lost in the haze of shock-induced memory loss. She's not exactly going to be coming in to the office for the rest of the work day today, is she?"

"You make a fair point," said Maya. "And I don't want to make this all about me. You're right. I should be there for her, however I can be." She shook her head. "But this...this changes things. It has to. I have to work for someone I can respect. Someone with some integrity and honor."

"I don't doubt for a minute that you will," Tom said. "You can do whatever you want, Maya. And maybe now's not really the time, but I hold to what I told you before. If you want to work for someone you respect, someone with integrity and honor, well...then what's wrong with working for yourself?"

"Yeah, definitely not the time for it." Maya said. "I mean, I appreciate the compliment, but I can't think about that right now. Nothing personal, no offense."

"None taken. Shall we get these two home now?" Tom gestured to Declan and Catherine, who were making their way over to them on the curb, looking tired, bruised, and about two inches tall. The ambulance had left, along with the tow truck that took Declan's car away. "I'll take Dec to a hotel, and you can escort Cath home. I think some time apart to think about what they've done would do them both some good."

"I totally agree," said Maya. While Tom put a hand on the back of Declan's neck and guided him towards the garage where his own car was parked, Maya put her arm around Catherine and walked her to the office building.

"Is your car here, Catherine? I can drive you home."

Catherine's eyes filled with tears. "Would you do that for me, please? Thank you, Maya. So much. For...for all of it. I'm so embarrassed, and you're being so kind. I don't deserve it. I'd like to go home, take some time to wrap my head around what happened today, but I don't trust myself to get myself there. Could you drive me? Please?"

"Of course. Your keys, please?" Maya followed Catherine to the parking structure behind the office building where her car was parked in the position of honor designated for the CEO. She had Catherine input her address into her phone's GPS, then put the car in gear and drove the two of them to Catherine's condo in silence.

•❤•❤•❤•❤•❤•

"We're here," Maya announced as she pulled up in front of Catherine's lakeview building. It had valet parking, naturally, so she was prepared to drop Catherine off, leave the car in the capable hands of the valet, and then take a bus back to the office. Catherine, however, had other plans.

"Will you come upstairs with me, please? I think I need to talk to someone." There was a vulnerability in her eyes Maya had never seen before. She was seeing through the armor Catherine wore every day, the battle gear that made her someone to be feared and respected, not someone who would share their feelings or even dream of shedding a tear.

"Yeah, I'll come up." Maya said, picking up her purse from the backseat and exiting the car with Catherine.

They rode up the elevator in silence, Catherine fidgeting with the keys in her hand while Maya said a silent prayer to whoever was listening that she'd be able to help Catherine. That she'd be able to be whoever Catherine needed her to be right now, rather than lecturing her once again about how stupid what she had done today was.

As she entered Catherine's condo, Maya was stunned by the view of the lake through the floor to ceiling windows that greeted them. This condo must have cost a fortune, and for that view alone, Maya understood why it was worth it. She stared in awe at Lake Michigan, grounding herself in the comfort of its gray-blue water as she followed Catherine to the living space that faced it. In answer to Catherine's gesture, she sat down next to her on the couch and waited for Catherine to speak.

Catherine was looking at her phone intently, as she had been throughout the ride home. She set it down on the couch in between them, looking up to make confident eye contact with Maya.

"I think I need to go to an AA meeting," she announced. "Tomorrow. Will you come with me?"

Maya blinked, unsure if she had heard Catherine correctly. "Really? Why? I mean...why me?"

"I have a problem. I would never have admitted it to myself before the last week. It didn't seem like a problem then, not really. I'd just have a glass of wine to unwind in the evening, and who doesn't do that? But then, reconnecting with Declan, it's like it flipped a switch. A switch I should have left unflipped. The drinking has been constant. Like I'm trying to keep up with him. Or prove that I'm as much fun as I used to be. Or... I don't know, numb myself to the fact that he's not who I once dreamed he was."

Maya was silent. She nodded to show Catherine she understood what she was talking about, but she stayed quiet, encouraging her to continue to speak her piece.

"Today was rock bottom. I don't want to go any lower than I did today. I made some really reckless decisions today, and I put everything I've built in my career on the line, too, showing up to work drunk like that. But I don't even care about that. This isn't about my business. This is about the fact that I could have died in that car or I could have been there, passed out drunk in that car while Declan killed someone else. And I would have never forgiven myself if that happened. I just keep playing it over and over again in my mind, how terribly it all could have gone today. I can't believe..." she trailed off.

It was time for Maya to speak up. She reached over and took Catherine's hand in her own. "You're so brave, Catherine. What you're saying...I didn't expect this. I was worried about you today, and then when I saw you in that car...I just...I got so angry. So angry at you for all that you almost threw away, all the risks that you took. Honestly, I was ready to walk away. I didn't even recognize you any more. I drove you home, ready to leave you here and hope that some day you'd have a revelation like this. But here you are, ninety minutes after the fact, having the breakthrough and revelation I could only have imagined for you. I'm so in awe of you right now. Your strength, your vulnerability to share this with me...just....thank you. Thank you."

It felt like healing, sharing this moment together. All the anger and rage that Maya had been carrying around for the driver who killed Nina had almost transferred itself to Catherine today. It had come damn close to severing any connection between them beyond repair. And yet now, in this moment of sharing such raw pain and honest truth, Maya felt herself cracking open, the ice wall that had erected itself the moment she saw the accident thawing in a gush of chilly water.

"You'll come with me then?" Catherine's voice was timid as she looked up at Maya. She had been staring at her hands in her lap once she started speaking and as she listened to Maya. Now, she was a scared little girl, asking another young child at school if they wanted to be her friend.

Maya squeezed her hand in both of hers. "I will. Of course. If it means something to you to have me there, then I wouldn't be anywhere else. Anything I can do to support you, I will. I hope you know I really mean that."

"I do. You've already done so much. I... I just left you. I left the whole company in your hands, and I disappeared. Declan's always had that effect on me. When he's on my radar, no one else exists, no other responsibilities matter. I just get so focused on him, on staying near him and staying shiny enough to keep his attention..." Her voice trailed off again as her eyes filled with tears.

"You shouldn't have to make yourself shiny and twinkly and entertaining just to keep the attention of someone. Not if that person really loves you," Maya told her. "If you have to dance and twirl and drink until you're sick to make him want to be with you, it's not love. It's something else."

"I know." Catherine sounded small when she spoke. "I think the best thing my younger self did for me was run away from him all those years ago. And then the worst thing my older, supposedly wiser self ever did was run right back to him. And why?"

"I was wondering that, too. Why *did* you reconnect with Declan after all this time?"

"I don't really know," Catherine shook her head. "Seeing Tom again...he's always been such a good friend to me, such a pillar of strength and integrity. But seeing him in person, not just chatting with him in an email, made a connection, I guess. Because in the past, it was never just me and Tom, it was always me and Tom and Declan. So being with Tom and that starting to feel so natural again…. it just felt like someone was missing, I guess. And I had to go and find him." Catherine hung her head. She looked small to Maya, smaller than she'd ever known it was possible for Catherine Andersen to look.

"I think that makes sense, Catherine. I don't know much about love, but I don't think there's anything wrong with you that you wanted to be with him. It sounds like you really care about him, like this wasn't just about him being fun to be around. And I'm sure it really hurts to realize that he's not exactly the man you dreamed he'd be."

Catherine shook her head, and her already sad expression dropped even lower. Her voice was quiet when she spoke again. "No, he isn't. And I need to straighten out my life for me. It's time to stop hoping that he'll change. That he'll be who I want him to be. We aren't good for each other now, and we probably never could be. I hope he gets the help he needs, but…I have to worry about me now. I can't save him, anyway."

It was profound to watch the transformation unfold in Catherine. In the span of a few hours, she had not only sobered up but begun to reevaluate her life and relationships at a deeper level than Maya would have even hoped for her.

"I know I don't really have a right to be, but… I'm really proud of you, Catherine. Can I give you a hug?"

Catherine choked back a sob. "Please," she said, as Maya scooted to her side and wrapped her in her arms. After that, there was no holding back the tears, and they flowed freely, soaking the shoulder of Maya's shirt.

When Catherine came up for air and wiped her eyes, she looked lighter. Clearer. Her eyes were bright, even if they were surrounded by puffy red, tear-soaked skin.

"When is this meeting we're going to?" Maya asked.

"It's tomorrow morning at eight o'clock," Catherine answered. "I found an early one, so I could go before work and then have the rest of the day to start making things right in the office again. I know it's early, but..."

"I'll be there," Maya reassured her. "I wouldn't miss it for anything."

Fifteen

T he next morning, just a few minutes before eight o'clock, Maya was waiting outside the church where the support group meeting was scheduled to take place. Catherine approached her, walking down the sidewalk with her hands in her pockets and a hunch to her shoulders that was unfamiliar.

Maya stepped towards her. "Catherine? How are you feeling today?" she asked, smiling at her boss.

Catherine smiled back. "Better in some ways, worse in others. I feel great physically—it's nice to be clear again after spending the last week fuzzy and/or hungover. But I think the shame-over is going to last a bit longer. I'm sorry for yesterday, and I'm sorry for dragging you here..."

"You're really going to have to stop apologizing for that," Maya made a concerted effort to keep her tone light even as her words were commanding. "I wouldn't be here if I didn't want to be. I want to support you, Catherine. This isn't going to be an easy journey for you, but I'd like to be there for you the whole way."

Catherine took Maya's hand. "Thank you, again," she said. "Shall we go in?"

They made their way into the meeting room in the basement of the church. Inside, there was a circle of chairs arranged, along with some tables by the back wall that held carafes of coffee and a couple of boxes of baked goods. A small group of people were milling around the room, a few of them already sitting in the chairs.

Maya followed Catherine's lead, and the two of them claimed two seats next to each other, facing the door. There was something comforting about sitting where you could watch the door, where no one could sneak up behind you, and Maya immediately felt more comfortable in this unfamiliar setting.

She turned to face Catherine. "Can I get you anything? Coffee?"

Catherine smiled kindly at her. "You've done enough already. Really."

"It's just coffee," said Maya. "I'm going to see if they have any hot water and tea bags. I'll get you a cup. Cream? Sugar?"

"Black is just fine. Thank you."

Maya headed over to the table, picking up two cardboard cups and filling them with her and Catherine's respective beverage choices. Before heading back to their seats, she peeked into the pastry selection. There were the standard blueberry muffins and yeast donuts, easy for her to say no to...but then her eyes landed on a small selection of cake donuts and her stomach rumbled, revealing its wishes. She rearranged the cups, so that one hand held Catherine's coffee and the other held her tea cup between her thumb and forefinger while her remaining fingers curled around the donut, pressing it tightly to the side of her cup.

Maya walked back to her chair, focusing intently on the cups in her hands—the last thing she needed to do was to make a terrible first impression at this meeting by pouring scalding hot beverages all over someone's knees. Because of her intense focus on the cups in her hands, she didn't notice the man who walked through the door, a man whose presence would normally attract her attention like it was magnetized to him.

She didn't notice him, in fact, until Catherine looked up, her eyes widened, and she whispered his name softly. "Tom."

Maya started then, thrusting Catherine's cup towards her as her eyes jerked towards the door. And there he was, standing frozen, staring back at her. She hadn't imagined him. Tom was here. But why?

Maya watched as Catherine stood and walked over to greet Tom with a hug. And then it all made sense. Of course, he was here to support Catherine. Of course, he felt bad about the negative influence his brother had on her, and he had come to make it right, in his own way. Of course Catherine had asked him to be here, just like she had asked Maya the same thing.

Tom gave Maya a small wave as he followed Catherine back to the chairs and seated himself on her other side. Maya was still frozen in place, donut and tea clasped in her left hand like a claw, something she only became aware of when Tom nodded towards them. "Looks like they have good taste in donuts here, eh?"

Maya startled as she looked down at her hand. "Oh, right. Yes." She smiled at Tom. "Sorry, I just didn't know you were coming this morning. I was surprised to see you. That's all. How are you?"

"I'm well, Maya. How are you? Did you come here to support our brave Lady Catherine?" He reached his arm across the back of Catherine's chair, smiling at her with the affection of a brother.

Maya sat down, shifting the contents of her hand, so that her cup was in her right and the donut remained in her left. "Of course." She smiled at Catherine. "Anything for Catherine."

The three of them sat together, the two women sipping their drinks. Catherine was staring at the floor in the middle of the circle, and Maya was sneaking glances at Tom over her head. She wanted to ask him what had happened with Declan yesterday—the two of them hadn't spoken or even texted. She'd been so busy with Catherine, work, and catching Andie and Luisa up on all the happenings of the last few days that she hadn't even noticed Tom hadn't been in touch until she was already in bed. But now wasn't the time to bring up Declan, not when Catherine was making such a valiant effort to get him out of her system. Maya resigned herself to being patient. Anything she had to say to Tom could wait until after the meeting was over.

The circle had gradually filled with the other people in the room, and a woman sitting across from Maya cleared her throat. "We're going to get started now, if that's alright with everyone." After nods and murmured agreement, the people in the room proceeded to read inspirational texts, taking turns and sharing their own stories in a display of vulnerability that left Maya humbled. As far as she could tell, no one was leading the meeting—they all seemed to be sharing in the responsibility, taking ownership of what was happening in this room in a beautiful display of co-operation and compassion.

When there was a lull in sharing, the silence was comfortable, stretching until the next person to speak felt the courage to do so. Catherine was fidgeting in her seat, and her face was creased with discomfort. Maya looked in her direction with compassion, meeting Tom's eyes when she did so. Something flashed across his face—he looked apologetic, almost—and then he cleared his throat and spoke to the circle.

"My name is Tom, and I'm an alcoholic."

As the rest of the circle murmured their greetings to Tom, Maya blinked rapidly, working to keep her expression open and neutral. Tom had never mentioned a problem with alcohol, not that he had been obligated to. But they had spoken about alcohol, and she had told him about losing Nina to a drunk driver. It seemed...odd...that he hadn't shared that with her. She shook her head once, clearing the thoughts that were scurrying across her mind like rodents, so that she could listen to what Tom was saying.

"It's been nine years since my last drink. I made some terrible choices when I was drinking, almost lost a lot of the relationships that matter most to me. But I'm proud of my sobriety—it's the most important thing I have. I get tempted, sure...don't we all? 'What's one drink? Surely I can just have one pint and then stop.' I don't want to take that risk, though. I just don't believe it's possible for me to be a casual drinker. That's why I'm here. It's hard, sure. We all know that. But when I think about what my life has become without alcohol in it....I wouldn't trade it for the world."

The circle thanked him for sharing, and Tom smiled humbly at the rest of them. His eyes darted to Maya's, then quickly away, and she found herself worrying what he had seen there. Had it been judgement? Disappointment? Disgust? Who could know what her face was conveying to him right now? It was a mystery even to her. She needed to talk to him about this, but...not now. Maybe not today at all. Catherine was her priority.

Speaking of which, Catherine was leaning forward in her chair, clearly on the verge of doing her own sharing. Maya reached over and squeezed her hand. "You can do it," she whispered.

Buoyed with courage, Catherine spoke up. "My name is Catherine, and I'm an alcoholic."

"Hi, Catherine," a chorus of voices responded.

"This is my first day of sobriety, and this is my first meeting. Yesterday...I hit rock bottom yesterday. I hadn't realized I'd had a problem until I woke up in the passenger seat of my ex-fiance's car after he crashed it into a streetlight downtown. Since getting back together with him, I've just made one dumb choice after the other. I guess seeking him out in the first place was the start of the dumb choices. We broke up almost a decade ago, because of his drinking problem and my fear of descending into codependency right alongside him. But I started to miss him. I wondered if things could be different...so I went looking for him. And I found him, of course. The universe never makes it hard to find the people and things we probably shouldn't be finding. It was a week of drinking and fun. Of course there were hard times in there too, as I look back at it now through the lens of sobriety. Some mornings we started the day with a drink just because the night before had ended so badly. There was no physical violence, but the shouting. The name-calling. It was just as bad as when I left him nine years ago. It was like nothing had ever changed. It's not his fault. It's my fault that I went after him again in the first place. I'm so grateful that no one got hurt yesterday, and I'm ready. I'm ready to change. I'm ready to be the version of myself that doesn't depend on alcohol to have fun or to numb the things I don't want to look at." By the end of her last sentence, Catherine looked lighter than she had when she had first begun speaking.

"Thank you for sharing, Catherine," one of the women in the circle said. "We're here for you."

Others nodded in agreement. Another woman spoke up, "Do you have a sponsor?"

Catherine looked at Tom, and he nodded in encouragement. "I think I could use one. Tom—" She gestured towards him. "—has been a great support to me, but I think he's too close to the situation. It's hard on both of us."

"Understood," the second woman said. "Let's talk after the meeting is over, and we'll help you get connected with someone who's just right for you."

"Thank you." Catherine smiled with relief and leaned back in her chair. Maya reached over again and squeezed her shoulder.

♥ · ♥ · ♥ · ♥ · ♥

When the meeting finished, Catherine excused herself to go talk with the women who had volunteered to help connect her with a sponsor. Maya remained in her seat, looking up when Tom moved from his seat to Catherine's vacant one.

"Hi," he said. "I didn't expect to see you here today." When had things felt this awkward between them? In a flash, Maya remembered their first meeting and the misunderstanding about the whiskey bottle, which made a lot more sense now.

She smiled at Tom. "I could say the same to you. I had no idea, Tom. I...I'm glad to know you a little better now. I'm just confused, I guess. I wish I'd known, but I totally get that I don't have any right to expect that of you."

"It's not that," said Tom. "I wasn't trying to hide it from you. I'm very proud of my sobriety, and I'm happy to share it. I didn't bring it up when our relationship was strictly professional, and when things started to develop between us personally, it just never seemed like the time. You don't drink yourself, so it's not like I was having to turn down glasses of wine or make excuses for not wanting to have a beer after work."

"That's true." She nodded. "It just seems like, if it's important to you, you'd share it with me. That's not fair though, and I'm sure you would have shared it, eventually. This isn't exactly the ideal venue for learning a big secret about someone you've got a crush on, you know? In a room full of strangers, learning it in real time along with the rest of them."

"So you've got a crush on me…is that it, then?" Tom's eyes twinkled.

"Something like that." She smiled back at him. "And by the way, I realize what you did here today. You sharing gave Catherine the courage to speak up. If not for you, she might have attended meetings for weeks, really leaning into the *anonymous* part of the support group. But because she shared today…look at her." She gestured with her head towards Catherine, who was accepting a slip of paper from a gray-haired woman with kind eyes. "She's going to get the help and support she needs."

"She is," Tom agreed. "I wrestled with speaking up today. I figured if I didn't say anything, you'd maybe think I was just here to support Catherine. I could fly under the radar. I certainly didn't intend to drop a bomb on you with the truth, and if I hadn't said anything in the meeting today, I still would have pulled you aside and shared the truth with you. But Catherine needed the encouragement, so I got over myself to give it to her."

"You're a good guy, Tom," she said. "You know that, right?"

He looked embarrassed. "I try to be…I try to make up for the years where I was a royal, drunk arse, at least. Some days are easier than others, that's for sure. The twelve steps of the program, my sponsor….they all help. When I'm having those days where I'm shame spiraling through the memories of everything I've ever done wrong, well…at least I know what to do next. One foot in front of the other, one day at a time."

Maya groaned. "Was it just yesterday I was telling you about the 12-step philosophy of taking things one day at a time? I talked about it like I knew what I was saying, and yet...this is the first time I've ever been anywhere near a meeting. It was beautiful...and humbling to see how they work. How everyone takes their turn sharing authentically, how it doesn't have a formal leader....I can't imagine this format working anywhere else—certainly not in the corporate world—but it's really inspiring."

"I'm glad you think so," said Tom. "It's definitely meant a lot to me. Can I ask you something, though?" Maya nodded. "Why is it you don't drink? If you're not one of us...if you don't have the slippery slope problem we addicts do, then what is it that made you step away? Is it about your friend? About Nina?"

Maya nodded again. "It is. I was so young when she died that I'd never really drank at that point. A stolen sip of wine at a family Christmas here and there, but I certainly never enjoyed it. When Nina died, I made the connection, I guess, that if alcohol wasn't part of our culture, things like that wouldn't happen. I know car crashes happen all over the world, and I'm not sure if there's a correlation between higher instances of crashes and higher consumption of alcohol, but I'd hazard a guess that there is. I never wanted to be a part of that. And even apart from getting behind the wheel of a car, I...I guess I just never really wanted to lose control. You hear these stories about the crazy things people do when they're drinking, or even about the things they say that they don't mean to...it just slips out. I just didn't want to have anything to do with that."

"That makes sense," Tom said. "In general, I'm not a huge proponent of trying to control every aspect of your life, you know. But of course, I make an exception for alcohol. Life is better off without it, frankly. When I miss having a beer to unwind or raising a champagne toast with friends in celebration, I'm reminded that there are substitutes. That I don't need it to mark an occasion as a special one or to help me relax."

"What do you do instead?" Maya asked. Her life didn't feel empty without alcohol, not by a long shot...but she could use all the pointers on how to unwind and celebrate unabashedly that she could get.

"This might sound stupid," Tom admitted, "But I usually just slow down and breathe. When I'm stressed and want to reach for a beer, I step back. I close my eyes, if I can do that without it being super weird, and I just breathe, slowly and deeply until I've gotten some perspective. And when I want to celebrate and have fun, I do pretty much the same thing. In that moment, though, I focus on what I'm grateful for. I let myself really feel how wonderful it is to have whatever that thing is in my life, and I just soak in it."

"That's really good." Maya nodded. "So often, when I get something I've really wanted, as soon as it's mine, I'm thinking about the next thing I want. The next goal to achieve. I don't even take two minutes to feel appreciative and happy to have gotten the thing I've been craving for so long."

Tom was shaking his head in agreement. "That's human nature, I'm afraid. I think it's evolutionary—if our ancestors got too comfortable with what they had, they'd probably have been eaten by a predator. The key to survival was to keep moving, keep striving. And we keep doing that today, even though there aren't any saber-tooth tigers out there around the next curve, waiting to pounce and eat us alive."

A soft chuckle escaped from Maya's lips. "You make a good point, my friend. You really do. Well, I'm going to take a moment today to be grateful for this...for Catherine's return, for her health, her friendship...for you, too. For your wisdom, for what I've learned from you...for the fact that you even give me the time of day."

Tom looked puzzled. "And why wouldn't I give you the time of day? Why is that something worth celebrating?"

"I wouldn't hold it against you if you admitted I'm more work than I'm worth, Tom." Maya shook her head. "It's not like this has been smooth sailing right out of the gate for you. Whether I'm trying to push whiskey on you or overthinking every little word you say to me, it's been...a journey so far."

Tom lifted her hand to his mouth and pressed a soft kiss across her knuckles. "And like any good journey," he murmured, "The thrill is not only in the destination. The journey itself is golden, and I wouldn't miss it for anything." He squeezed her hand tightly one more time before releasing it. "I suppose we should get to work, eh?" he asked, checking his watch.

Catherine was making her way back over to them, a spring in her step and a lightness in her eyes Maya hadn't seen since before Tom turned up at the office. "My people," she said, pulling them both towards her for a group hug. "Is this the best day ever, or is this the best day ever?

I'm so glad you joined me here, Maya. And Tom!" She stepped back and gazed up at him. "Thank you for inviting me and for encouraging me to come here. I wouldn't have been able to do it on my own. You are my actual hero, you know that?"

Tom shook his head. "I just made the invitation, Catherine. You saved yourself. Or, rather, you asking for help from the group, from whatever you believe in that's greater than you... it wasn't me. I'd love to claim credit and be the savior of women everywhere, but—" He cringed at his own words. "—that just doesn't sit right with me. Not at all."

Catherine linked her arms through both of theirs, and the three of them walked towards the door, squeezing through it in a comical attempt at not breaking the chain until Tom stepped aside and let the two women through. Outside, they blinked in the morning sun and then began the short walk from the church to the office, just a few blocks away.

Sixteen

"Ugh, it feels like it's been *forever* since we did this," groaned Luisa. She, Maya, and Andie were sharing a beach towel on the shore of Lake Michigan and an after-work beverage. It was too chilly for any of them to chance taking a dip in the water, but it was still beautiful, and between sips and conversation, they frequently found themselves slipping into the lull that comes when staring at a large body of water.

"It's definitely been an eventful few days," agreed Maya. "I'm sorry for not keeping the two of you as real-time updated as possible, but I think we're all caught up now?"

"Almost," said Andie. "You've dodged most of our eyebrow raises and questioning looks about Tom, so I guess I'm going to have to come right out and say it. What's going on with the two of you? It seemed like things were gearing up to be...well...*something* around Sunday evening, and then all of your time and energy got consumed by his brother and Catherine. Have you two talked about what's going on between you? Or even *if* something is going on?"

Maya sighed. "Honestly, no. We haven't talked. I mean, we *have* talked, quite a lot, of course. But it's all been about Catherine's recovery and Declan's relapse. If that's even the right word for it—I don't think you can really have a relapse unless you've stopped using in the first place."

Andie winced at Maya's words. "Be careful, love. It's not fair for those of us who don't battle with addiction to judge those who do. It's easy for you and I not to do drugs, you know? The temptation, heck, even the option, has never really been there for us. But for people who are wrestling with addiction every day—and even if they're losing that battle, there's still a war going on, trust me—it feels like the only peace they get. The only respite from the pain of life. I know it's just as hard for the ones who love them to watch them go through it, but...still. I'd caution against judgment."

Maya felt chastened by Andie's words. "You're right," she said. "I'd never really thought of it that way. Honestly, I think I've been feeling morally superior, even at that support group meeting, because I don't have a problem with alcohol. But, come on. It's not like that's a hard-won victory. I've never even touched the stuff, so it's not exactly a challenge to avoid it."

Luisa chimed in. "These are all excellent points, and I promise we will all do the required soul-searching regarding our own journeys with alcohol and blah blah blah." She gestured to the two of them to wrap it up. "Now, can we *please* talk about what's going on with you and Tom? I'm growing old here."

"I don't know if he has the time or the energy to even think about a relationship right now," admitted Maya.

"Or maybe relationship is too big of a word. But even a date...doesn't that feel like a luxury we can't have? He's trying to help his brother, and I want to be available for Catherine if she needs me, and it's just...I'm a lot of work, you know? He probably wants to avoid that whole situation."

Luisa scoffed. "That is utter crap, and you know it. No man who's as interested in you as Tom seems to be looks at a beautiful woman like you and thinks, 'eh...too much work. I think I'll just stay alone for ever.' What are you even talking about? The man has made it abundantly clear that he is into you."

Before Maya could respond, Andie interjected. "While I—surprise, surprise—don't agree with her delivery, I think Luisa is right. Are you using the situation with Declan and Catherine as an easy way out of exploring what's going on with you and Tom? Ask yourself, honestly...when this all happened, was there a little part of you that felt relieved, like you wouldn't have to be vulnerable or take a chance on intimacy?"

Now *that*, Maya had to think about. She remembered the day of the accident, the interruption from the peace and calm she had been enjoying with Tom. And then, seeing Catherine and rushing to her side...there was something to it. A feeling of being needed, of being too busy to think about herself—was that sacrificial love, or was it some kind of martyr nonsense? She asked Andie just that. "Is this normal? What's wrong with me?"

Andie shook her head. "It's not just you, Maya. I think it's a combination of human nature and, frankly, the patriarchy."

Maya laughed out loud. "Could you explain that, please?"

"Sure. I mean, it's human nature to avoid what's uncomfortable. So, your ego jumped at the chance to think about something else. To take the focus off the thing that was making you stretch and grow and put it on something that you already know how to do—care about someone who's safe to care about. A friend, a coworker...these are safe bets for you. It's the romantic relationship—or rather, the potential of one—that makes you want to run screaming in the other direction."

"That makes sense," Maya agreed. "But what about the patriarchy? I'm just dying to hear how you explain that one."

"I'm not ranting about the system or suggesting men are the enemy," Andie began. "It's more about the culture that we live in. That most of the world lives in, honestly. A culture that, more often than not, assigns caregiving tasks to women, rewards them for selfless behavior, and reviles them for selfish behavior. We celebrate mothers, not for who they are as people, but for what they give up for their children. For how well they take care of them. We celebrate fathers for the bare minimum tasks they do, the same things that we take for granted that mothers will do. So, in your training and programming as a member of a patriarchal culture, you saw someone who needed care, and you jumped at the chance to abandon yourself."

Maya blinked rapidly. "Information overload. I need to sit with that one for a minute to make sense of it."

In the silence, Luisa spoke up. "That's a really wild way of looking at it, Andie. I'll be honest, I'm rethinking some things right now, too, after hearing you say that. How often do we celebrate women for taking up space? I think it's the opposite, more often than not. When we see women speaking up or drawing attention to themselves for any reason at all, we judge them, criticize them, find fault with what they're doing. It's like we're the other crabs in the bucket, trying to pull them back down rather than letting them escape to freedom."

"I'm glad you used that metaphor," said Andie. "It's a really poignant illustration of exactly what's happening. We think we're trying to keep each other safe, but really, we don't want someone else to have what we think we can't have either. Not that that's what the crabs are doing. I honestly know nothing about crab psychology."

"Who does?" Maya laughed. "The metaphor doesn't have to be perfect. It just has to start the conversation. And it worked in this case."

"So," Luisa said, "What are you going to do with all of this? I mean, with Tom? Do you have an action plan?"

Maya smiled. "I know you probably won't approve of this, but I'm trying *not* to have too much of a plan, actually. I just know that I need to talk with him, and I need to be as honest as I can let myself be."

"That's amazing," said Andie, reaching over to stroke Maya's arm. "And it sounds like more than enough of a plan to me. Trust yourself, follow your guidance, and when the next step reveals itself, take it."

"I'll do my best," said Maya.

•❤•❤•❤•❤•❤•

Maya called Tom when she got home. Without letting herself think too much about what she was about to say, she picked up the phone while she was gathering ingredients for her dinner and she dialed.

He answered on the second ring. "Maya, love! How are you?" His deep voice was soothing, like liquid caramel pouring through the phone directly to her ears.

"Hi, Tom," she greeted him. "I'm doing well. I was just thinking of you and wanted to call and say hi. It's been a minute since we got to chat."

"We've seen quite a bit of each other lately, Maya," said Tom, making her laugh.

"That's definitely true. And I'm not complaining about it at all. But we haven't had a conversation without Catherine in the room or without talking about her and/or Declan the entire time, and it seemed like it was about time we fixed that."

"I totally agree. What are you doing right now?"

"Now?" Maya sputtered. She was already in her comfy after-work clothes, with tonight's dinner recipe queued up and ready to go, and there was no chance she was going anywhere again until tomorrow morning. "I...well, I just got home from seeing my friends, and now I'm getting ready to make dinner."

"I see," said Tom. "And what are you making?"

Maya relaxed a little. He was just making conversation; he wasn't suggesting that they meet up or anything like that. "I'm making pasta with..." She scrolled through the recipe to double check the ingredients. "...shrimp for protein. Veggies in there too, lots of garlic and olive oil. All the good stuff."

"That sounds absolutely delicious," said Tom.

"I thought so, too," Maya said. "What about you? Have you eaten yet?"

She heard the smile in Tom's voice before he even started speaking. "Well, you see...I was thinking that if I played my cards just right, that the beautiful lady I fancy might invite me over for pasta and shrimp."

Maya laughed out loud. "I see how it is. Well, you're in luck. This is probably the easiest dish to double, especially since I haven't even started chopping veggies or boiling pasta yet."

"I'll leave straight away," said Tom. "If that's alright with you, of course."

"It is. It'll be nice to have company."

"Especially if it's me, right?"

"...especially if it's you," she agreed.

"What can I bring? I'll stop at the corner market on my way to catch a cab."

"I think dinner's under control, actually," she said.

"Got it," Tom replied. "Dessert it is, then. See you in fifteen."

Fifteen minutes later on the dot, there was a knock on Maya's door. In the intervening minutes, she had traded her sweatpants for her comfiest, stretchiest jeans, thrown her hair in a ponytail, and thrown on lip gloss. Maya was pleased with herself for not making too big a deal of this visit—she didn't shower, put on a full face of makeup, or douse herself in perfume. But she still didn't want to leave on her grungiest sweats with the mysterious stain on the left knee.

"Coming!" she called, as she slid across the wood floor in her socks to open the door. When she did, there was Tom, holding up a large paper bag and grinning from ear to ear.

"Hello there!" he said, leaning in to give her a kiss on the cheek. He walked into her apartment, setting the paper bag on the counter. "I didn't know your dessert preference as well as I know your breakfast pastry preference, so I got—" He began pulling things out of the bag, setting them on the counter next to it. "—a little of everything. Cake, cookies, ice cream, and even an apple pie."

Maya threw her head back to laugh. "How many people did you think we were feeding tonight? This is way too much for the two of us?"

Tom shook his head, an exaggerated, sad smile on his face. "Maya Maya Maya...have you no faith in us?"

Maya rolled her eyes at him. "We'll try our best. That's about all I can promise to do."

"Fair enough." Tom nodded. "I certainly couldn't ask more than that."

While Maya finished cooking, they fell into step finishing up the preparations together. Tom set plates and utensils out on the small table in Maya's kitchen, and he filled both of their glasses with filtered water from a pitcher she kept on the counter. When he didn't know where to find something, she seemed to anticipate his needs or know what a raised eyebrow meant before he could even ask the question. It was nice—if strange—to share the responsibility with someone else, and in no time at all they were ready to dig in to their meal.

Tom took the pot from Maya when she offered it, serving a mound of penne, vegetables, and shrimp onto both of their plates before placing the pot on a trivet between them. Maya sprinkled fresh parmesan cheese on top of both of the mounds as they took their seats.

"This looks wonderful, Maya," said Tom. "And the smell! Delicious. I can't wait to try it. Where did you learn to cook?" He lifted his fork to his mouth, closing his eyes as he drew in a breath and then took a bite.

"Honestly, I'm more into cooking for practicality than to try to create something gourmet," admitted Maya, as she loaded her own fork up with all of her favorite flavors. "One-pot meals, and all that. Sometimes, though, it's nice to destress with a new recipe at the end of the day. Something about having directions to follow is very comforting to me. Like if I just follow every step exactly right, the end result will be exactly the same as the picture at the top of the webpage."

They both chewed in silence for a moment, contemplating her answer. Maya was wondering about what her need to control things in order to be stress free said about her, when Tom asked the question she hadn't been expecting.

"So what exactly was causing you stress today?" Off her look, he chuckled. "Come on, this recipe has 'Maya's favorite cooking show' written all over it. It's not that I don't doubt your creativity. I'm just pretty sure you stashed away a tablet with the recipe on it right before I walked in the door."

Maya had to laugh. "You got me. Admittedly, I don't cook shrimp all that often, and I was up for the challenge of something different today. Things have been...a lot lately, you know?"

Tom nodded as he finished chewing his mouthful of food. "With Declan and Catherine? Of course. It's never easy being the primary support person during a relapse. How are you holding up?"

"Pretty well, I think. This is unfamiliar territory for me, but I'm trying to pick up slack at work where I can and be there for Catherine if she needs me. It's a bit strange, being let into this part of her life, considering that a week ago I didn't even know where she lived. Now, I've been to her home, hugged her on her couch while she's crying...it's surreal. I don't want to cross lines I'm not supposed to cross, and it's just hard to know how to be her colleague—her employee, actually—and part of her support team."

"Absolutely." Tom nodded again. "For what it's worth, I think you're handling it all really well. But do you know what I've just realized? You and I are alone again for the first time in what feels like an age and what are we talking about? Catherine and Declan. It's like they're in the room with us, even if we don't want them to be."

"You read my mind," said Maya. "I was talking about just that with my friends today."

"Were you?" Tom's eyes twinkled. "You told your friends about me?"

"Of course! I tell them everything. Even if I don't want to, they get it out of me."

"You're lucky to have good friends," said Tom. "I hope to meet them one of these days, if you'd like me to."

"I'd love that!" Maya responded too quickly, though Tom's grin told her he didn't mind. "That's...sort of the thing, actually. Getting clearer on what it is we want from each other, I mean. It seemed like things were...well, progressing. In one direction or another. And then everything happened with Declan and Catherine and it's like we haven't had a minute to even check in with each other. I was wondering if you were even still interested or if it just wasn't a good time anymore..." she trailed off, staring at the table and refusing to meet his eyes. She hadn't intended to say all of that, but once she started talking, it just came out.

"Hey," Tom reached across the table, tapping his hand in front of her until she lifted her hand from her lap and put it in his open palm. "Maya, look at me. If I've done anything to make you think now isn't a good time, I am sincerely sorry for it. I...I've been focused solely on Declan. And Catherine, too. I felt responsible, because it was probably me coming here that made her want to reconnect with him in the first place. I got so focused on the two of them, and I think I thought things between the two of us would just stay the same until I had a minute to focus my attention on them again."

"That...makes sense," said Maya. "I'm sorry if I overreacted..."

"Not at all," said Tom. "It wasn't ideal, what I was doing anyway. You're a human, you're not a crossword puzzle."

A laugh croaked out of Maya before she could stop it. "What does that even mean?"

"I mean...well, you can put a crossword puzzle down if you don't have time to finish it and pick it up again later. But you can't really do the same thing with humans. If you set one aside, even for a short time, there's no guarantee that they'll still be where you left them when you come back to pick them up again."

Maya nodded. "That's...a pretty good way of looking at it. So. Did you set me down? Is that what happened?"

"It wasn't what I wanted to do, but I'm afraid I may have." His eyes were apologetic as his thumb stroked the back of her hand. "Will you accept my apology?" Maya smiled as she shook her head in the affirmative. "Good. And will you let me pick you back up again if I promise to be more careful this time?"

"I'd like that," Maya admitted. She smiled, then looked back down at the table when the intensity of Tom's eyes was too much to hold.

"Good," he said. "Now, where shall we begin?"

Maya looked at the nearly empty plates in front of them. "We've got two choices, the way I see it. We can sit here at this table and eat more pasta until we can't possibly move..."

"...or?" Tom asked, wiggling his eyebrows.

"Okay, it's not a super sexy second option, so don't get too excited. Remember, this gal is going to require some majorly slow moves." She pointed at herself with her thumb.

"I know it," Tom said, "And that's just fine with me. Now, what's the second option?"

"A movie and dessert on the couch?" She cringed as she asked it, bracing herself for Tom's disappointed reaction.

"Absolutely perfect," he said. "Why don't you go pick something out, and I'll clean up here?"

Maya tried to protest, but he ushered her out of the kitchen and refused to let her come back. Who was she to put up too much a fight if it meant not having to do dishes for once? She made her way to the couch and flipped on the television, scrolling through the new releases.

"How do you feel about chick flicks?" she called into the kitchen, teasing Tom.

Except that his response surprised her. "Just great. Why do you ask?" He walked over to the couch, drying the pot in his hands with a dish towel.

"I was kind of messing with you, actually," she admitted. "The last time I watched a movie with a guy my age I was living in a dorm, and anything other than an action-adventure flick always got two enthusiastic thumbs down."

Tom shook his head. "That's a boy talking. Men, at least in my experience, don't have to reaffirm their masculinity with every single choice they make. I can enjoy a rom com or even a 'gal on her own finding her way in the world' kind of movie without forgetting that I am, in fact, a manly, virile male."

"Ooh, 'virile!' Excellent word choice. And...uh...good to know, I guess," Maya said.

Tom winked. "It just may come in handy one of these days. If all goes well."

"Indeed," Maya agreed. "Now hurry up and get back here. I've got just the movie picked for us."

A few short minutes later, Tom returned with two plates, each filled with a small portion of every single dessert he had bought. Maya's eyes almost bugged out of her head as she looked at the plate he handed her, but she only thanked him and scooted aside to make room for him. The two of them sat, shoulder to shoulder, tucking into their dessert smorgasbord as they settled in for the duration of the evening.

"Thanks for being up for this," Maya said, just before she hit the 'play' button. "I know vegging out on the couch isn't probably what you had in mind."

"It's even better," Tom said, his eyes dropping to her mouth and then back up to her eyes. "There's no place else I'd rather be."

Seventeen

After a week of attending daily support group meet-ings, Catherine seemed to be feeling more herself again. She was consistently at work early, on top of every project the firm was handling, and Maya felt the stress of being in charge easing from her shoulders—almost. Even though it was no longer hers to carry, it was hard to put down the burden of responsibility that she had gotten used to in her tenure as the stand-in boss. She found herself checking in with Catherine far more often than she ever would have before, not only to talk about her own project, but also to double check that the firm's other clients were being taken care of.

"Knock knock, hi there," she called to Catherine as she poked her head into her boss's office. "Can I come in?"

"Please do," Catherine replied. Her words were clipped, and Maya resigned herself to keeping this meeting brief and to the point.

"I was just checking to make sure that the Koalify A/B test was on track to choose a winning campaign. I believe that's scheduled for today…" She stopped herself from leaning over Catherine's desk to check her agenda, but only barely.

"Maya, sit down. Please." Catherine said, gesturing to the chair across from her desk. "We need to talk, and not about Koalify."

"Would you like an update on the Conley Corp results so far?" Maya asked as she sat down. "I can run and get my laptop really quickly so I can give you the latest update..."

"No."

"What is it then?"

"I don't know how to say this, Maya. Not really. I'm incredibly grateful for all the support you've given me with my recent troubles—"

"Of course," Maya interjected.

Catherine continued. "—But, I think we need to talk about how this is going to work moving forward. I need to resume control of my company, and that means I need you to trust me to do it. I was running this business before you were ever even hired, Maya, and I can certainly do it again without your hovering."

"Oh." Maya looked down. "I—I'm sorry, I..."

"I don't mean to chastise you, Maya. Not at all. I appreciate your help so much, and I know stepping up to fill my shoes when I was gone must have been so stressful for you. But now I need you to refocus—your project with Conley Corp, well...that's all I need you to worry about right now. I can handle managing the company, I really can. And you deserve to go home at the end of the day and not take all the stress of this office with you. Can you try that? For me?"

It was all Maya could do to stop herself from hanging her head in her hands. "Of course. I understand," she told

Catherine. "I'm a little embarrassed, to be honest. I didn't realize I was doing that, and I can assure you I'll make a concerted effort to, er, back off a bit."

"It's an unusual and honestly a rather beautiful position I find myself in, Maya. You have to believe me." Catherine's tone was gentle. "Most of my cohorts are complaining about their employees not caring enough, and I might be the only one who's ever had to convince a member of my team that it's okay to care a little bit less."

Maya smiled weakly. "I see. Yes. That *is* rather unusual. Well, I think I'll go back to my desk and dive into my project. *Only* my project, I promise." She excused herself and left the room before Catherine could get in another word.

If she was only "allowed" to work on her project with Tom, then, by golly, she was going to do the absolute best job that could be done. Maya pulled out her phone and dialed Tom's number before she even got back to her desk.

"Maya! To what do I owe the pleasure?" Tom answered her call. "I don't have a meeting scheduled with you until tomorrow, so don't tell me you're bending the rules and making a personal call during business hours?" He gasped in exaggerated horror at the idea.

"As if I would do such a thing." Maya bit back a smile. "I just suddenly found myself with a rather large amount of free time during my work day. I don't suppose there's any chance you could use my help today? Or that you'd be interested in moving our meeting up?"

"I tell you what," Tom said. "I'd like to keep our one-on-one on the books for tomorrow..."

"Oh, okay," Maya said. "Never mind then..."

"...but, I'm just about to leave for a site tour of one of our production partners, and I'd love your company if you'd like to join," he finished.

Maya brightened up. "I'd love that! How interesting. Maybe I can capture some content today too—at least B-roll for one of the video ads..." She began picking up the things she'd need—a notebook, a portable charger for capturing footage on her phone's high quality camera—while mentally making a list of the shots she'd love to have when Tom cut into her thoughts.

"I won't tell you *not* to do that," he began. "But that wasn't my intention in inviting you. You're more than welcome just to come see how the sausage gets made, meet some members of the production chain, enjoy hanging out with me during work hours and getting paid to enjoy the pleasure of my company..."

Maya laughed. "I will do all of those things, Tom. And if I happen to capture some golden footage today too, then would that be so bad?"

"I suppose not," he agreed. "I'll pick you up on my way out of town. Be there in about twenty minutes."

"See you then!"

The factory that Tom was taking them to was in Gary, Indiana—not exactly Maya's favorite place on earth. They smelled the city before they could see it, and for just a moment Maya regretted not asking where they were going. But, when she turned to Tom to make just that joke, it died on her lips. This man...this handsome, patient, compassionate man was all hers today. And complaining about that, or wishing any part of it away, just didn't make sense.

Tom lifted his eyes from the road—this was the first time he had driven the two of them anywhere on his own without his trusty driver in sight—and glanced at Maya. "What? What's that look? What are you thinking?"

Maya smiled and looked out the passenger window. "Oh, nothing," she said. "I was just thinking of how nice it is to spend this time together....even if you didn't tell me we'd be spending it in Gary, Indiana, of all places."

"Hey now," said Tom. "Don't knock Gary, Indiana, *or* the hardworking people of Gary, Indiana. It might not be Disneyland, but I've found a great little factory here to produce the water filtration system. We're keeping jobs in America, and close enough that we won't spend a fortune on shipping, either. Plus, you and I are taking a road trip together." He glanced at her again, wiggling his eyebrows. "Could you have guessed that would happen today when you woke up this morning?"

"I certainly could not." Maya chuckled. "But, uh...watch the road, okay? I know I'm irresistible to look at, but it makes me a little nervous."

Tom adjusted his grip on the steering wheel, repositioning his hands at the ten and two position. "You've got it, ma'am. And sorry about that, I didn't mean to make you nervous."

"It's okay," said Maya. "It's just, you know..."

"Anxiety from how you lost Nina that never really leaves you?" She nodded in response. "That's perfectly normal, love. And it's not something I'd ever intentionally trigger. I should be more careful, I know. I got a little carried away in the fun of it all, but I won't do anything to make you uncomfortable."

"It's really okay," Maya said. "I could very well be over-reacting. That's why I try to keep these things to myself. I don't know why I even said something to you. Usually I just grin and bear it and eat myself alive from the inside."

"Well, that *does* sound like a much better plan of action," Tom teased. "But I don't need to tell you it's good to express these things, do I? In case I do, I'll say it: it's good to express yourself rather than letting it eat you alive from the inside. Even if it's uncomfortable. Even if people judge you for it. Better to say something than nothing. Otherwise...well, you usually end up regretting what you *don't* say more than what you do." Tom shifted in his seat but kept both eyes locked on the road. He looked uncomfortable, but he didn't say more.

The curiosity got the better of Maya. "What is it, Tom? We've talked plenty about my demons...and about Catherine and Declan's, too. But we never really talk about you. You know you can share if you want to, right? I'd love to return the favor when you've already been such a good listener and support to me."

Tom was breezy but evasive. "Oh no, that's not necessary. If something comes up, I'll definitely share it with you. But as I think about it now...no, there's not anything in particular that's bothering me. Nothing to share today." He reached his hand over without looking and patted her on the knee—or tried to. Using only his peripheral vision, his aim was terrible, but Maya was sure the chair appreciated the reassuring pats Tom gave it.

Maya decided not to push. If things were going to work between her and Tom, they'd both have to learn how to be open with each other about their feelings. And if there was something on Tom's mind or some skeleton in his closet—though it seemed laughable to imagine some dark secret past—he'd reveal it when he was ready. Maya put her hand over his and gave a gentle squeeze.

Tom pulled off the highway and nodded towards the building off to their left. "There it is," he said. "Smith Plastics. It looks a bit bigger and more intimidating in person than it does on the website, I don't mind admitting."

"You haven't been here before?" Maya asked.

Tom shook his head. "We've done all our business on the phone up to this point. But if production is going to be starting here soon, then it was unavoidable for me to come here and check it out."

"Makes sense," said Maya. "Are you...*nervous*, Tom?" He had started to chew at the edge of his right thumbnail, something Maya hadn't seen him do yet.

"Seems like it," said Tom. "I'm surprised too, trust me. I think it's just that coming here, taking this step...well, it's making it all real. If all goes well today, then we're just a few months out from seeing our product travel all over the globe. That's the part that's a bit scary to me."

"But Tom!" Maya crowed with excitement. "That's the part where all the good stuff happens. Think of all the people who are going to have access to clean water, like, *all* the time, just because of you. I know it's a little intimidating, going to the next level, but in this case the next level is *seriously* cool and also seriously doing a lot of good for people who need it."

"You're right about that," Tom said. "I imagine there's some work I need to do on myself before we get there. Something to get to the bottom of, eh? Though if I were a betting man, I'd wager it's something to do with the potential for things to go wrong, for attention to be directed my way that I'd rather not have...you know. The usual."

The attention—or even *fame*, in some circles—that would go along with this development were taking the fear and potential for self-sabotage to a level Maya had never considered. She had yet to be contacted by any of the news networks for any changes in her own life, and yet she still let the fear of them hold her back. But here was Tom, about to launch something that was definitely going to be getting him more attention than he had right now. Any advice that she could offer felt silly—what did she know about navigating fame and success?

While Maya had been lost in thought, Tom had steered them into the factory parking lot. "You ready?" he asked. To her firm nod, he responded, "Here goes nothing," and then the two of them walked side-by-side, pacing each other, to the visitor's entrance of the building.

"How can I help you?" asked the disinterested young man at the reception desk, barely glancing up from his phone.

"Yeah, I'm Tom Conley from Conley Corp, and I'm here to check out the facilities. I believe Leann is expecting me."

At the name—seemingly of his supervisor, or at least someone he'd like to impress—the young man looked up at Tom with wide eyes. "Absolutely, sir. If you'll just wait here for a moment, I'll call Ms. Smith."

Tom winked at Maya. "Never underestimate the power of using the right names," he said.

"Does that mean you don't actually have a meeting scheduled?" Maya was horrified by the thought.

"Not technically." There was that mischievous glimmer in Tom's eye again. "But I'm sure Leann won't say no to seeing me here. I'm about to write her a rather large check, and it wouldn't be a great idea to turn me away, now would it?"

Maya shook her head. "This is definitely a situation I would *only* be in with you."

"Aren't you glad you're here and not sitting in that boring office of yours?" Tom asked, moving closer to her but stopping himself before they found themselves in an unprofessional position.

"I'm definitely happier to be with you than at work," said Maya, "But I'd better not hear you call my office boring again."

Tom chuckled. "Or else?"

"Or else I'll have to show you what the word 'boring' really means," threatened Maya. "And you don't want to find out."

"Bring it on, love. I'm guessing anything you think is too boring for words would actually be quite delightful if I were experiencing it with you."

Maya rolled her eyes. "You say that now, but we'll see how you feel during hour three of my shipwreck documentary marathon."

"I am almost certain we could think of something more exciting to do than that." Tom's voice was low, so low she had to lean forward slightly to hear him.

Before Maya could respond, but while she was still feeling her cheeks flush brighter and brighter red, they were interrupted by a melodious voice.

"Tom! What a delightful surprise!" The speaker, who must be Leann, stepped towards them with a broad grin, hand extended to shake Tom's and then Maya's.

"Hi, Leann," said Tom. "This is my colleague, Maya, and we just stopped by today to check out your production here. I hope you don't mind; it was a little spontaneous. Maya needed to get out of the office, and I had to think of something quickly. You know how it is." He winked at Leann, who threw her head back and laughed. As relieved as Maya was that Leann didn't seem to be upset, she wasn't sure she appreciated Tom throwing her under the bus to explain their presence here...unless it was true? Had he spontaneously planned this excursion just to give her something to do? That was a sweet thought...

....but not one she had time to think about too much right now.

Leann was smiling at her, reassuring the two of them they were indeed most welcome. "We're always happy to have visitors here."

"Grand," said Tom. "We're quite eager to get the work underway. It just seemed wrong to move ahead without actually coming here, without actually meeting face to face. Especially when we're so near to each other."

Leann shook her head, looking chagrined. "That's life in the digital age, I'm afraid. It's easier to communicate via email than get in the car and have a face-to-face meeting. We feel a bit like dinosaurs here, sometimes, with the work we do. But they can't replace all of us humans with robots, you know. There are some things that a machine is just no good for at all."

"Isn't that always the truth?" Tom asked. "At least today the three of us are making a little effort to not lose the battle to our robot overlords." Maya heard the teasing tone in his voice, but it didn't seem to land with Leann, who was nodding along seriously.

"That we are, Mr. Conley. That we are. Now, if you don't mind, are you ready to begin the tour?"

Three long hours later, Tom and Maya knew everything there was to know about Smith Plastics, with a hefty helping of facts about Leann Smith, too. Witnessing the production line for the Conley Corp components was surreal and exciting, though she hadn't been able to capture any footage—Leann was concerned about privacy, integrity, and intellectual property, and she didn't want any video evidence of the layout of the inside of her factory. Even if it was a bit old-fashioned for the modern age, where showing the behind-the-scenes footage was a cornerstone of most good marketing campaigns, Maya respected her wishes. It wouldn't do Tom any good if the marketing side of his business started a feud with the production side, and the last thing Maya wanted to do was make his life and his work any more complicated than it already was.

"Well!" Tom breathed deeply as they stepped outside for the first time in what felt like an age. "That was incredibly informative, and—" He checked his watch. "—*really* long. I think I can hear my stomach starting to digest itself. What do you say to a late lunch? Or an early dinner? Linner? Dunch?"

Maya laughed. "As long as you don't call it either of those made-up words, I'm game. Do you have a place in mind?"

Tom shook his head. "Believe it or not, I don't know Gary, Indiana that well. Do you?"

"Not Gary, but..." She pulled out her phone to check something. "Okay, hear me out. In this traffic, we're only about an hour away from the place I'm thinking of. I know, I know...I *swear* I know what you're thinking. And we can stop to get a snack at a gas station and then drive there. I promise it'll be worth it. You just have to trust me."

"Maya Maya Maya." Tom was shaking his head. "You should know better than to think you have to *beg* me to give you anything you want. Especially since you so wisely suggested stopping for snacks. If you'd opened with that, I would already be in the car with the engine running."

The excitement overcame her, and Maya barely suppressed a squeal. "I'm so excited. What a perfect day this is turning out to be. You're in for such a treat, Tom..."

"I know I am," he said, looking at her with heat in his eyes that made it hard for her to hold his gaze. "Now, are you going to tell me where we're going, or...?

"I'll tell you what turns to take, but no. It's going to be a surprise. A good one."

Eighteen

"Wow," Tom breathed. "It was definitely worth the drive." The two of them were sitting on the beach in New Buffalo, Michigan, with a picnic spread out between them on the sand. Maya had called ahead to her favorite restaurant, a pub on the edge of the marina, and placed a to-go order, which they were digging into now. Burgers, crispy fries, dill spears...it was all taking her right back to her childhood.

"We used to come here every summer when I was younger," Maya said. Before Tom could even ask, she found the explanation for their unexpected jaunt to Michigan pouring out of her. "Just for a week, but it was always the best week. Swimming in the lake, walking the beach, spending time with my family...it was just different than being at home, you know? Life is better at the lake, and all that."

"I think I saw that cross-stitched on a pillow once," Tom teased.

"Definitely," Maya chuckled. "But cliches like that, they become cliches because they're true. And it wasn't just my family here. When I got older, some years I'd bring a friend along, and that was another level of fun. Nothing makes or breaks a friendship like traveling together."

"That is definitely the truth," Tom said. Based on the knowing look in his eyes, Maya suspected he'd experienced both the "make" *and* the "break" of traveling with friends. "Did Nina come here with you, too?"

Maya nodded.

"I'm guessing it didn't end your friendship." He smiled.

"Not at all. After that, it was like we were more sisters than friends."

"That sounds really nice." Tom looked wistful.

"Do you have any more siblings?" Maya blurted out, startling Tom. "I just thought, you know…"

He waved away her concerns. "I know. I got a little far away there. And you're perceptive—it *was* about not feeling like Declan is my brother, friend, or anything else. Sometimes he feels like a total stranger to me, in fact. And when you talk about Nina, it makes me wonder what it would feel like to have that connection with someone."

Maya was stunned by the honesty of his confession. "I'm sorry, Tom. Do you not have many close friends?"

"No, I do. I guess I was just thinking specifically of my brother." He was quiet, looking out at the water. It was a calm day, and the waves were gently lapping the shore. This was always a place that had grounded Maya as a child, and that remained true into her adulthood. Looking further out, it was just blue as far as she could see. As a child, she'd squinted to see Chicago on the horizon, sometimes convincing herself that she could make out the skyscrapers. Now, she reveled in the feeling that the lake just might be neverending, her own personal ocean. There was a comfort in its bigness, a perspective about the magnitude of her own problems. The water went further and stretched deeper than she could even fathom; facing that truth, how big could any of her problems really be?

Maya turned to face Tom. "I think I understand. There are people we want to feel close to, and no matter how many other relationships we have that can fill that void or meet that need, we won't let them. We want to have that closeness, that connection with *that* person, and nothing else—or no one else—is really good enough." Tom started to protest, but Maya kept speaking. "I felt that way after Nina died. My mom tried to be there for me, and my other friends, too. But I couldn't accept their love or support; I just wanted my friend back. And even when I met my friends Andie and Luisa...it took a long time before I could just love them without comparing them to her."

"It's not fair, is it?" Tom asked quietly.

"No," she said. "It isn't fair. *Life* isn't fair. But it is full of special people we get to share it with. Sometimes we can't see them because we get too focused on one specific person—it's like the same thing that happens with a crush. You get this dumb, hopeless crush on someone who doesn't even know you exist, and then you can't even see all the other cute guys who would be happy to take a spin around the dancefloor with you at homecoming?"

Tom choked on the sip he had just taken from his soda. "Well, that was oddly specific. Though I don't remember there being a lot of cute guys who wanted to dance with me. We don't really do homecoming dances in Ireland, though, so maybe that was the problem."

"You know what I mean," said Maya.

"I do," he agreed. "But just to be clear, were you thinking of me when you were talking about crushes? Because I definitely do have one on you."

Maya smiled. "Well, I was talking about unrequited crushes. So...no. Definitely not. I'm well aware that you like me..."

"...and?" Tom asked.

"...and I like you too, of course." Tom put his arm around Maya, and she leaned into him. The two of them continued to stare out at the water, both quiet as they thought about all they had revealed to each other and all they were still striving to understand about themselves. It was a comfortable in-between, both wanting to become the best version of themselves for each other, and both continually surprising themselves by the level of honesty they were willing to share.

Tom put the car in park in front of Maya's apartment, but kept the engine running. They had spent a record-breaking amount of time together today, but Maya wasn't ready for it to be over yet.

"This isn't really a parking spot, you know," she said. "But if you want to come up and hang out for a bit, I'm sure we can find one in the structure nearby."

Tom winced. "I really wish I could. Declan promised me he'd go to a support group meeting tonight, and even though there's a very good chance he's not going to keep that promise, I still need to be there."

Maya felt the corners of her mouth turn down against her will. "Yeah, I guess you can't be the one to break that promise, can you?" She tried to keep her tone light and failed.

"Hey," said Tom, tipping up her chin. "I wouldn't want to say goodbye to me either if I were you, but I promise you'll see me again soon."

"How soon?" she asked.

"Tomorrow," he said. "Or did you forget we've got a meeting scheduled?"

Maya facepalmed. Hard. "Of course not. But I did forget I have some slides to prep for it. And that I left my computer at the office. It's fine. I'll…I'll just go in early tomorrow."

"Are you sure? I can drop you there on my way home."

A few more minutes with Tom sounded like heaven right now, even if it meant that Maya would have more work to do tonight. She told herself it was better to do it tonight than to leave it for her future self to do tomorrow, so she nodded. "Let's go."

Entirely too soon, they were saying goodbye again. Maya waved at Tom's car, then made for the entrance of Andersen Consulting. It was after five now, so most of the team members who worked in the office had left.

But not everyone was gone. As she rounded the corner to her cubicle, she came face to face with Catherine Andersen.

"Maya!" Catherine crowed, putting her hands on Maya's arms, either to stop the two of them from colliding or to stop herself from giving Maya a hug. Who could say with her?

"Hi Catherine," Maya smiled. "I just came back to get my computer. I'm not staying long."

"By all means, don't let me keep you. Did you… have a productive day today? I noticed you weren't around this afternoon."

"I did, thanks," said Maya. "I accompanied Tom to the production site to get some more background on the water filtration system. I think the fact that it's all produced here in the States—and so locally—will be another strong selling point."

"That's great." Catherine smiled. "Thanks for being so understanding this morning. Things went well here today, all things considered, and it feels good to be back in the routine."

"I'm glad to hear it. Well, I guess I'll see you tomorrow…."

"Maya, I don't know if you saw my email, but…well, we're going to have a little staff meeting tomorrow morning. I sat down with the board of directors on a video conference today, and…well, they had some suggestions. And I've taken them to heart. There are going to be some changes announced tomorrow, some restructuring. I shouldn't say any more, but it would be really good if you could be there."

Maya was stunned, nearly to silence. "Of course I'll be there. That sounds big." Before reason could creep in and temper it, her mind was already racing with what this could mean. Surely the ways she had gone above and beyond during Catherine's absence had been noticed. Would she be getting a raise? A promotion? She'd have to wait until tomorrow to find out, but she was already sure it was going to be a sleepless night. Maya fought to keep the grin from her face. It would be tactless to celebrate what she didn't yet have. Best to keep it all buttoned up and save her reveries for a more private setting.

And maybe for a time when you know it's actually yours, a voice in her head reminded her. *Don't count your chickens before they've hatched, and all that.*

Maya waved the voice away. Something good was coming her way. She could feel it. And *that* right there was reason to celebrate. She had gone from only ever having premonitions of doom to having one that told her, beyond a shadow of a doubt, that something good was coming. Something to be excited about. Something that was about to change her life.

She wished Catherine a nice evening, collected her laptop from her work station, and went back outside to hail a taxi. A bus would be the more economical option, but an occasion like this—possibly the last time she'd leave Andersen Consulting with her current job title—called for a splurge.

Maya texted Andie and Luisa when she got home.

"Guess who's probably (definitely) getting a promotion?" she wrote.

Luisa responded first. "Well, if it's not you, then I really don't care. But congrats! That's really exciting. What's the new role?"

Maya groaned as she began typing. "Okay, well, I might be celebrating a little prematurely. Because, technically, no one has told me I'm getting a promotion. But there's a meeting tomorrow morning, and the board convinced Catherine to do some restructuring and...I mean...come on. Who else would they be promoting right now?"

Text bubbles from both of her friends took turns popping up and then disappearing before one from Andie finally came through.

"You know I believe in you, Maya. Whatever happens, this is going to be for your best. I'm sure of it."

"You don't think I'm getting the promotion?" Maya wrote back.

"I wouldn't even dare begin to guess what the board suggested to Catherine. Or how much she actually shared with them about her 'leave of absence' and your role in keeping the whole company afloat. I think we're both just worried about you getting your hopes too high about something that isn't a sure thing." Luisa responded.

"Well, here's something wild." Maya typed. "For the first time in...oh...FOREVER, I actually have a good feeling about something. That's got to count for something, right?"

Andie responded to that. "It counts for everything. And I'm inclined to trust in that feeling, too. Just remember, no matter what happens, this is somehow a good thing. Even if it's not immediately obvious."

"Honestly, the two of you are a bit of a buzzkill right now." Maya wrote. "But it's probably what I needed. I'll let you know what I learn tomorrow. Got some work to do now."

Maya put down her phone before she could read either of her friends' responses. She didn't need reminders to temper her excitement or look for the good in every circumstance; she needed to finish her slides for tomorrow's meeting with Tom and then pick out her outfit for the morning staff meeting. And then maybe do a sheet mask and take a bath. Possibly paint her nails. Definitely wash her hair. She had a lot of work cut out for her tonight, and it was time to get started.

Maya strutted into Andersen Consulting the next morning feeling like a million bucks. She was wearing her lucky pantsuit—she had decided it was lucky last night after she tried it on again and saw how good she looked—and she could feel a confidence in her step, a lift in her posture that were familiar like déjà vu. Like she must have experienced them at some point, but she just couldn't put her finger on it.

Her coworkers were responding to her lifted chin and ready smile. Greetings and compliments were flying every which way as Maya made her way into the conference room. The staff meeting had been scheduled for nine o'clock on the dot, and at just ten minutes before starting time, the room was already filling up. Everyone was eagerly awaiting whatever Catherine was going to announce today, or else just anxious to be in the same room as her again. Many of the team members hadn't had any face time with Catherine since she'd come back to work, and today was their chance to see how she was really doing and if everything was really back to normal.

As the last few stragglers filed in and took their seats, Catherine made her big entrance. She walked as if she were aware of all the eyes following her and stood in the front of the room, waiting for the inevitable silence to fall. She was in front of the projection screen where presentations were normally shown in the conference room, though the screen was dark today. Catherine wasn't relying on the support of a visual aid to command any attention today; she was going to do it through the sheer impact of what she was about to say.

"Thank you all for coming today," she began. "I realize it's been a strange couple of weeks here at Andersen, and it was important to me to hold this meeting today. To clear the air, to talk about things to come, and to address any questions you might have."

Catherine paused and turned to Maya, who was sitting towards the front of the room. "First things first, I think you've all noticed I've been a bit...absent lately. Without going in to too much detail, I had a bit of a personal crisis, and it took me away from the office. That's all in the past now, and I am back here, with all of you, with no plans of something like that ever happening again. What you may have also noticed in my absence is that our very own Maya Jefferson stepped in, seamlessly keeping the ship that is Andersen Consulting running. I am deeply grateful to Maya, and I want all of you to know that. Anything that happened in the time I was gone only happened because of the skill and attention of Maya. If you haven't yet thanked her personally for that, I'd highly encourage it. Taking the lead on that, let me be the first to say thank you to Maya publicly. You are an invaluable member of this team, and we are all better off for having you here."

As Catherine paused, a smattering of applause echoed in the room. Maya felt herself blushing and willed herself to keep a straight face—if the promotion that she *knew* was coming was about to be announced, she wanted to be in control of her face when it was. Not looking too pleased with herself, too unsurprised, or too outright gleeful, like she was rubbing it in others' faces.

As much as she was thinking of what to do with her various facial muscles, Maya almost missed Catherine's next words. "Another major reason we're gathered here today is to announce some exciting changes the board of directors and I have decided on. We had an unplanned meeting the other day, where they understandably shared their concerns about what my absence had revealed about the organization of the company. There is a great deal of information that only I have had access to, and it is no doubt a significant part of what made the time that I was gone so very stressful. For all of you, I'm sure."

Catherine paused, taking in the murmurs the people in the room were sharing with those around them. Then she continued, "That's why it's become obvious that I need to have another member of the leadership team, another person at the management level to share the responsibility that I've borne alone up to this point. Now, it's never easy to choose who gets moved up to a position like this, but in looking back at the events of the past two weeks, one obvious choice has risen to the top, again and again..."

Maya's pulse was racing. This was it. The moment where her career trajectory changed irrevocably. She hoped the people around here couldn't hear her heart pounding in her chest. *Keep calm, Jefferson. Just a few more seconds...*

"And that is why I'm so pleased to tell you all that our very own Chris is going to be joining me as the Assistant Director of Marketing. It was such an easy choice to make, as he already has the most access to the work I'm doing, the contacts I'm responsible for, and the inner workings of my office..."

Catherine probably kept speaking, but Maya couldn't be sure. In her mind, she heard static growing to a roar. Like a massive wave of sound was coming, about to knock her under the water far longer than she'd be able to hold her breath. She felt cold, yet sweaty, exhausted yet so, so wired. Thankfully, some wise words of Andie's popped into her head at just the right time, reminding her to breathe, in and out, in and out. Most likely, that's the only thing that kept her from passing out right then and there.

Breathe in. Breathe out. Now do it again.

Maya couldn't wait for the meeting to be finished, but she had to. She kept a smile—it might look more like a grimace, but it was the best she could do—plastered to her face, as she stared at the notebook on the table, doodling spirals in the margin. When Catherine finally finished speaking, Maya made a beeline for the door. If anyone wanted to talk with her, now was not the time. She especially didn't want to talk with Catherine, who was heading her way. Maya sprinted to the restroom and locked the door behind her. The tears started to flow before she'd even taken her hand off the door.

Nineteen

Maya was still in the bathroom, trying to get a grip on the emotions that had already spiraled well out of control when her phone pinged with a new message in the group chat with Andie and Luisa.

"Well? Is the meeting over? We want details. Spill!" Luisa had written.

Maya choked on a sob. As much as she didn't want to admit her failure to her friends, she could definitely use some moral support right now.

She pounded out a quick message back to them. "I guessed wrong. There was a promotion, but it went to Chris."

"Oh, honey." That was Andie. "Are you okay?"

"What in the world is wrong with Catherine? With the board? I get that Chris is great. Talented. Blah blah blah. And I'm all about celebrating other people's success and not thinking this is all a zero-sum game. But after all you've done, the way you kept the company afloat single-handedly...I just don't get it." That was Luisa.

"I don't get it either," typed Maya. "And to answer your question, Andie, no. I'm really not okay. I've been hiding in the bathroom since the meeting finished."

"I'm so sorry, Maya. What can we do to support you?" Andie wrote.

As Maya started to type a response, her phone rang with a call from Luisa.

Before Maya could even greet her, Luisa was speaking. "Listen to me, Maya. Now isn't the time for a long extended text message conversation while everyone wonders why you're still in the bathroom. You don't need them thinking you've got a nasty case of food poisoning any more than you want them to start wondering why you might be feeling a little emotional about the meeting today."

"I—" Maya started, but Luisa wasn't done speaking yet.

"This is definitely, *definitely* a situation that calls for rising above. You know that, right?"

"I do..."

"Pull yourself together, splash some cold water on your face, and get back out there and do your job. Don't let anyone see the cracks in the badass exterior you're putting out there today. Be good at what you do and save *all* the emotions you want to express for when the workday ends at five o'clock. Andie and I will come over this evening, and you can feel it all then. That's Andie's area of expertise, obviously. And I can help you start taking action. Whatever you want to do, I'll support you. We'll get your resume together, draft a few different variations of a cover letter...or we'll have a serious conversation about starting out on your own. Your call, of course."

"Thanks, Lu," Maya managed. "I think I can make it through the rest of the day here…"

"Don't think you can," said Luisa. "You've got to know it. This is not the place to fall apart. This is not the place to show weakness. Heck, it's not even the place to be nice a lot of the time. Just do your job, do it well, and make it to five o'clock. After that, you're all ours."

"I can do that. Thank you. Again. Really."

The two friends hung up, with Luisa promising to update Andie on their after-work plans and Maya promising to exit the bathroom within the next forty seconds. Then Maya splashed cold water on her face and patted it dry with a paper towel. Amazingly, her eyes weren't red-rimmed or puffy—something she'd hated in her dramatic teenage years when she'd locked herself in her room crying for hours, and then there was no evidence of it to garner her sympathy. But the resilience of her skin was something she was grateful for today. Because Luisa was right—no one needed to know she'd been crying. And even if they'd detected it, she could always spin it. Say she was just so happy for Chris. Or that her dog was sick. Or she was just really, really glad Catherine was back.

No, all of those things sounded bogus. And honesty really was the best policy, so removing all evidence of the tears was the way to go. Once Maya was satisfied with what she saw in the mirror, she left the bathroom, making her way back to her work station and smiling at everyone who crossed her path.

The thing about pretending—it got easier the longer you did it. Those first smiles felt half-hearted, but by the time she'd given ten or fifteen of them, she had almost—almost—forgotten what she was so upset about.

For the rest of the day, Maya settled into a comfortable routine of keeping her head low and smiling when she was forced to interact. Either because she was sensitive to Maya's feelings—or more likely because she was oblivious to their existence—Catherine gave her a wide berth. While she was working on creative projects, in the zone, Maya popped in her ear buds, tuning out the rest of her colleagues while sending the "do not disturb" message at the same time. At lunch, she didn't linger so as to avoid any invitations to join a group ordering takeout or heading to a local restaurant. Instead, she went to the nearest convenience store, picked up the first things that caught her eye—a sandwich, a bag of chips, and a bottle of chocolate milk—and headed for a bench far enough away from the office that she was unlikely to cross paths with anyone familiar.

Back at the office, a notification from Maya's online calendar reminded her she had a meeting with Tom starting in half an hour. She groaned as she swiped the alert aside. Hiding her true feelings from Tom was likely going to be an order of magnitude more difficult than hiding them from anyone else in the building. And if he took it upon himself to right the wrongs that had been done to her...well, that could get messy.

Maya preemptively texted him. "Hi Tom, just a heads up. I can't really talk about this because it's still kind of raw. But Catherine announced a promotion today, a new Assistant Director. I really thought I would get it, stupidly, after she was gone and everything. But I didn't. And I don't want you to do anything. Or say anything. Not at work. We can talk about it later, though. Okay?"

His response was quick. "I'm on my way there right now. I won't say a thing. I'm really sorry Catherine has her head so far up her arse."

Maya laughed for the first time in hours. She agreed with Tom's assessment, but more than anything, she was grateful that he wasn't about to swoop in here and take up the cause of defending her honor. That wouldn't help anything.

When Tom arrived, Maya almost hugged him before she remembered where she was. His kind eyes, searching hers for evidence of what she was feeling but couldn't say, his comforting presence, his ready wit... it was all a balm for her wounded ego.

"How are you?" he asked, delivering the question like a greeting rather than something he hoped to hear an answer to.

Maya knew better, though. "I'm hanging in there. Thanks for being here."

"I'd never miss a chance to spend some time with you." Tom winked at her. "Shall we head to the conference room?"

Maya made a face before she could stop herself. The scene of the crime. She hated that damn room now.

Tom caught on quickly. "Actually, why don't you grab your laptop and we'll head to the café? It's a nice day, and we don't need to be in that stuffy room."

The look Maya gave him conveyed all the gratitude she was feeling. She wished she could hug him now, but she remembered Luisa's words about not showing weakness in the office. She supposed that included hugs too, and not just bathroom crying. Maya wasn't sure she wanted to work in a place that didn't allow those things, but she also wasn't sure what the alternative was.

Tom escorted Maya to her work station to pick up what she needed and then out of the office and across the street to Beans Café.

"Why don't you grab a table and I'll get the drinks?" he asked. "What would you like?"

"That sounds perfect. Thank you, Tom," Maya replied. "I'd really like a nice comfort beverage right about now. Maybe a chai latte?"

Tom's eyes widened. "Black tea? You really aren't kidding around, are you?" He gave her a warm smile and left to order their drinks.

Maya set up her laptop and opened the presentation with the results from Conley Corp's latest ad campaign. She flipped briefly through the slides, willing herself to get back in the game, to be professional enough to spend this time with Tom actually talking about his company and not just whining to him about her boss.

But her mind wouldn't stop coming back to it.

How could she do this to me? Is she oblivious to all I've done for her...or is she cruel? Chris is great...of course he is. But he didn't single-handedly keep the office running while

Catherine was gone. Though to be fair, I had help too...from Chris. So why couldn't the two of us both have risen together? I mean...I got a public thank you, and he got a promotion and a raise. That hardly seems fair. I feel so dumb. I was so sure this was it. My big break...

Her thoughts were interrupted by the sound of Tom's chair scraping against the floor as a steaming to-go cup was placed on the table in front of her.

"Do you want to talk about it?" Tom asked as he sat down. "I know you didn't want to in the office, but we're here now, so..."

Maya shook her head. "Honestly, no. I mean yes...but no. I'm so in my head right now, and if I spend your valuable time—as a client, of all things—lamenting that I didn't get a promotion, I might start to believe that I didn't deserve it. Does that make sense? Like...at least while I'm on the clock I should probably act as if I'm a really great employee who deserves the promotion she didn't get. But if you want to come over after work and meet my friends, well...then I will definitely be playing the role of the very disappointed gal who didn't get the promotion she one hundred percent deserved more than anyone else in the office. Deal?"

Tom smiled at her. "Deal. Especially because it means I get to meet your friends."

"They'll be happy to meet you, too. That'll be a nice surprise for them, actually....a great way to thank them for their years of loyal service, finally letting them meet my new boyfriend—"

Maya stopped herself as soon as she realized what she'd said, but it wasn't soon enough to keep Tom's eyes from turning into saucers and the grin from spreading wide across his face.

"Your boyfriend, eh?" he asked. "No, I'm not complaining. It's a nice role, and honestly, I'm just grateful to be considered for the part. But I don't want it to be too much too soon. Are you okay with that? Or do you want to rewind and pretend it never happened?"

"I...I don't think I want to take it back, actually," Maya said, surprising herself. "As long as you're okay with it, I think I'd like to keep it. Try it on. Play around with it and see if it sticks."

"That sounds fair enough," said Tom. "If it doesn't, I'm sure we can find a different label you feel better with. Just not 'boy toy,' okay? Promise me you won't ever refer to me as your 'boy toy.'"

The laugh that barked out of Maya's lips surprised her. "I can absolutely promise you that I will never refer to you as my 'boy toy.' Now that we've got that cleared up, shall we get down to business?"

Tom scooted closer as she turned to her laptop and the open presentation. "We shall. Lead the way, Ms. Jefferson."

The meeting with Tom went smoothly, and it had the added benefit of transforming Maya's mood. By the time she returned to the office—after a promise from Tom to pick her up after work so that the two of them could meet Andie and Luisa as soon as possible—she had almost forgotten what had put her in such a foul mood that morning.

Almost.

But of course, when she saw Catherine and Chris with their heads together, looking down at something on Chris's desk, it all came streaming back into her mind.

Embarrassment. Betrayal. Jealousy. More embarrassment for caring more about her own career advancement than Catherine's health, the company's future, or Chris's success. Shame. So, so much shame.

The next few hours ticked by as Maya fought and lost battles with the thoughts and emotions raging in her mind. Just when she'd slain one thought monster, another two would pop up. Inside her head, she was fighting the veritable hydra of being unacknowledged in the workplace, and by the time five o'clock rolled around, the monster had at least forty heads.

"Well, that's a problem for another day," she muttered under her breath. Tom would be here any moment, and the promise of time off the clock with him and her two dear friends was driving her towards the door like metal shavings to a magnet.

Maya said her goodbyes to the two colleagues whose paths she crossed on her way to the door. She had done a masterful job today of minimizing her human contact in the workplace, and she had no plans to change that now, just because the workday was over.

Outside, before she could even scan the street for his car, her eyes landed on Tom. He was leaning up against the side of his car—with a driver again, today—which was parked on the street right in front of the building. Snagging that spot was a rarity, and Maya couldn't help but wonder if he'd been circling the block ever since their coffee shop meeting ended just to get the best possible parking spot.

Maya's pace quickened the closer she got to Tom, and her smile widened proportionally. "Hi, boyfriend," she said, trying out the word again. "Thanks for picking me up." She leaned in for a quick peck on the lips before Tom opened the door and let her into the backseat of his town car.

"Hi, girlfriend," he said as he gestured towards the leather seat, a frown crossing his forehead. "People don't really call each other 'boyfriend' and 'girlfriend,' do they? It makes me feel like a child."

"Hmm," said Maya. "You make a good point. It also reminds me of my grandma. She'd always refer to her friends as 'my girlfriend, so and so.' So no, maybe it's not super sexy for you to address me as 'girlfriend.' Let's try something else."

"What do you suggest?" asked Tom. "I'm all ears."

"Well, it's probably too soon for 'lover,'" said Maya. She felt her ears turn red as soon as she said the word. "But I'm definitely fond of 'your grace.' What do you think of that one?"

Tom's eyes had heat in them when they contacted with hers. "I can't lie. I liked that first suggestion of yours. In the meantime, while I'm waiting to earn that title, I'd be honored to refer to you as your grace. Your grace." He winked as he lifted her hand to his mouth and kissed her knuckles.

Maya giggled. "I was definitely joking when I suggested it, but now I'm very pleased with the result, so I think I'll keep it. Oh! Do you mind if we stop at the store before we go to my apartment? I should get some snacks for all of us."

"We can certainly stop at the store," said Tom, at the same time he reached for a paper bag on the floor Maya hadn't noticed. "But first, you should check what's in here. If anything's missing, we'll go buy it straightaway."

Maya opened the bag and immediately started laughing. Inside were all of her favorite donuts, and lots of them. Eyeballing it, she'd guess there were four of each kind. "Did you buy all the donuts at the bakery?" she asked.

"Something like that," he said. "I also got some hummus, with chips and veggies to dip in it. French onion dip, too. I'm not sure what that is, but it was prominently displayed at the grocery store near the potato chips and...well I guess I impulse bought it. I'm not entirely sure how to be a supportive boyfriend in this situation, especially when I've only known for sure that I even *am* a boyfriend for, like, three hours. But I figured it meant buying snacks and giving you a range of options for how healthy said snacks are. How did I do?"

He looked nervous, like he was truly unsure if he'd done a good job, and the vulnerability of it made Maya's heart do a somersault. She leaned over and kissed him, longer than a peck this time, and she didn't pull back until she was confident he'd no longer have that uncertain expression on his face. When she opened her eyes and looked at him, she saw she was right. His pupils were dilated, he was breathing faster, and he was staring at her with a question in his eyes that she desperately wanted to answer.

Except obviously she wasn't going to make out with him, let alone take things any further than that, when they were in the back seat of a car and only a few blocks from her apartment. And nothing was going to happen when they arrived there, either, for a couple of reasons. For one thing, her friends were going to show up any minute. And for another, far more significant thing, this was going to be a big deal when it happened. And playing it cool or pretending it didn't happen would seriously mess with Maya's head. That was the last thing this day needed.

Considering all of that, it was time to be like a cold shower on this whole situation. She smiled at Tom and shook her head. "Now is not the time, boyfriend. Soon, I hope. But not in the backseat of your car. Not on the worst day of my career. And not when we have to meet my friends in, like, fifteen minutes."

"Those are all very valid reasons," said Tom, shaking his head. "And I knew all of that. I really did. Just...if you had needed, you know, to use my body to comfort yourself over all the nonsense of this day, well...I wouldn't have minded providing that help to you."

Maya laughed and punched him lightly on the arm. "Oh, I'm sure you 'wouldn't have minded' it. But we've already established that I'm very much not a 'rushing into anything' kind of gal. And I'm okay with that, and I really hope you are, too."

He lifted her hand and kissed her knuckles again. "For you, your grace, I would be okay with absolutely anything. That sounded wrong. I mean, I do make a rule of always respecting a woman's wishes, especially as regards her body. But, like, even more so for royalty. Your grace."

"Thanks for clarifying that," Maya teased. The car pulled to a stop in front of her apartment building then, and she and Tom gathered all of the snacks from the backseat and trunk—he had undersold just how many he had bought—and headed inside. Tom smiled at Maya as she fumbled with her keys in the lock, and she felt the faintest glimmer for the first time that day that things just might turn out alright.

Twenty

Tom and Maya had just finished setting up the array of snacks in the living room when there was a knock on the door.

"Yoo hoo! It's us! Let us in!" crowed Luisa's voice through the wood.

Maya grabbed Tom's hand and squeezed. "You ready to meet my friends?" she whispered. He nodded with a confident grin, and Maya felt herself flush with excitement. It turned out this day, which had been all gray clouds since about ten minutes into the workday, had a silver lining. Her two dear friends and her boyfriend—that was another silver lining—were about to meet each other. She had no reason to expect it wouldn't all go well, and she rushed to the door, flinging it open with Tom right at her heels.

In a flurry of hellos, hugs, and introductions, Andie and Luisa entered the apartment. They were bearing gifts of their own—food, flowers (from Andie), and a stack of books about entrepreneurship from Luisa—which Maya readily received, placing them on the counter before ushering her friends into the living room.

Once they were all seated around the loaded coffee table, the conversation started to flow.

"So Tom! What's your deal?" Luisa got right to the point, but she stopped herself before she could turn on her inquisitive skill at full power. "Sorry...are we grilling Tom, talking about Maya's job, or a bit of both?"

Tom chuckled. "I'm definitely voting for talking about Maya's job, as much as I love grilling."

"I think we need to let Maya steer this evening," said Andie. "So, love? What's it going to be?"

Maya looked around the room. "As much as today sucked...and as much as I just wanted to come home and cry or yell or rant and rave... well, now that you're all here—together, no less—I'm not really feeling that ragey. Or that sad. I'm just grateful you're all here. And I'm not opposed to having a nice evening together. I think I might need it."

Andie exchanged a glance with Luisa, and it didn't go unnoticed by Maya. She continued speaking. "I promise if any work-related feelings come up, I will address them. Okay? It just feels like a total waste of friend time and boyfriend time to spend it all complaining about how I spend my forty hours a week."

"I'm sorry...did you say *boyfriend*?" Luisa had to pick her jaw up off the floor. "When did this happen?" She turned to Tom. "You there! Explain yourself."

Diplomatic as ever, Andie jumped in to temper Luisa's enthusiasm. "I think what Luisa means to say—" She made eye contact with Maya and Tom in turn. "—is that we're both happy and excited for you in this new development of your relationship. But yes, if there's a story, please don't hold out on us. How long has this been, like, *official* official?"

"Oh, it's quite a recent development," Tom said, eyes twinkling. He looked at Maya, giving her the opportunity to jump in and explain before he made a mess of it.

She took the opportunity gladly. "Yeah, I mean...don't blow this up into a big thing, you two." She glared at Luisa, softening her expression slightly before directing it at Andie. "We actually just had the conversation today. Maybe...an hour ago?"

"Oh wow, so we've missed *nothing*," said Luisa. "And we're all caught up then. Awesome. Then how about you tell us about yourself, Tom?"

"Happy to oblige," he replied. "What would you like to know?"

Maya leaned back into the sofa and enjoyed watching her friends get to know her new boyfriend. They learned about each other's careers, families, and even their childhood pets. If Maya didn't know better, she'd think her friends—and especially Luisa—were gathering information to be able to crack Tom's passwords. But considering none of them knew, or even bothered to ask, what his mother's maiden name was, she figured he was safe.

In this position, Maya was mostly an observer, and she found herself reveling in it. She was learning things about everyone in the room, from stories she'd never heard before to bizarre and random personal facts she never would have even thought to ask about. The most profound part? She felt completely and totally at ease and secure watching it all unfold. She wasn't worried she'd be forgotten about or squeezed out of the circle—both fears that had cropped up in her past relationships for as long as she could remember. It was as if, every time she got close to someone, she became terrified that it was all too good to be true and she was about to lose that person forever. *Hmm...three guesses where that particular fear came from*, she thought to herself. *And the first two don't count.*

❥ · ❥ · ❤ · ❥ · ❥

By the time it was dark out, the four of them had polished off a massive thin crust pizza loaded with everyone's favorite toppings—a wonderful surprise was discovering how well they all complimented each other—and made a significant dent in the coffee table of snacks. Maya packed up to-go containers in the kitchen with Luisa and Andie's respective favorite treats, keeping another container aside for Tom to choose whatever he'd like.

Andie wandered in ahead of everyone else and helped Maya finish wrapping everything up. "I really like him," she said quietly. "I think Tom is just what you need...and I can't even tell you how good it is to see you finally letting yourself enjoy having someone special in your life."

Maya blushed. "It still feels strange to me, honestly, especially the part where I'm letting other people see it. When you all were here, I felt like I needed to sit on the other side of the room or something. Like I didn't want you to know that I like him. How dumb is that? Of course you two know I like him—I should hope so!"

Andie stroked her arm. "You already know what I'm going to say, but it's not dumb at all. Why do you think you're afraid of letting us see how you feel about Tom?"

Maya said the first thing that came to her mind. "Maybe because if you see it, then that means it's real. And if it's real...then I'm in the prime position to get hurt. If no one knows I have feelings, then no one can hurt them."

"Is that really true, though? Or do you still get hurt, even if you hide your feelings?" Andie asked, her eyes searching Maya's.

Maya shook her head. "Oh, I definitely still get hurt. It's just that no one knows I'm in pain because I did such a good job of hiding it." She held up her hand before Andie could get a word in. "Okay, okay. You don't have to say it. I can accept that this...whatever happened here today...this was progress. Not a setback. This was good. Thank you." She pulled Andie into a quick hug just as Luisa and Tom joined them in the kitchen.

"Ooh, are we all hugging?" Tom asked, walking up behind Maya and encircling her with his arms. "I like that."

Maya felt her cheeks burning with all the blood that had rushed to them, but she pushed through her sudden urge to leap away from Tom and make herself busy loading the dishwasher. Or unloading it, whatever was needed at the moment. Whatever would get her more than an arm's length away from him.

"Aww, you two are cute!" Luisa crowed, taking it all in. Off Andie's exaggerated pout, she continued. "You're cute too, Andie, but this is not your moment. You may be excused." Luisa yawned then, loudly and proudly. "I'm beat. Time to go for me. Andie, you want a ride? I'll drop you off. Let's leave these two alone. *Finally*, I'm sure they're both thinking."

Andie picked up the cues Luisa had been putting down and gave her own yawn and stretch combo. "You're right, it's late. I'd really love a ride home. Thanks, Lu!"

Before Maya could put up a protest, the two women were at the door, doggie bags in hand. They were saying their goodbyes, and then...they were gone.

And she and Tom were alone. And all that heat from the car ride earlier...well, now there was nothing to keep it from roaring to life.

And that scared the heck out of Maya. She busied herself with the rest of the tidying up, even wiping down all the counter tops in the kitchen. She never did that, but she was on a roll with the cleaning, so why stop now?

Only, Tom stopped her when he stepped in front of her, blocking her way. He reached out to take the sponge from her and placed it gently in the sink. "Maya," he said, eyes focused on hers. "Why do I get the feeling that I'm making you nervous just by being here? Do you want me to go?"

Maya shook her head. No words would come out. She didn't know what she wanted from Tom—or maybe she did, but she was too scared to say it—but she only knew that she *didn't* want him to leave. Whatever was about to happen, he needed to be here. She felt that, deep in the core of her being.

"Okay, that's a good start. You want me to be here, for right now, at least. Should we go sit down? Maybe back in the living room? We could just talk, just get comfortable with it being the two of us again. Would you like that?"

Maya nodded again.

"Good," he said. "We can debrief the visit with your friends." He led her by the hand back into the living room, where they sat down shoulder to shoulder. Maya could feel Tom's gaze on the side of her face, but she was still stuck, too nervous to move. Or too...*something*...to move. It felt like if she said or did whatever was coming to her, things might spiral out of control very quickly. Whatever was about to happen next might happen from one instant to the next.

She was pretty sure that was what she wanted...but the implications of taking things to the next level with Tom were overwhelming her. Swirling in her mind and over-powering her senses. She hadn't even realized Tom was talking...

"...really great. I'm glad I met them. Luisa is such a character. Did you know she threatened me? I'm not going to lie, I got a little scared..."

Maya pulled herself back from the thoughts she'd gotten lost in enough to realize that Tom was talking about her friends. "I'm sorry...what? She threatened you? What did she say?"

"It was just at the end there, when you were in the kitchen with Andie. Luisa stayed behind, and she told me she liked me...so far...but that if I did anything at all to hurt you..."

Maya's eyes widened. "Wait, what did she say she would do? That sounds intense. Scary, even."

"Oh, it was." Tom was nodding. "And what made it even more intense was that she didn't actually say what she would do if I hurt you. She just left it open-ended like that. Hanging out in the open. Like, maybe she meant she'd never speak to me again. Or maybe she meant no one would ever speak to me again because I'd be at the bottom of Lake Michigan. Who's to say?" He threw up his hands in a comical shrug.

Maya laughed. "Well, I don't know anything about any violent tendencies of Luisa's, so I think you're safe there. Though maybe to be on the safe side, you could think about just...not hurting me?"

She looked up at Tom, and he leaned down to kiss her then. "That would *never* be my intention, Maya."

Whatever thoughts had been playing in Maya's mind, the kiss stopped them. It was slow and gentle, deepening to an intensity that sent sparks traveling up her spine. It wasn't as if she'd never been touched before...but when Tom touched her like this, it felt like that was the truth. Like she'd never been touched by someone who treasured her as much as he seemed to. Like she'd never been handled with this much care. And yet, at the same time, like she'd never been wanted this much.

Maya pulled back when she needed to breathe, and she gazed up into Tom's dark eyes. "What are we doing?" she asked.

"We're doing whatever you want, Maya," he said. "We're saying good night and sending me home...or we're not doing that. Either way, it's your call."

"I don't want you to go. At least...not yet," she said, smiling shyly at him. "That's not usually the kind of thing I'd just admit outright, but, I mean...it's you. So I guess I feel like I can actually try being honest about my feelings."

Tom pulled her close again, stroking her back with his chin rested on top of her head. "That's exactly what I'd wish for, if I were a wishing man."

After an age passed—or what seemed like an age, at least—of the two of them sitting on the couch, talking and kissing, it had gotten late. Well past Maya's normal bedtime.

Tom looked at her with a question in his eyes. "Well, love, we're approaching the time when I turn in to a pumpkin. As much as I'd love to sit with you on this couch until the sun rises in the east, I'm afraid I'm going to need to get some sleep before the work day starts tomorrow. Not as young as I was once, and all that other nonsense. So unless you object, I think it's time for me to be going."

Maya held his gaze. "What if you stayed?" she asked.

His eyes widened almost imperceptibly as the question landed.

"I will if you want me to," he said. "I can sleep on the couch."

Maya patted the couch seat next to her. "This couch is terrible for sleeping on. Trust me, when I first moved in here, it took me a month to get a bed. And that was plenty of time for me to do all sorts of damage to my neck and back from sleeping on this thing."

"What do you suggest instead?" he asked.

"Don't be coy with me, Conley," Maya said, through the blood rushing to her cheeks. "You know I'm not asking you to sleep in my non-existent bath tub. That leaves one piece of furniture big enough for your body. I'll wait while you figure it out."

"Really? Are you ready for that?"

"I honestly haven't decided yet how far things are going to go tonight. As long as you're okay with that uncertainty—and you'd better be, because it's my body after all—you're welcome to stay. It's been a long time since I didn't sleep alone."

Tom nodded in agreement, and Maya made herself busy finding toiletries for her overnight guest—a spare towel, of course, and a toothbrush were definitely a necessity. When she came back and delivered those things to Tom, he laughed out loud.

"I wasn't expecting this level of service," he said. "Usually if I have to crash at a mate's flat or something, I just squeeze toothpaste on my finger and call it good."

"Welcome to midwestern hospitality, then, I guess," Maya smiled. "Do you want me to look for some...pajamas or something you can wear?"

It was Tom's turn to blush. "It won't do great things for my self-confidence if I can wear anything you own, I hate to admit. I'm good with my t-shirt and boxers, if that's alright with you."

Maya chuckled nervously. "As much as I wish we had adorable matching pajamas for our first sleepover, I think that will work just fine."

"Good," he said, standing up from the couch with his towel and toothbrush in hand. He approached her again, lifting his hand to her cheek and ducking down to place a soft kiss on her lips. "Thank you for the hospitality and thank you for letting me stay."

The kiss left her breathless. "You're welcome," she said, when she regained control. "Let me know if there's anything else I can do for you."

He winked at her. "I'm going to leave that one entirely up to you, love. Just know that there is literally nothing you could want from me right now that I would hesitate to give you."

"Hmm," she teased. "Even the code for your bank card? Or access to your private email?"

He kissed her again to stop her from making another joke. "I know you're messing with me," he said between kisses, "And I also know that you got my meaning. If you need to make jokes to avoid the topic that scares you, that's fine. Just know that you don't *have* to do that. I promise I won't think less of you if you admit you want me."

"I want you," she said, without even thinking. "I mean..."

"That's good." Tom smiled against her mouth, and she felt his teeth touching her lip. "We're on the same page then. What do you want to do next?"

"I think... I think I'd like to just kiss you for a while longer," she said. "And then maybe we can move to the bedroom."

Tom granted her wishes and didn't stop kissing her. "Do you have any preferences for what happens in the bedroom?" he asked.

"Oh no, you don't," she chuckled. "You're not tricking me into dirty talking you on our first over night. No. I promise to give plenty of guidance when the moment comes...and not a moment sooner."

"That's fair enough," he said. "I'm a very quick learner."

It wasn't long before Maya's prediction came true and making out on the sofa was no longer enough. When she stood and tugged Tom's hand, trying to pull him toward the bedroom, he hesitated one last time. "Are you sure...?"

he asked. The heat in her eyes and the firm nod of her head answered his question, and he tumbled readily after her.

The door slammed shut behind them.

In the morning, Maya woke with a smile on her face. Last night had been unexpected in all the best ways—it had more than made up for the unfortunate things that had happened at work, and today truly felt like a new day. As she shuffled out into the kitchen, she found Tom there and the smile on her face grew wider and wider. He was here. In the morning. He was here, in her apartment, in the morning, filling her electric kettle with water to make them both nice, warm beverages to start the day.

"Good morning, Maya," he said, kissing her on the cheek. "What kind of tea would you like this morning?"

"I can make it," she said. "I don't want to keep you—the work day is going to start soon, and we can't have you doing the walk of shame without any clean clothes."

He threw his head back and laughed. "I never understood why they called it the walk of shame. There's certainly nothing to feel ashamed of as far as I'm concerned."

"Would walk of awkwardness be a better name?" Maya asked, not quite making eye contact. "Is this weird? Being here? The whole morning after thing?"

Tom reached for her and pulled her into an embrace. "Not at all," he said, kissing the top of her head. "It's perfectly lovely getting to see you first thing in the morning." He checked his watch and groaned. "Even if there's barely any time to actually enjoy it. Would you mind terribly if I jumped in the shower? I can have my driver bring a change of clothes, but I'm afraid even Derek can't manage to squeeze a shower into the backseat of a sedan."

"Go for it," said Maya. "The towels are in the linen closet." Off the look Tom gave her, she raised her eyebrows. "Oh right, yeah. You already have your very own towel. Welcome, again, to Chez Maya."

"Thanks, love." He smiled. "I'll be out in a jiffy."

Once Tom was out of the kitchen, Maya started getting her things ready for the day—packing her lunch, making sure all the papers she'd brought home and not looked at the day before were still in her briefcase, and getting dressed. Tom's phone rang once, but she ignored it. Sure, the two of them were closer today than they'd been yesterday morning, but she wasn't sure if they were "calling through the bathroom door" close yet.

When it rang again soon after, she second guessed herself. Should she...? Without even thinking about it, she glanced at the screen and saw that it was Declan calling. That could be important, right? Maybe Tom needed to know...

Just as she was walking to the bathroom door with his ringing phone in hand, there was a knock at the door. Apart from feeling like she might suddenly be living in a horror movie, Maya didn't let herself get too freaked out. After all, there was a man in her shower. If someone was here to axe murder her at eight o'clock in the morning, at least she wouldn't be alone.

Glancing through the peephole, Maya spotted a familiar face on the other side of the door. Without thinking twice, she pulled it open and greeted the man standing there.

"Declan," she said. "What a surprise! What in the world are you doing at my apartment?"

Twenty-One

Declan looked like he'd been out all night, Maya was disheartened to notice. She had only seen him at the scene of the accident, when he had been practically unconscious. This morning, though, he looked like he hadn't showered or eaten a vegetable since at least the previous page on the calendar, and his eyes were glassy and unfocused.

"*Your* apartment?" he said. "Mary, was it? Is my brother here?"

Maya barred the door with her body. She wasn't sure what mental state Declan was in right now, and she also wasn't sure, as a result, that she wanted him to come inside. "Yes, this is my apartment. How...*why* are you here?"

"I needed my little bro's help, didn't I? I couldn't get a peep out of him, and Derek was useless, too. Well, until I *borrowed* his phone and tracked the last address on his GPS."

"I'm sorry...so you *stalked* him here, essentially?" Maya was incredulous.

"Um, I'm pretty sure the word 'stalking' is only used when you're talking about people who don't know each other. Tom is my brother, and I was just worried about him."

"Like hell you were," boomed Tom's voice, as he entered the room from behind Maya, dropping the towel he had been using to dry his hair onto his shoulder. "What is it, Dec? What do you need?"

Declan's eyes filled with disdain as they set sight on his brother. "Always so full of judgement. You think you're better than me, don't you? You're just ready to swoop in on your white horse and save the day again, aren't you?"

Tom sighed. "Nobody's doing any swooping, Dec. We're all just trying to get on with our days. And if you could help, that'd be just grand."

"What's the matter, little brother?" Declan sneered. "Am I cramping your style? Are you, perhaps, afraid some of the skeletons in your closet won't stay hidden? Afraid I'll make you look bad—or worse, reveal you for who you really are?"

"Declan, none of us have time for this right now. Maya and I both have jobs, and we don't have the spare time to try to figure out what on earth it is that you're even talking about. What do you want? Money? Drama? Attention? I don't have time for this. Not now, not ever."

"Amazing how you're so above drama these days. I remember a time when it wasn't that way. When you and I were troublemakers together. Life was fun then. I bet your girlfriend doesn't know much about those days, does she?" Declan jerked his head in Maya's direction.

Maya had heard enough. "I know plenty about Tom's past, though I don't believe any of it is relevant with regard to who he is today. Let that give you some hope if you want it to, Declan. There will always be people who will love and accept you in the future, and who'll be more than happy to forgive and forget who you used to be."

Declan's lip curled at Maya's words. "Well, I *definitely* didn't ask for your input. And I'd be willing to guess Tom hasn't told you *everything* about his sordid past. Sure, you probably know he used to drink a lot...but do you know what kind of things he did when he was drinking?"

"I find specifics incredibly dull," said Maya. "So if you're trying to drum up interest for Story Time with Declan, I'm going to have to pass."

"That's enough, Dec," said Tom. "Now is definitely not the time. I'll get my driver to take you home, and if you want to meet Maya again when you're sober...well, we can talk about that then."

Tom escorted Declan toward the door, but just before he could push him through it, Declan broke loose from his arms and spun around.

"Tom was more dangerous than I've ever been," he said. "Me, I know I've got a problem, but it's only ever put *me* in danger. Tom...well, Tom used to just love driving his car when he'd been drinking. He said it made the Dublin traffic more tolerable if he'd had a pint or two. Of course, it wasn't always just a pint or two—sometimes he was absolutely pissed. That's what happened when you lost your license, right brother? If I remember correctly, that was the day you almost crashed into a minivan with a young family inside it. As it was, you just ran them off the road a little.

But I can still see that shaken mother's face. She almost lost everything that day, thanks to you."

Maya was silent, taking it all in. The color had drained from Tom's face, and his eyes were searching hers, pleading for her to just give him a minute. Give him a minute to get Declan out the door so that he could explain what she was hearing.

Maya's vision narrowed in at the same time that her ears filled with the sound of static. The things Declan had said, they painted a new picture of Tom that she didn't want to see, that she didn't want to believe. And yet, she was frozen to the spot—leaving, without giving Tom a chance to explain what his brother was saying, wasn't an option. She wanted to believe that Declan had it all wrong, or that he was making things up just to make Tom look bad. She stayed rooted to the floor of her kitchen as Tom closed the door behind Declan. It had to be wrong. Tom was going to explain, and then everything was going to be okay.

Tom approached her slowly and reached his hands out to rub the sides of her arms. "Maya? Are you with me? Are you alright?"

Maya shook her head to clear her mind and bring herself back to the moment. "Is it true? It can't be. He was wrong, wasn't he? You...you wouldn't..."

Tom was looking at the floor, refusing to meet her eyes. "I wouldn't. Not anymore. You know I would never do something like that today."

"But that doesn't answer the question, Tom. Did you do that? Did you get behind the wheel of a car and...my God, did you really come that close to killing someone? And a whole family, no less?"

He hung his head, his shame evident in all his features. "I...I did. That was my rock bottom. That was what turned it all around for me. I couldn't believe what I had done and how reckless my actions had been. It was that same week that I stopped drinking and found my support group."

"Tom, I don't know what to say." Maya wrapped her arms around her stomach, holding herself together. "I'm...well of course I'm glad that no one was hurt. But I feel sick. I can't believe you didn't tell me this, that I had to find out from Declan. Of all the ways to learn something like this, something this big, this serious. You set me up. You could have told me. You could have trusted me. But it's like you assumed I'd just never find out, and so it was enough to keep it to yourself." Maya turned away from Tom. "I don't even know how to face you right now. I feel like I don't know you."

"Maya, please." Tom sounded desperate as he reached for her, but Maya pulled away, out of his grasp. "Of course I was going to tell you. I...I want to share everything with you. I want you to know everything there is about me. I want to know everything about you. There just hasn't been the right moment. but it would have come up. I know it would have. Declan just sped things up faster than I'd intended today. I'm sorry he did that."

Maya shook her head. "This isn't about Declan, and you don't need to apologize on his behalf. This is about you and me. It's about how much I've shared with you, the way I've practically bled in front of you as I've shared my pain, my open wounds, everything I'm feeling...I share all of that with you, and yet, getting personal information out of you, the kind that *really* matters...it's like I have to be a master codebreaker. And I'm not skilled enough to do it. And I'm not thick skinned enough to do it ether." She wiped her eyes quickly and sniffed. "Because it really hurts to be ambushed like this. I feel like a fool for having let it happen this time, especially after you didn't even tell me you were an alcoholic until we were literally sitting in a support group meeting. This isn't going to happen again, Tom."

Tom reached for her again, desperation in his eyes. "It won't happen again, Maya. I swear it. There aren't any other skeletons in my closet, I promise you. This...this was the thing I didn't know how to tell you. But I knew I was going to tell you...somehow, someday. There's nothing else. You know it all. I'm deeply, deeply sorry that I kept this from you. Can you forgive me? Please?"

Maya had let Tom put his hands on her arms while he spoke, but as he came to the end of his confession, she shrugged away from him. "That's not what I meant, Tom. This isn't going to happen again because...because I made a mistake being vulnerable like this in the first place. This is more than I can handle right now. I never should have let things evolve between us...and I definitely shouldn't have invited you to stay last night. Can we pretend I didn't do that? Can we go back to how things were before? Of course I'll still manage your marketing efforts, but...just...life is better, easier for me if I don't put myself in a position like this. I hope you understand."

"Please, Maya," Tom said. "Don't do this. Punish me if you want to. I know I deserve it for not being honest with you. But you closing yourself off...that's a tragedy. That's not good for anyone, and especially not you." There were tears in his eyes as he reached over, just stopping himself from placing his hand over Maya's heart. "You have such a special, beautiful heart. I know I must seem like an irredeemable fool to you right now...but I'm better for having known you, for having gotten to touch your heart. To be touched by it. It's the same for your friends, for Catherine, for your family...everyone you let in, they're blessed by it. Please, please, *please* don't close yourself off to everyone. Don't let me be the reason that you do it."

Maya felt the tears shining in her own eyes and batted them away again. "Don't give yourself that much credit, Tom," she said. "It's my default setting to remember that closeness causes pain. I would have gotten back to this point sooner or later. Thank you for making it sooner and for not wasting too much of my time. Now, if you don't mind, I think we both need to be getting started with our days."

Tom looked shell-shocked, but he nodded. "You're right. I know you don't want to hear me say it again, but I really am deeply, deeply sorry. I hope we can talk about this again someday. Not today, I know better than that...I'll stop. For now. That doesn't mean I'm giving up on you."

"It would be better if you did," said Maya, walking to the door and holding it open until Tom went through it. "We don't have another meeting scheduled until next week, so I'll be in touch via email if you need anything before then. I'll send you daily updates on the campaign results."

"Thank you," said Tom. It was clear he didn't want to leave, that he was afraid of what would happen once the door closed between them. But he respected Maya's wishes, and he let her close the door.

It wasn't as if her heart wasn't breaking too. She just couldn't show it—that was the problem, wasn't it? Pain always begets more pain. You grieve and mourn, and when you bring others into it, it amplifies as you grieve and mourn together. But Tom was the reason she was grieving today—grieving the loss of a promise she'd only really dared believe in the night before. It had been such a cruel tease, that one night of hope. Now it was gone with the morning sun, vanished like a dream, slipping away more and more with every second that she was awake.

"This is ridiculous," she said out loud to herself. "What is there to mourn? We were barely together, if you can even call it that. It happened, it was a mistake, and I've learned my lesson. I do better on my own, so on my own I shall be. It's that simple."

But Maya's pep talk wasn't working. The more she reasoned with herself about why she shouldn't bother being sad, the more the gaping hole of sadness grew. That little bit of hope that she'd let herself experience had been fatal. Once she had tasted it, knowing she couldn't have it, that it had never really been hers...well, that was what hurt the most.

Maya went through the remainder of the motions of preparing herself for work. She finished putting on makeup and styling her hair, barely recognizing the expressionless face staring back at her. Touching up the exterior helped create the façade of putting on her professional disguise, an armor of sorts. Because there was no way that all she was feeling right now was going to have any place at the office. If she had learned anything in the last twelve hours, it was that mixing emotions and business was messy

and painful and not a mistake worth repeating anytime
soon.

♥ • ♥ • ♥ • ♥ • ♥

It was a quiet morning in the Andersen Consulting office,
and Maya was relieved by the relative peace and calm from
the moment she'd walked through the doors. She'd been
able to put her head down and focus on her work without
having to make any small talk or invent a response for
anyone who asked how her evening had been or comment-
ed on what a beautiful day it was. If Maya was sure of
anything, it was that this day was an irredeemable waste of
life. Nothing good had happened yet today, and nothing
good was likely to happen for the rest of it. Heck, if she
thought back to the work news that had rocked her world
yesterday, she might as well write off the whole week.

The other frustrating thing—and there were so many
today, weren't there?—was that everywhere she looked in
the office, she saw Tom. No, of course he wasn't foolish
enough to come to Andersen and make a grand gesture
to try to get her back. But notes about his project were
tacked up all over her workspace, and of course his project
was the only thing she'd been thinking about for the past
months. Even seeing Catherine striding across the office
floor reminded Maya of Tom because of their personal
connection. Maya didn't have a lot of experience with
getting over someone in the romantic sense, but she was
pretty sure that being bombarded with reminders of them
all day long was a terrible strategy for managing it.

It was a relief when, a few long hours later, Catherine summoned Maya into her office for a meeting. It wasn't until Maya was actually face to face with her boss that she recalled they hadn't spoken since the fateful meeting yesterday, where nothing at all had changed in Maya's career. But she remembered her own words of wisdom about keeping her feelings separate from her work, and she pasted on a smile before Catherine could see through to what she was feeling.

"Maya, I wanted to have this meeting with you today…well, actually I wanted to have it before we announced Chris's new role, but you know we were really trying to keep that under wraps. Now that it's out in the open, I'd love it if the three of us could have a proper chat." Before Maya could respond, Catherine reached for the phone on her desk and paged Chris at his table outside the office. "Chris, could you join us, please?" She hung up before a response came, but the door opened a few seconds later in answer.

"Maya, hello! How are you?" Chris was as friendly and warm as ever, and Maya couldn't help herself from feeling happy for him, just for a second before she remembered how miserable she was for herself.

"I'm well, thanks. Congratulations on the promotion. This must be so exciting for you!" She forced a smile, and Chris returned it tenfold.

"It really is! I admit I do feel a bit overwhelmed when I think about it—"

Catherine interrupted then. "Yes, that's why we asked you here, Maya. Naturally, you are aware that you have more experience here at Andersen Consulting than Chris here. And that's why, especially in light of the really top-notch work you did while I was gone, I'd love to see the two of you working as a team. I can't think of anyone better—other than myself, of course, but I really don't have the time for that—than you to help Chris settle into his new role here. What do you say, Maya?"

Maya stared at the two of them, both waiting for her response with open grins spreading across their faces. She wanted to say a lot of things to them—more than anything else, she wanted to ask Catherine why this role was being given to someone less qualified than her, especially if she was qualified enough to *train* that someone for the job. But instead of saying any of it, she simply shoved it all back down. "Sure. I'm happy to help. Just let me know what you need from me, and I'll do it."

Catherine nodded, and Chris clapped his hands. They talked over each other in their efforts to thank her properly, and Maya gritted her teeth and waited for it to be over. She was running out of patience with this place. She was done making excuses for why things were done the way they were, and always assuming that Catherine had a grand plan in place that was better than anything she, Maya, could even imagine. She had seen the flaws and humanity of her boss, and it was clear to her now that they were made of the same stuff. Her boss might have the business cards to impress a room full of C-level executives, but she didn't have any grand vision for Maya's career that Maya herself couldn't even see. She had simply taken Maya for granted. To her, Maya was like wallpaper—maybe Catherine had noticed it once upon a time, but after weeks and months and years of staring at it, it just blended into the background anymore. There was nothing special about it, or about her.

This was too much—too much emotion, threatening to drag her down too deep. Maya stood abruptly. "Would it be alright if I went back to my desk?" she asked. "I've...got a lot of work to do."

Catherine searched her face, her eyes hunting for the answer to a question she didn't speak. "Of course. We'll talk another time," she said.

Twenty-Two

The rest of the workday, Maya went through the motions of all that was expected of her. She completed the work that came across her desk, she joined a couple of coworkers in ordering food from a local sushi restaurant they all liked, and she even sent Tom an update on the marketing campaigns they were running for Conley Corp.

Her email had been professional and to the point, simply telling him that there was a spreadsheet attached. She had even remembered to actually attach it, so there wasn't even the need to send a "cute" follow up email with the whole "oops, I forgot to attach the attachment" message.

Tom had responded quickly, thanking her for sending the information and asking how she was. She knew he was genuinely asking the question, without risking getting too personal and scaring her away, and yet she let herself pretend he'd asked it as a greeting and left the message unanswered.

By the time Maya got back to her apartment and dropped her keys on the counter, she felt like she was about eight hours too late for crawling into her bed and putting a lighthearted movie on the TV to numb out her mind a bit. Or maybe a tearjerker...it could be nice to have something to feel emotions about that wasn't actually directly impacting her life, happiness, or career.

She saw the remnants from last night in the kitchen—pizza boxes waiting to be recycled, and empty glasses on the counter she hadn't gotten around to washing yet. Maya felt a pang of something low in her stomach at the sight. At the same time, she wished she could go back to the innocence and ignorance of last night...and she also wished it had never happened. Or at least that Tom had never been there. Maybe she even wished Tom had just left his ex-future-sister-in-law alone and found a marketing agency to work with in Ireland like a normal human. Thinking of the exquisite torture it had been knowing him thus far made it all worse—if she could take away the part where she fell in love with him and got hurt as a result, it had been a lot of fun knowing him. He'd made her laugh, he'd challenged her, and he'd even been the one to support her career potential, the most of anyone she knew.

She groaned.

And then, as if in response to her groan, her phone rang. Maya was almost afraid to look at the screen, fearing and hoping that Tom had been telepathically summoned by her thoughts about him and was calling her now. But when she peeked with one eye, she breathed a sigh of relief—it was her mom. And if there was anyone Maya wanted to talk to when her heart was breaking, it was her mom.

"Hi, Mom." Maya sighed into the phone, not bothering to mask her exhaustion and emotion.

"Hi, honey," Janice answered. "What's going on? Are you okay? You don't sound like yourself."

"Not really," she said. "I mean, I'm fine, physically or whatever. It's just been a hard couple of days emotionally."

"What happened?" Janice asked. "Was it something with that boy you liked? I'd been waiting for a newsy update, but I finally realized I'd have to call you myself if I wanted to hear it."

Maya groaned. "I'm sorry. I meant to call you, I really did. Things were going well between us, honestly, until yesterday. First, I *didn't* get a promotion at work despite being publicly recognized for basically saving the company while Catherine was gone. And then this morning, Tom's brother showed up here drunk. And that's when I learned something Tom had never bothered to tell me...that he got arrested for drunk driving and nearly hit a family in a minivan."

"...wow. That's a lot." Janice was quiet, waiting for Maya to continue.

"It was. *Too* much, actually. I ended things, right then and there. It felt like a betrayal, him not sharing that with me. It felt like an ambush, finding out from his brother like that. And it just made me realize how much pain can come from letting people get close enough to hurt you, and I just don't think I'm interested in that."

"Maya..."

"I know you're going to try to talk me out of this, Mom," Maya responded. "But I don't know if this is something that you can make okay. I don't really believe this is something you can just fix with a different perspective or a better attitude."

Janice chuckled. "You know me well, my daughter. But I'm not going to give you any affirmations or suggest a different way of looking at things if you don't want it. I know sometimes you just need someone to listen, and I'm here for that, too."

"Thanks," said Maya. "It just really sucks. It feels like I'm being punished or tested or something. I mean, seriously, it's the first time I've really let myself get close to someone since Nina died...not like this is the same as my friendship with Nina. I just mean, I've not exactly been doing a lot of dating..."

"I noticed," Janice said. "I just assumed you had decided that, since it hurt so much to lose her, that you didn't dare let anyone get even closer to you than she had been."

Maya exhaled all the air in her lungs. "That's exactly it. It felt safer to keep people a little further away. Which makes no sense, since I'm just as close with Andie and Luisa as I was with Nina."

"It makes perfect sense. You survived loving someone at that level, but maybe it felt like you only barely survived it. So you didn't dare love someone even more than that."

"Yeah."

"And what do you feel about Tom now?" Janice asked.

"I was hurt, at first...but I think now I'm mostly just angry. I can't believe he set me up like that. He didn't trust me with the truth about himself, so he set me up perfectly to get blindsided by it. I never imagined he would do something like that. I wish he had told me, and I don't know if I can ever move past the fact that he didn't."

"So if he came to you today and begged you to forgive him...you wouldn't be able to do it?"

Maya groaned. "I don't know. I mean…I can't imagine that. It's easy to say I wouldn't even budge on it, but he's not standing in front of me giving me puppy dog eyes right now. I like to think I'd hold true to my values and, like, I'd say, 'Yeah, I can forgive you, but I'm not going to forget this. And I think that means we can't go back to the way we were before, either.'"

"I see," said Janice. "I know you're not looking for a solution right now, but do you want me to tell you what exactly it is that I see?"

"Ugh, I guess so," Maya groaned.

"I know how important your values are to you, and I respect that immensely. I really do. I've never had to worry about you getting behind the wheel under the influence, and that's been a great weight off my mind. But I think that holding too firmly too your values, to the absolute adhesion to your values, might make it a little difficult for you to let yourself be close to people. You can hold people to a standard for their behavior today, but it's completely unfair to hold them to that same standard for their past behavior. Do you know what I mean?"

"I mean, I think so…but also, ouch."

"I'm not trying to hurt your feelings, love. But this is important." Janice's tone was gentle but firm. "Have you ever done something in the past that you wouldn't do again if you had the chance? Think about the conversation we had when you were home…about the stress and worry I went through when you were in college. That made you feel awful, right? So, if you could go back to the eighteen-year-old version of yourself, would you do things exactly the same, or would you try to be a little different?"

"I'd try to be different," Maya said, "Though I'm sure I'd fail. I already failed at calling you this week to tell you about Tom."

"I didn't bring up that example to make you feel bad," Janice said. "But I did bring it up to make a point. It's easy to hold other people to impossible standards while we make allowances for ourselves. It's a great way to justify keeping them at arm's length, which is usually just what we do when we're feeling too scared about being vulnerable."

"Oof," said Maya. "You're making some excellent points. Giving me a lot to think about. It doesn't mean I'm going to call Tom or that I believe I can forgive him, but thanks for saying all of this, anyway."

"Well, I'm not quite done, honey," said Janice. "Why is it you think you can't forgive him?"

"I just can't believe that he would do something like that. That he *did* something like that. It was so stupid. So dangerous. So selfish."

"If you had the assurance that he would never do something like that again, would you forgive him? If you could be one hundred percent confident about it?"

"...I mean...maybe?"

"Why maybe? If that's your objection, then knowing that it would never happen again seems like it would definitely help ease your mind."

"For sure...I mean, it would definitely make it easier to trust him for the future. But it doesn't change the past."

"Ahh," Janice said. "So we're back to holding the past version of someone to a higher standard than what they already proven themselves capable of living up to. It's a no-win game."

"It's just…you don't get it. You couldn't possibly…"

"I do understand it. I think anyone who has ever had to forgive someone…forgive them genuinely and not just going through the motions…understands it."

Maya exhaled deeply. "Sorry. I didn't mean to assume."

"Not at all. But let me ask you a question. If Tom came to you tomorrow and said everything you want to hear him say…if he told you he was deeply, deeply sorry, he was totally in the wrong, totally stupid, berated himself for all the wrong he had done and promised it would never, ever, ever happen again and then begged your forgiveness…would you be satisfied?"

"What do you mean?"

"I mean, would that change anything? Would you really be able to move on past it?"

Something clicked into place in Maya's mind. "Whoa. Or would I still want to hold it over his head and remind him of how he messed up in the past?"

"Yep, that's it." Janice's voice was small. "Most of us think forgiveness is all about the other person truly repenting and saying all the things we long to hear them say. But there's another big part of it, and that's what we do with what they tell us. Are we able to move past it and really let it go? Or do we want to keep bringing up the past every time we think they get a little too big for their britches? Knock them down a peg when they get too full of themselves?"

"Yeah, that…" Maya began. "I think I have to sit with that one for a while. I've been rehearsing over and over in my mind today, replaying everything that he did wrong. I've thought of all the things I'd like to hear him say, which ones would be good enough to even consider seeing him outside of work again. But the idea that I wouldn't be able to move past it, that I'd be the one continuing to bring it up and never letting him forget...well that stings a little."

"Good," said Janice. "That means it struck a nerve that needed to be struck. Don't feel like you have to act on this right away, but do let it marinate. Forgiveness works best when it's from a place of genuine understanding, not one of grasping and urgency and rushing to the conclusion before you're really feeling it. Are you ready to forgive him and move on today?"

Maya answered quickly. "No. Not yet. I...I think I need to stew in it some more."

"There's a good girl." Maya could hear the smile in her mom's voice. "You're being honest with yourself and with me. I'm so proud I could cry. Do you think you might be ready to forgive Tom at some undetermined point in the future?"

Maya thought for a moment. "I'm open to considering it. And that's more than I could have said half an hour ago."

"That's all I could have ever hoped to hear you say," said Janice. "Are you alright, apart from that? What's this about work?"

Maya waved away the question, even though her mom couldn't see her through the phone. "Honestly? Let's save that conversation for another time. You've already worked your Mom magic on one part of my life, so how about I just sit with this one for a while? We can talk about work on a different day. And I promise I'll actually call you this time. Deal?"

"It's a deal. I love you, Maya."

"I love you, too, Mom."

Maya spent the rest of the evening alone with her thoughts. She didn't call Andie and Luisa to talk the whole thing through with them, even though she wanted to. Because something inside her was urging her to be quiet, to be alone, and to go against her normal way of processing.

She had always been one to process through her feelings out loud, and there was nothing wrong with that. But she felt a vague nagging that perhaps sometimes the processing turned into rehearsing. The first time that she talked through what was bothering her, she was likely to have revelations about what she needed to change or learn from the incident. That had certainly been true while talking with her mom today.

But often, after that first, impactful journey through the feelings, beliefs, and motivations that were causing her pain, she'd still keep talking. Keep telling the same old story. Looking for the reactions from her audience, letting herself feel the same righteous indignation or incredulity with every time that she told—or performed—the story again.

It was hard to explain how Maya knew this about herself. It wasn't that she'd had a mystical download of new information about herself; it was more that she was following one intuitive nudge at a time and this was what was being revealed. First, there was the urge to be quiet and still, and she honored that. Then, there was the question that arose: why do I want to talk about this again with my friends when I've already got something to digest from my mom? The answer to that question, which Maya felt arise as if from within her belly was a harsher, uglier truth.

Maybe you want a second opinion. Maybe you want to be justified in doing the cowardly thing and cutting Tom off. Or maybe it's just that sitting here alone with your thoughts and feelings is scaring the crap out of you. Either way, does it really matter? You've never been one to shy away from a challenge, so right now, your challenge is to be alone. To notice what you're thinking and feeling and just sit with it. Can you do that? Or do you need to numb it?

It was the idea of numbing her discomfort that sat with Maya the deepest. It had been easy for her to judge Tom's actions, which were the result of his addiction. But she hadn't even considered what was at the root of those actions. Had he been in pain? Suffering? Trying to numb himself from something? And was that any different from the ways that she numbed herself? Sure, her vices of choice didn't make it unsafe to operate a motor vehicle, but they kept her from working through the pain and suffering in just the same way.

All of this poured out of Maya into her journal, words flowing faster onto the page than she could even feel them bubbling up. She wanted to remember this, everything that she was coming to understand tonight, for the first time in her life. And the act of writing it down, well, it seemed to leave peace in its wake. The more she wrote, the calmer and more settled she felt. The clearer her head. The more clarity she gained about her next steps forward.

And so, knowing what she needed to do, Maya prepared herself as if it was the night before a grand battle. But she did it in the "self care" way, and not in the "sharpening my sword" way. She made herself a healthy meal, turned off the television, and read a few pages from one of her go-to favorite books. Then she treated herself to a bath, dropping a few splashes of lavender oil into the tub. Between the heavenly smell and the hot water easing her tense muscles, by the time she emerged, she was ready to sleep like a baby. Or not actually like a baby, since crying and waking up every few hours demanding to be fed didn't sound like the rest of champions.

Maya went to bed that night knowing that the next day she was going to start out on a new path that was going to change everything. And with that knowledge in her heart, she fell asleep as soon as her head touched the pillow and her dreams were every bit as hopeful and exciting as the new reality ahead of her.

Twenty-Three

"**I**'m sorry if this sounds rude, but what in the world are you doing calling us at seven in the freaking morning?" Luisa didn't sound thrilled when Maya video called the next morning, but Andie's warm smile made up for it.

"What's going on?" Andie asked. "You look happy..."

"I am, and I'm sorry, Lu," said Maya. "This just really couldn't wait. I think you're going to want to hear it, and I think you'd be angrier at me if I didn't tell you than if I did. If that makes sense."

"Okay..." said Luisa. "I'm listening, but I'm also going to, you know, keep getting ready for work while I do that. Because, as you might be aware, it's seven o'clock in the morning, Maya."

Maya chuckled. "Yes, I'm aware. I just...today is going to be big. Last night was huge, and I need to tell you two all about it."

"Tell us, tell us!" crowed Andie. "We're both just dying to know; ignore Luisa's attitude and carry on, please."

"Is it about Tom? I bet it's about Tom. Did things, ahem *progress* between you two?" asked Luisa.

"Tom definitely plays a part in this story, and if you'll let me tell it, you'll find out just as soon as I can get the words out," promised Maya. "So actually...Tom stayed over after the two of you left the other night..."

"I knew it!" cried Luisa.

"I mean, yeah...I think we all knew that," said Andie. "I'm still happy to hear you confirm it, but I'm not exactly surprised by it."

"Well, that's not at all the end of the story," said Maya. "Because the next morning his brother turned up here and everything pretty much fell apart."

"What do you mean? His brother? How does he even know where you live?"

"All good questions. But the point of his brother's unwanted visit is that he revealed something about Tom that totally changed the way I see him. Tom...when he used to drink, he made some terrible decisions. He drove drunk, and he almost hit a car with a family in it."

"Oh my god," said Andie. "What happened to them?"

"They were all okay, by some miracle," said Maya. "I just can't get over the fact that he did it in the first place. Or at least, it really shocked me in the moment and I basically ended things between us."

"Wow," said Luisa. "That happened really fast. I mean, I definitely understand. I know this is, like, the most serious betrayal someone could do to you. I'm just shocked, is all."

"I was, too," said Maya. "That's actually why I didn't tell the two of you yesterday, though. I talked it through with my mom, and then I realized I just needed to be alone with it. To work through it on my own. Not to do what I'm doing right now, gossiping with my two best friends—"

"Aww, we're your best friends?" asked Luisa.

"You know you are. Now let me keep telling the story." Maya shook her head. "Anyway, the point is that all of this brought up a lot of...stuff...for me. And it made me realize my options are basically either to focus on what Tom did wrong and punish him for the rest of eternity because of it...or to bless and release him and focus on myself. On what I can work on and work through. Maybe even to forgive him at some point, though I'm still not entirely sure what that entails."

"I love it," said Andie. "Of course you know I'm always going to be in favor of any option that involves a lot of personal development work, though."

"Me, too," said Luisa. "What do you have in mind?"

"I'm not entirely sure yet. I spent the evening just being quiet, writing in my journal, doing self care type things..."

"That's beautiful," said Andie. "And I think it's the way to go. Follow your own intuition and listen to what you need in the moment. You don't really need to have a detailed plan to follow on how to improve yourself."

"Well, I take some offense to that," said Luisa. "You know I love a good plan, after all. But yeah...sometimes we do over-plan and then immediately fail. So you're doing it the right way, taking small steps now rather than promising yourself you'll start taking big steps on January 1st or next Monday or something like that."

"Thanks, you two," said Maya. "I think what I'm really going to need from the two of you is some tough love.

Like…if you see me misstepping in how I'm handling this, will you tell me?"

"Absolutely," said Luisa with conviction. "Sorry. You probably didn't want me to say that quite so enthusiastically. But yes, I will definitely tell you the truth."

Maya laughed. "Duly noted. Andie? What do you think?"

"We can tell the truth in love, always. I think that's what we've been doing for each other already, Maya. This doesn't have to feel like a giant momentous change. It can just be a gradual sliding from one stage of your life into the next one."

"You're right," said Maya. "So one thing I'm thinking is that I really need to just spend a lot of time working on myself. Like, alone, you know? Daily meditation and journaling…exercise would be good, too, I think. Just really focusing on my own development, putting aside this whole relationship thing because I'm clearly not ready for it."

Luisa laughed. "Okay, it's tough love time. Don't you think you've spent enough time alone, just focusing on yourself? Isn't that what your entire life has been up to this point?"

"Well, I mean…I *was* alone, that's true. But I wasn't, like, consciously working on myself…"

"Maya, the idea that you have to be actively working on yourself in order to grow and evolve as a human being was sold to you by personal development gurus. No offense, Luisa. But whether you are devoting study time to it every day or not, you are growing and evolving as a human being. and life is giving you opportunities to stretch and grow even more... telling yourself that you're not ready for those life-brought opportunities yet but that you will be someday...that's a major fallacy." Andie was gentle, as promised, but her words still had a bite to them.

"But Andie," protested Maya, "There's no way I'm ready to figure out how to be in a relationship. I'm way too much of a mess on my own."

"But when you were on your own, were you aware of the things that you're working through right now? If not for Tom coming into your life, would you have known that you needed to grow in these areas? Or were you doing just fine avoiding them?"

Maya was quiet, so Luisa chimed in. "Andie is right. Relationships...and life, for that matter...have a way of revealing things to us about ourselves that we need to work on. It's super inconvenient, honestly. I'd much rather prefer being on a deserted island with just a stack of personal development books to work through. I'm pretty sure by the end of a year or two, I'd have achieved enlightenment. But if that enlightenment only works when I'm on a deserted island all alone without the joys and challenges that other people provide...is it really even real? If it doesn't work in the real world, does it even matter?"

"Oof," said Maya. "You two are destroying all of my big self improvement plans before I can really even get them off the ground. I mean, I already got up early this morning and meditated before I even called you. Now it feels like I'm doing it all wrong."

"That's not what we're saying, Maya love," said Andie. "You can still do all of those things. Meditating, journaling, exercise, breathwork...it's all really, really wonderful.

Just don't do those things in a vacuum, without any other people in your life. Don't tell yourself you can't date until you've mastered all of them. Do those things *and* go out to dinner with an attractive man. Or..." She paused.

"What? I'm afraid to even ask," said Maya.

"Or do all of those things and put them into practice with Tom. Learn about forgiveness, and then offer it freely to someone who deserves it," said Andie.

Maya couldn't speak. She felt a lump of emotion in her throat that she couldn't quite identify—it was like a mixture of fear, sadness, and anger all at once. Her friends waited, giving her the time she needed to find her next words.

"Does he?" she asked. "Does he deserve to be forgiven?"

"What do you think?" asked Luisa.

"I don't know," Maya admitted. "I really believe what he did was wrong, and I just don't know if I can move past it..."

"Let's look at this a different way," said Andie. "Let's focus on what forgiving him would do for you, not what it would do for him. Forgiveness is never really about the other person. It's not a way to try to force or convince them to change their behavior...it's about you deciding that you no longer want to carry it around anymore—the anger, the hurt, any of it. So, that's the question then. How long do you want to carry around these feelings? The betrayal? The hurt? The disbelief? The anger? Is it serving any purpose for you?"

"You sound like my mom." Maya groaned. "But I think, actually, that all of these feelings *are* giving me something."

Andie cocked her head. "What's that?"

"It makes me feel justified. Self righteous. Like I'm better than him."

"I know that feeling well," said Luisa. "It's an old friend, and honestly, I'm quite fond of it."

"Yeah, it's been strangely comforting," admitted Maya. "But I don't think I want to keep it forever. I don't think I want to keep stoking this fire of anger. I bet it's not very good for me."

"No, it's not," said Andie. "And you'd have to do a *lot* more meditation to counteract it than if you just dropped it in the first place."

Maya groaned. "You're probably right, and I kind of hate you for it. Not really, but...I wish I *could* hate you for it and just move on from this without having to do any of the hard stuff. But I'm pretty sure you're going to win this round, Andie, even if I'm not quite ready to admit it yet."

"Take your time, love," said Andie. "I promise I won't rub your face in it or say, 'I told you so.'"

"And that right there is why Andie is better than all of us," Luisa said, "because I would *relish* the opportunity to say, 'I told you so.' Wouldn't you?"

They all laughed, then said their goodbyes and prepared to start their days. Maya wasn't sure what was waiting for her at Andersen Consulting today, but the pit in her stomach told her she might need to be honest with Catherine about her feelings. That was definitely not a pleasant thought, but she'd never been good at moving past something without actually talking about it first. If there was any chance she was going to keep working for Catherine and not feeling resentful about it, she'd need to speak up for herself. It might even have the added benefit of making it a little more difficult to overlook her in the future, but Maya wasn't going to hold her breath about that.

As it turned out, Maya didn't have much time to overthink her conversation with Catherine. Before she had even put her mug down on her table, Chris was there with a smile on his face and a sticky note in his hand. The note was written in Catherine's familiar handwriting, and it was asking if Maya would have time for a "quick chat first thing." Maya gulped down the anxiety that wording gave her—it sounded too much like her boss was asking, "Can we talk later?" which always made her feel like a naughty school-child—and followed Chris to Catherine's office with her travel mug still in hand.

Maya knocked on Catherine's door and opened it as soon as she heard Catherine's voice say, "Come on in!" Upon entering the room, she saw her boss sitting at her desk, staring intently at her computer monitor, glasses resting halfway down her nose. "Maya! Good morning," she smiled. "You got my note. I'm glad you're here so early. I really wanted to speak with you before everyone got here."

"I did get your note," Maya said, forcing a smile back. "I was curious what it was about, so I came before I even logged into my computer."

"There's that work ethic I admire so much." Catherine beamed.

As Maya felt the bile rise in her throat, she realized it was now or never—if she had something to say to Catherine, it needed to be said and not just thought forcefully in her direction.

"Catherine, I have to say something to you," she said. "Or ask you something, maybe. I...I'm confused. I appreciated the acknowledgement of the work I did while you were gone. But I was a little surprised, I guess, that I wasn't considered for the promotion. If I'm being honest."

Catherine blinked in surprise. "You...you would have wanted to be promoted? Wow, I...I honestly hadn't even considered it. It's not that you aren't talented enough—of course, you know I appreciate your talent more than anyone else does." She shook her head. "I had no idea, Maya. Why didn't you say something? You never asked."

She looked genuinely sorry, and Maya didn't know what to say. So it hadn't been intentional? Catherine wasn't trying to slight her? Maya sighed. Of course she wasn't. Catherine was trying to do the right thing in every area of her life, and she wasn't a mind reader.

"I'm sorry, Catherine," Maya said. "I should have said something. I can't expect you to know what I'm thinking. I just thought that since you left me in charge when you were gone that you might have seen some leadership potential in me." She shrugged. "That was silly of me."

Catherine shook her head. "Don't say that. It's not silly to want something, and it's not silly to ask for it." She lifted the corners of her mouth in a small smile. "And I'll keep it in mind for the future."

"Thank you." Maya smiled back at her boss. "What was it you wanted to see me about this morning?"

A blush spread across Catherine's cheeks. "Oh, well...that feels a bit inappropriate now. I was going to work with you and Chris on setting up a plan for his training period." She waved a dismissive hand. "Never mind that now."

"No, it's okay," Maya offered. "I still care about you, about Chris, and about the company as a whole. I'm happy for Chris, and if there's anything I can do to help set him up for success in his new position, I'm here to help."

Catherine looked surprised. "That's...wonderful news! Really! Thank you, Maya. I really do owe you one."

Maya chuckled lightly. "You said it, not me. I'll leave you to your work, and I'll talk with Chris to get our schedules coordinated. Have a good day, Catherine."

And with that, she left.

Twenty-Four

"**I**'m not going to lie, Maya," said Luisa, taking a sip of her drink. "I'm very proud of you, but I'm also completely and utterly shocked by all the words coming out of your mouth."

Andie nodded. "It's more than a little surprising, I agree. Especially considering all the pep talks we've given you...to see you go from finding it hard to believe the words we were saying to suddenly standing up for yourself to your boss's face is, like, very cool and also has me wondering where the hidden cameras are."

"I get it," said Maya. "I've been a bit of a slow learner. And you're probably both exhausted by how many times you've had to tell me more or less the same thing in the time that we've been friends. Well, for some reason, things were different this time. It's like all the things that I'd heard over and over again finally made sense. Something clicked into place. And that changed things."

Andie and Luisa exchanged a glance before Andie spoke up again. "For some reason, huh? Any ideas what was different this time?"

Maya shook her head. "I think the easy answer would be to say that it has something to do with Tom, and I'm pretty sure that's what both of you are thinking. But I don't believe it's that simple. I think maybe it's just that the timing is right, so it finally became clear to me that I've been taken for granted at work and that if I want that to change, then I'm the only one who can do anything about it. It probably doesn't hurt that in the last few weeks, I've seen a very human side of Catherine that I never had before. So now that I know she's human and makes mistakes, it's actually possible for me to believe that her overlooking me could be just that—a mistake—and not part of some grand master plan or, even worse, an intentional slight."

"That's not bad insight," admitted Luisa. "You're getting pretty good at this self awareness thing."

"Thanks," said Maya. "So far it's been a whole lot of work. I kept having to talk myself back into having the conversation with Catherine this morning. Reminding myself why it *wasn't* actually a better plan to just gloss over it and pretend nothing happened and that nothing was wrong."

"Did you feel better after it was over?" Andie asked.

Maya nodded. "Absolutely. *So* much better. I actually even felt better just as soon as I started talking to her. As soon as I started having a spine and standing up for myself. It was like this exhilaration was just rushing through my body and the whole thing took on a life of its own."

"Like an out-of-body experience?" Luisa asked.

"I think so," said Maya. "I mean, I've never had something like that happen to compare it to. But yeah, as I think back on it now, it did sort of feel like I was up on the ceiling watching the whole thing happen. Cheering on the little figure who looked like me as she went into conversational battle with the little figure who looked like my boss. I was *exhausted* when it was over. Is that normal?"

"Sure," said Andie. "Just think about all the emotional excitement that takes. All the energy you're using. Now if only you could have taken the rest of the day off and gone home to sleep it off."

Maya laughed. "Yeah, I can't imagine we'll ever live in a world where that's a possibility. But it's okay. I think I'm going to get better at this standing up for myself thing as I practice doing it more. It probably won't always be quite that big of a shock to the system, right?"

Luisa shrugged. "It definitely has gotten easier for me, but we aren't all wired the same, so I don't want to make you a promise I can't keep."

"It's a part of being human," said Andie, "And like all the other parts, it doesn't necessarily get easier but you *can* get better at it with practice. You can get better at anything if you practice doing it enough."

"That's good to know," said Maya.

"Doesn't it already seem like it's getting more natural?" Andie asked. "Checking in with your emotions, acting on your intuitive nudges...is it starting to feel easier?"

Maya laughed. "Well, it's been almost twelve hours since I started, so I'll let you know after I've at least slept on it. But, I mean, my hunch is that you're right. We'll see, I guess."

"We will." Andie smiled. "If it's not too annoying for you, could we talk about Tom? I have a question, but I don't want to ask it unless you're cool with it."

Maya groaned. "I guess it's fine. I'm still a mess of emotions about him. Part of me wants to write him out of my life forever, and part of me just wants things to go back to the way they used to be. And all of me knows that neither of those options is really entirely possible." She waved away that train of thought. "Anyway, I'm rambling. What's your question?"

"It was just something you said about Catherine," said Andie. "About realizing that she was human and therefore capable of making mistakes."

"Yes...I do recall saying that," said Maya.

"I just thought that was a particularly profound statement," said Andie. "And I wondered if it could be applied to anyone else?"

Maya rolled her eyes until she could see her eyebrows. "Sure. It could probably be applied to anyone and everyone. So this could go either way. Maybe I apply that logic to Tom and realize that he's a human man who made a human mistake and deserves human forgiveness. Or maybe I apply that logic to myself and accept that pursuing the relationship with Tom like I did is simply an example of how *I'm* a human capable of making human mistakes. And that was a mistake and I can forgive myself for it and move on."

"I love to give Andie a hard time just as much as you do," said Luisa. "But even I think you're maybe being intentionally obtuse about this one, Maya. No one is going to force you to forgive Tom. But we aren't asking you to do it for us. We're suggesting it—over and over, I'd like to point out—probably because we think it's the best possible thing you could do." She shrugged. "Or else because we're jerks who want to control you. You'll have to figure out which one it is."

Maya was quiet. She took a long drink from her glass and stared out at the horizon. Once again, they'd managed to get a table with a stellar view of the lake, and she was grateful to have something to stare at that didn't make it quite as obvious that she was trying to avoid meeting her friends' eyes. They were right, she knew. She was being childish about this whole mess with Tom, distracting herself with twisting her friends' words or willfully misunderstanding them just to prove a point. She knew all that, and at the same time, she felt powerless to stop herself from continuing the same trajectory.

"I know, Lu," she said. "And I'm sorry. To both of you. I know you're both speaking from a place of care and concern for me, and I haven't received it as well as I could. Honestly, I get it. I know that forgiveness and moving past all of this is the only real option for me moving forward. But there's been a comfort in being, like, the jilted ex-lover. And I know I'm going to lose that when I forgive him and move on. I won't have him in my life, and I won't have him to complain about, either. Because I'm going to have to be the bigger person and move on, and I'm not sure how good I am at playing that role."

Andie scooted over to put her arm around the back of Maya's chair, at the same time Luisa reached over and grabbed Maya's hand. Feeling their support—literally *feeling* it, in the form of their pats on the back and squeezes of her hand—brought a lump to Maya's throat. She couldn't say anything to thank them, only lean in to Andie's arm and squeeze Luisa's hand back. She really had the best friends, even when she was being stubborn and obstinate and probably didn't deserve them.

They were all silent for a few minutes, holding the position they'd found themselves in. Maya was absorbing her friends' strength and support, and all three of them enjoyed a moment of unspoken gratitude—for the beautiful place that they lived, for the special friendships that they had formed, and for the moment that they were sharing.

After what felt like a very long silence, Andie's gentle voice broke in with a question. "How do you know you don't get to keep him?" she asked.

The silence came back and continued for a few more minutes as Maya tried to find the words and the ability to speak them without her voice breaking. "Because I think I was greedy. I asked for too much, or...I didn't ask for it, really, but when I got it I was too comfortable too quickly. I took it for granted. But look at my life. Look at this moment. I have the best friends in the world. My family is super supportive. I live in the city I always dreamed of living in. My career is going well, even if it has its little hiccups. And all I do is take it for granted. That's the irony, actually. I complained about being overlooked at work, but all I do all day long is overlook all the blessings in my life. I mean, I have to write a sticky note to myself to remind me to call my mom. I should be so grateful to have a mom like her that I just call her to share news or ask her how she's doing without even thinking about it. But no, that's not how I work. If I don't write a sticky note, goodness knows how long it'll be before I'm actually the one to pick up the phone."

"I think you're being too hard on yourself," said Luisa. "Or at least, the things that you're talking about don't make you special. You're not the only person to forget to be grateful for what they already have. And you're *definitely* not the only person to be less than stellar at calling their parents regularly. So by that same logic, you can't possibly be the only person who doesn't deserve to have a loving partnership."

"Maybe it's not about deserving at all," said Andie. "If we all got what we deserved all the time, the world would look very different. But I think a lot of what we get—all of us—is more like random chance. The roll of the dice. So when good things come our way, we don't need to doubt whether or not we deserve them, just like we don't need to assume that we've earned every bad thing that comes our way, either. Good, bad, or otherwise, life happens. Hold on to what's good while it's in your life, and take deep breaths through the bad, until it passes."

"That's your whole philosophy?" asked Maya.

Andie nodded. "That's my whole philosophy. It's not easy to be human sometimes. But love helps, whatever form it comes in. Maybe it's friends, family, or a handsome Irishman who can't take his eyes off you."

"Thank you two," said Maya. "I don't deserve you, but I'm grateful for you. For tonight. For your friendship, always. Thank you."

The following Monday, Maya woke with a renewed feeling of purpose. She had rested well over the weekend, and she was rocking life as a confident, hardworking single woman. As she got ready to go to work, she mentally walked herself through all that the day held in store. She would need to check in with Conley Corp's results again, as usual, though if the last week of data were any predictor of the current results, things were looking good. It might not be much longer that she would need to take point on Tom's product. Or at least not daily. Maya resolved to suggest passing the account down to a more junior marketing associate today, so that she could be freed up to take on some new projects and clients.

The thought of passing off her account with Tom stirred up a mix of emotions. Maya would be glad to end the awkward dance they had been doing—he had done an excellent job of respecting her boundaries and had let Maya take the lead on any and all interactions they had had. But at the same time, it was hard not to miss the way things had been—the friendly banter, the sharing, and, of course, the sparks. She hadn't felt those sparks since just before Declan turned up in her apartment that fateful morning, and she supposed they were extinguished for good.

It was for the best, though. Tom would be moving on, and who knew how much longer he would need to stay in Chicago, anyway? The last thing someone with Maya's anxiety about intimacy needed was a romantic connection with someone on the other side of an ocean. It hadn't turned out well for Catherine and Declan, after all. Better to avoid that whole mess entirely.

Maya nodded to herself, agreeing with her own thoughts. She was doing a stellar job on her own. She really was. She wondered, not for the first time, if she was just the kind of person who handled being single better and with more ease than anyone else. It wasn't a flaw of other people, necessarily, that they needed someone in their life to love and support them. She was just pretty sure that she wasn't missing her other half, and she didn't actually need a relationship the way the world insisted she did. She was surrounded by love, in the form of her family and friends, and she was living a very fulfilled life.

Yes, it was true it had been nice to spend those weeks with Tom. But she saw it for what it was now—a fleeting gift. She had enjoyed it while it lasted, but it had never been meant to stay. After all, most people in long-term relationships ended up resenting their partners at some point, or at least getting bored with them. That wasn't possible if the whole thing only lasted a couple of weeks.

She let that thought buoy her spirits. She was young, single, and the star of her own story, darn it! Maya finished getting ready for the day, a vague feeling that she was the character in a movie coming over her. With that feeling came the idea that teenage girls all over the world were watching her, envying her, dreaming of becoming her when they grew up. That definitely added a little extra bounce to her step—and inspired her to choose a fun lipstick color for that main character pop of personality.

Locking the door behind her, she smiled to herself. "Here we go," she said. "Time to go be the star of my own story today."

Twenty-Five

When she arrived, the office at Andersen Consulting was full of more hustle and bustle than Maya had ever seen it. She checked the clock to make sure she hadn't missed turning the clocks ahead an hour, even though it was not the appropriate time of the year to be doing that. Still, it didn't feel like it was barely nine o'clock on a Monday morning in the building—if anything, it felt like the "all hands on deck" staff meeting that happened in person once a year when employees from all over the globe were welcomed to the Andersen offices.

Maya grabbed Chris as he bustled past. "What's going on here?"

Chris looked flustered. "Your guess is as good as mine. Catherine called me at seven thirty this morning to pick up coffee and pastries for thirty people, but didn't bother to say what the occasion was. I haven't seen her yet today, but I think she's here in her office. Preparing for...whatever this is." He gestured around himself vaguely.

Maya went to her desk to set her things down. She recognized a few board members making their way to the conference room, but there were plenty of unfamiliar faces, too, and no clues to be found anywhere in the room.

Maya's colleagues were gathering in clusters around their cubicles, whispering to each other. Did no one have any idea what was about to happen?

She toyed with the idea of going to Catherine herself to get the inside scoop on what was going on, but then remembered that it wasn't her job to take responsibility for the entire office. Especially when Catherine had made it clear that wasn't what she wanted from her. So, like the rest of her coworkers, she waited.

The wait didn't last long. Within a few moments, one of the board members asked everyone to join them in the conference room. As she filed in with the rest of the staff, Maya felt a sinking feeling in her stomach. The fact that Catherine hadn't been the one to summon them—the fact that she hadn't even seen her boss yet—was doing nothing to diminish her anxiety. Something big was about to happen, and the last time she had felt that way at work had been the day Chris's promotion was announced. Was this going to be even bigger than that had been?

Once they were all inside, Catherine was the last to enter. She closed the door and sat down in the back of the room, while Rob, the chairman of the board, took Catherine's usual position of power in the front.

"Thank you all for being here," said Rob. "If we haven't had the pleasure of meeting yet, I'm Rob Richmond, chairman of the board here at Andersen Consulting. We called this meeting today to share with you some changes that are going to be taking effect very soon here at Andersen. I know that likely sounds scary to many of you—none of us like change, after all—but it is my sincere hope, which I share with the rest of the board, that you will see this as an opportunity."

Maya looked at the back of the room where Catherine was sitting. She seemed smaller today, like some of the spark had gone out of her normally luminescent being. She was dressed in a plain black blazer and slacks, with no pop of color or funky accessory to make her stand out in the normally male-dominant spaces she was accustomed to occupying. Catherine glanced in Maya's direction just then, and their eyes locked. Something passed between them, too quickly for Maya to put a name on it. Was it an apology? Asking for support? Understanding? She couldn't be sure, but she felt some of the resentment she'd been feeling towards Catherine dissolve as she gave her the slightest of nods back.

"You're no doubt aware of the changes that Ms. Andersen implemented here during her lapse of judgement," Rob continued. "You may have been told that some of those changes were done at the suggestion of the board, but I can assure you they were not. It's only been recently that the board and I have grasped the full extent of the damage that has been done to our company's reputation in the past month, and we have spent the last several days in near constant meetings to determine the appropriate plan of action moving forward.

"Catherine, if you wouldn't mind joining me up here, I think it would be comforting to your staff to hear directly from you." Rob nodded to Catherine, who stood and found her way to the head of the table.

She looked around, surveying the faces of the many staff members she had hired, including those who were joining remotely. "Thanks, Rob," she said. "And thank you all for sticking with me during this tumultuous time. I owe you all a debt of gratitude, and I won't forget how you stepped up in my absence. As Rob said, there is a need for some major changes to take effect here at Andersen, one of which being that I'll be stepping down. In the interest of focusing on my own health and well being—and I'll come right out and say it, my sobriety—I'm going to be moving back to New York where my family is. That's where I have the strongest support system, where I've been the healthiest, and where I see the most potential for a bright future."

The room was silent until one of the junior executives spoke up. "What does that mean for the company? We're going to miss you, Catherine, don't get me wrong. But what's going to happen to everyone else here? Is Chris getting another promotion already?" At the mention of his name, Chris blushed and dipped his head to look at something under the table, giving away his true feelings about being assigned even more responsibility than had already been piled on him.

Rob spoke again. "Things are going to look different here, too. For one thing, we already have a massive remote workforce, as I'm sure you're all aware. We've had great success with that, and Catherine's cross-country move has inspired us to consider another way of doing things. Rather than Catherine leaving us entirely—the company *is* named after her family, after all—we're going to take the entire business remote."

The room erupted in whispers, the collective volume of which was enough to force Rob to pause his speech. He held up his hands, pleading with the staff to let him finish his explanation.

"It's a big change, I know, but we truly believe it's in the best interest of not only the company but all of you as well. Hours will be more flexible, with your responsibilities being performance-based rather than requiring a set number of hours in the office. We'll also be providing a stipend to each of you to help you get set up. So if you don't have a desk at home, or if you just want to use that stipend to buy cups of coffee at the local coffee shop and work from there, that'll be up to you."

Someone near the front of the room—Maya couldn't see who it was, but her guess was that it was a new hire—raised a hand. After being acknowledged by Rob, they asked, "Are our jobs going to stay the same? Full time, with benefits?"

There was the faintest crack in the façade of Rob's expression before he regained complete control of his face. "That's the last thing I wanted to mention, so I thank you for your question. Your employment terms are also going to be changing. As the job responsibilities are going to be task and performance-based rather than tied to an hourly schedule, it makes financial sense for us as a company to rehire our staff on a contract basis."

"What does that mean?" The same person near the front of the room asked their follow up question.

"In plain English, it means that you will be hired on as freelance employees, and you'll be paid by the contracts that you are assigned to. And other than the work-from-home stipend we will be providing, there will be no other benefits. Health insurance and tax withholdings are going to be your responsibility. Look at it on the bright side, please—the freedom that you are going to have as a result of this restructuring could change your entire career. If you've always been wanting to work for yourself, but never quite knew how to take the first step, this is the prime opportunity. There will be nothing in your new contracts to prevent you from working on your own or for other companies at the same time. So, for our very motivated staff members, you could easily be seeing a significant increase in your yearly income."

Rob grinned out at the room but was met with blank stares. The murmuring and frowns lining the faces of everyone around her suggested to Maya that Rob's bombshell announcement had been received about as well by everyone else as it had by her.

But one thing he had said had stuck with her—something about "If you've been dreaming about working for yourself..." and she felt something click into place and a sense of peace wash over her. When the meeting was over, she knew what she needed to do.

Though Rob had clearly established himself as the one in charge in the conference room, he wasn't the person Maya wanted to talk to. As the meeting ended and her colleagues crowded around Rob and the other board members, dissatisfied with the answers they'd received to their questions thus far, Maya stepped outside just in time to catch Catherine.

Catherine had been trying to slip away unnoticed, it seemed, but Maya didn't let her out of her sight. She followed her boss down the hall until they were out of earshot of anyone in the conference room, and then Maya called out. "Catherine! Wait!"

Catherine wheeled around, her face looking pale. The tension in her eyes faded as she saw it was Maya approaching her.

"Maya," she said, forcing a smile. "Pretty wild stuff, huh? What do you think about all that back there?"

"I'm not too worried about it for myself," Maya answered. "I don't think I'll be working here much longer. I just wanted to make sure that you're okay and also to thank you for everything you've taught me. I think I'm going to be striking out on my own—*totally* on my own, not as a contractor for Andersen - and everything I know about marketing I learned from you."

Catherine shook her head. "That's not true, Maya. You're very talented. If I ever made you feel like you were nothing before you met me, I apologize." She took Maya's hands in her own. "You're brilliant, and you're going to do just fine on your own. I have a feeling you've already got your first client lined up."

"Who, Tom?" Maya asked. "I haven't spoken to him about this, but I suppose if he was interested and it was alright with you I could continue to work with him…"

"It's more than alright with me," said Catherine. "This isn't about the bottom line. This is solely about getting *all* of the Conleys—even the really good ones—out of my system. Let me tell you something, Maya. This whole change here? It might look like they're doing it *to* me, like they're trying to squeeze me out or make me look incompetent." She shook her head. "But I want this change. Heck, it was my idea. For the first time in a long time, or maybe ever, I need to prioritize myself. My mental health, my relationships, my sobriety...that's all true. So this conversation we're having now? I'm not thinking about how it's going to affect Andersen Consulting or about client contracts or any of that. I'm sorry but that's probably exactly what I've done in every previous interaction we've had." She lifted the corners of her mouth in a sad smile. "But I really do care about you as a person, Maya. I want you to be happy, not just to do well. I *know* you'll do well in business, I'm not worried about that. Just don't do what I did and put it ahead of everything else."

Maya was startled into silence, but managed to find her voice eventually. "Thank you, Catherine. That means a lot."

"It's the least I can do, and it's a long time coming. Anything that you need in the future, you let me know, alright? A reference, a referral of a client or two to get you started. I owe you, and I *will* make good on that debt."

Without thinking twice, Maya reached out and pulled Catherine in for a hug. The older woman resisted at first, but Maya felt her settle into the hug and squeeze her back after a few seconds.

"I'm actually going to miss you, Catherine," Maya said when she pulled away. "We've definitely had a complicated working relationship, but that doesn't mean I don't admire and respect you. I wish we could have gotten a little more time to connect on a personal level, but I guess that's how life goes."

"Actually," said Catherine, a sparkle appearing in her eye. "If you want to spend a little more time together, what do you think about getting out of here? You could accompany me to the airport and then...well, I don't know what you'll do after that. You could go home. Or you could get on a flight yourself. Or anything in between. The sky's the limit, kiddo."

"Really? Do you need a ride to the airport? You don't have to check in with the board or anything like that?"

Catherine waved the suggestion away. "They'll be cleaning up their mess here for a while, and everything we need to say to each other for now has already been said. I was just going to get a taxi by myself, and I can still do that. I just thought maybe..."

Maya shook her head. "No, it's a great idea. I'd be honored to see you off. Let me just get my things and we can go."

Because it wasn't rush hour, the drive to the airport only took about half an hour. Maya and Catherine sat together in the back seat, reminiscing about the fond memories they had shared at Andersen Consulting and talking about what the future held for each of them.

"My parents and my brother all live in Buffalo," explained Catherine. "These last few years that I've been in Chicago, I've barely made it home once a year to see them. With everything that has happened, it only makes sense to be near my family. Not only to lean on them for support, but, well, maybe for once to actually be a support to them, too. I think I've got some trust to earn back, and I intend to make it my mission to do it."

"If there's anything I know about you," said Maya, "It's that when you set your mind to something, you accomplish it. Just look at the way you grew your family's business. If you can do that in just a few years, I'm sure you can take that same energy and determination to your family and create whatever kind of reality you want to together."

"Thanks," said Catherine, giving Maya a grateful smile. "What about you? What's the next step for you?"

Maya shrugged. "I didn't know until this morning that I was going to actually give the idea of working for myself a try. Don't get me wrong, it wasn't like I made a super impulsive decision back there; I've been playing around with this idea for...well, a long time. I've been thinking about it, feeling pulled to it, being encouraged to do it...and just not taking action."

"Why is that?" Catherine asked.

"Great question," said Maya. "And if I knew, I probably could have avoided the whole thing. I mean, I know it's fear, but that hasn't helped me get to the root cause of that fear and eliminate it."

Catherine nodded. "I've been there. Let me just tell you one thing that helped me when I was taking over the business. We all think that working for someone else is the key to financial security, right? But businesses fail all the time—small ones, large ones, new ones, old ones. I don't say that to discourage you from starting your own, just to say that whatever other business you can work for, it has a possibility of failing. So the decision ultimately comes down to one question. Who do you want to put your faith in? Whose dream do you want to invest in? Working for someone else is just putting your faith in them and investing in their dream." She shrugged. "You saw it with me, I'm sure, when I disappeared. I'll bet Andersen didn't feel like the most secure place to be working when that happened." Catherine looked down at her hands, studying her fingernails.

"That helps, actually. Thanks, Catherine. And don't feel bad about anything that happened while I was working for you. I learned from all of it, and we wouldn't be here having this conversation right now if things had happened any differently."

"You're probably right," admitted Catherine. "Without having a breakdown of my own, I doubt I would have made any of the changes I needed to make. I doubt I could have connected with you on a human level without that happening."

Their taxi pulled up in front of the domestic terminal at O'Hare airport, and Catherine tipped the driver. Maya got out with her, the two of them following the driver around to the trunk of the car, where Catherine's suitcases had been stowed. There were two of them, and they were large and heavy, so Maya insisted on helping Catherine take them inside. She followed her former boss to the check-in counter for American Airlines, looking down at her phone as she walked. She'd need to request a ride back downtown after she and Catherine said goodbye, so she was checking the rideshare app to see how long her wait would be.

As Maya waited for the city map to populate with available drivers and their distances from the airport, Catherine stopped short in front of her. Maya tripped over the suitcase Catherine was wheeling and felt herself losing balance, about to execute a perfectly disastrous spill in front of all the people in the terminal. Just before she reached the point of no return and faceplanted on the floor, two strong hands wrapped around her arms and set her back on her feet.

"Maya." She heard the familiar voice and looked up into Tom Conley's warm green eyes that were smiling down on her. Behind him, with his gaze locked on Catherine's shocked face, was Declan.

Twenty-Six

"What are you doing here?" Maya asked Tom, her eyes darting to where Declan was standing a few feet away. Catherine was still frozen in place, looking at Declan as if she had seen a ghost.

"We're flying back to Dublin," said Tom. "Not direct, of course. I'm well aware that this is the domestic terminal. But we're leaving for New York and then on to Dublin. Be there by morning." Tom looked at Declan, and Maya took the opportunity to survey the two men. They both had suitcases and were both wearing travel-appropriate clothes, jeans and sweatshirts. "Hi Catherine," said Tom, shifting his gaze in her direction. "How are you?"

Catherine snapped to attention, pasting on a smile and walking over to join Maya and Tom. Declan mirrored her movements, and the four of them stood in an awkward and uncomfortable huddle of sorts. "Tom, Declan," said Catherine, nodding at the men. "What a delightful surprise to see you again."

Tom's smile was genuine, though the expression on Declan's face was hard for Maya to read. He was studying

Catherine's face like it was on display in an art museum, like he was willing her to look back at him, something she was pointedly not doing. Finally, he darted out a hand, lightly touching her on the arm before jerking his hand back like she had burned him. "Sorry," he said. "Catherine, could we have a word?"

Maya and Catherine exchanged a look, Maya offering a silent vow of support and Catherine assuring her that she didn't need it yet...but if she did, she would let her know. Tom was studying Declan with a scowl on his face, and Maya knew that if Catherine needed rescuing, he'd be more than happy to oblige.

As Declan and Catherine walked over to a bank of empty chairs, Maya looked up into Tom's eyes. "So," she said, forcing brightness into her voice that she didn't feel. "You're leaving?"

"We are," Tom nodded.

"How's Declan doing?" Maya asked. "He looks...different from the last time I saw him." She cringed inwardly at the memory of the last time she and Declan had been in the same space and all that had changed between her and Tom after that.

"He's doing really well, actually," said Tom. "I'm proud of him, and it's been a long time since I could say that. He's agreed to go to rehab, which is a first. He wanted to do it back home, in Ireland, so I'm accompanying him. I believe him this time, that he wants to clean up his act, though I understand well enough how addiction works that I'm not investing all my hope and happiness in him turning his life around 180 degrees on his first try."

"That's great," said Maya. "Both things, I mean. I'm really glad to hear that Declan is trying to make a change for himself, and I'm glad you're guarding your heart or managing your expectations. I'm not really sure how to say that."

Tom smiled. "I think 'managing your expectations' is a great way to put it. If he relapses, I'll definitely be sorry, so I wouldn't say I'm guarding my heart. I'm still open to being hurt by him, I've just got some boundaries in place, too."

Maya nodded. "That's love, isn't it? Giving someone the opportunity to hurt you and hoping that they won't. Not holding back, regardless."

"That's right. But don't forget the boundaries either. Without them, you're just asking for pain."

"I'm trying to learn that one still," Maya admitted. "Sometimes I'm a little too good at boundaries, but I'm still working on the being vulnerable part."

Tom stepped closer and lowered his voice. "Is that what happened to us?"

Maya felt a lump rise in her throat. "I...I think so," she said. "And it's been easy enough while I haven't been seeing you. But now, with you here, I'm actually feeling a little sad that you're leaving and we never got a chance to fix this."

"You're wondering what could have been?" asked Tom.

She nodded. "Yeah. And I know it's dumb. Too little too late and all that. But I'm sorry. I'm still figuring a lot of this out."

Tom gave her a small smile. "Figuring what out?"

She shrugged. "Life? Vulnerability? Love?"

Tom's eyes widened. "Love? That's a big word. Are you sure it's the one you wanted to say?"

"I think so," she said. "What's the point of hiding how you feel, especially when someone is about to walk out of your life forever?"

Tom reached up a hand and stroked her cheek. "Is this the time where we're supposed to have a big dramatic airport scene? With vows and declarations and everything ending in a happy ever after?"

"That's not how it works in real life," she answered. "And that's not why I'm sharing these feelings with you. I'm trying to be braver, and that felt like the right next thing to do. I'm not trying to ask you to stay or anything like that. I didn't share it with the expectation of changing anything."

"Would you...would you *want* me to stay?" Tom asked, his eyes darting back and forth between each of hers.

"I..." Maya fumbled as she tried to find the right words. Before she could get any more of a response out, Catherine appeared at her side. She was smiling, but there were tears in her eyes. "Is everything okay?" Maya asked her.

Catherine nodded, turning to Tom. "Tom, thank you for being such a wonderful friend to me and brother to Declan. You were the one to help him turn this around, and I'm just so grateful that I got to see you both one last time."

Tom smiled warmly at Catherine. "I always had a soft spot for you, you know. And I heard you're moving back home, too. Good for you. I'd offer to help anytime you need it..."

Catherine shook her head, waving her arms. "It's time for a clean break for me and the whole Conley clan. I said goodbye to Dec already." She gestured toward the chairs where she had spoken with Declan, where he was still sitting, waiting for his brother. "I don't know if Maya has told you all her big career plans yet, but you'll be in good hands if you keep working with her. I give it—and whatever else there is between the two of you—my blessing."

Tom pulled Catherine in for a hug and dropped a kiss on the top of her head. "Take care of yourself, okay? There's a whole world out there ready to help you. You just have to ask. Don't forget that."

"I won't," she promised before turning to Maya. "I'll say goodbye to you now too, dear Maya. I can take my bags from here. Don't forget my offer and please take it seriously. Anything you need, I owe you." She hugged Maya before taking her suitcase from her and walking away towards the check-in counter without looking back again.

"Wow," said Tom, turning back to Maya. "This day is just full of surprises, isn't it?"

"I think I owe you an explanation about all the career stuff she mentioned," said Maya.

Tom shook his head. "You don't owe me anything, but I'd love to hear about it. It sounds like some exciting changes are in store for you, and I'm all about that." He stepped closer to her again. "But no, that wasn't what I was going to ask you about. I believe I already asked you a question before we were interrupted."

"You did?" Maya asked, stalling for time.

"I did," said Tom. "So tell me, please. Would you like me to stay, if that were an option?"

"It's too selfish to even consider it, Tom," said Maya. "Declan needs you. If you're not there with him, supporting him, who knows what will happen when that plane lands in Dublin?"

Tom nodded. "I agree. I definitely do need to accompany Declan on this flight and help him settle in to his rehab program."

"Yeah," said Maya. "So that pretty much settles it. Maybe in the next life..." She shrugged, forcing a levity into her voice that she didn't feel.

Tom was shaking his head. "You know it doesn't have to be all or nothing, right? The flights go both ways, so conceivably, I could actually come back..."

It was a sweet offer, but it was more than Maya could ask for. She had practically driven Tom away, so who was she to ask him to give them another chance?

"I can't ask you to do that, Tom," she said. "So I should just thank you for a wonderful time and wish you a safe flight. If our paths cross again one day, maybe things will be different. Let's just leave it at that."

"Why are you so stubborn?" Tom asked, grabbing her hand as she turned to walk away and pulling her back. "For one thing, you don't get to single-handedly decide if our relationship is worth giving a chance or not. If I want to be in Chicago, there's nothing you can do to stop me from it. You realize you aren't the mayor of this city, right? And I'm fairly confident no one else has the right to bar an individual from being here."

"Of course," Maya said. "I didn't mean you can't be here or that I don't want you to be here...I just meant I couldn't handle you choosing to be here for me. That's too much pressure...too much pressure on us, whatever we even are, and I think it might be more than we could take."

"I agree," said Tom.

"You...you do?" she asked, looking up into his eyes. Why were they even having this conversation if they both agreed he shouldn't come back to Chicago for her?

"Absolutely," he said. "Which is why I should probably show you this." He reached into his pocket and pulled out his phone. He spent a few long seconds tapping around on the screen until he found what he was looking for and handed her the phone.

There, on the screen, were Tom's flight details. Today's date, followed by the flight number for his flight from Chicago to New York and then on to Dublin. She looked at him again, confused why he was showing her what she already knew.

He exhaled a laugh through his nose. "You're a smart person, Maya. I think you're being willfully obtuse right now. Use your pretty finger to scroll a little further down in the email..." He reached over and swiped up the screen until she saw it. Two weeks later, he had two more flights booked. From Dublin to New York and then on to Chicago. *Oh. Right.*

"You...you were already planning to come back?" she asked.

"Of course I was," he said. "You didn't even know I was flying out today, and the only reason for that is that I'm coming back in two weeks. I was hoping by the time I came back you might be ready to talk to me again, but I figured in the meantime you wouldn't miss me since we were doing all our—very professional, if I may say—communication via email. You didn't really think I'd leave without telling you, did you?" His sad eyes searched hers, willing her to give him an answer.

"I...I don't know," she admitted. "Not really, I guess. But I had made it so clear I didn't want to see you anymore, that I wouldn't have blamed you if you had decided to just get the heck out of here and never talk to me again."

"That would be a pretty strange thing to do to my marketing manager," Tom said. "A pretty poor business decision, I mean."

Maya nodded. "Sure. But I also wouldn't have been surprised if you excused me from occupying that role the same way I excused you from occupying the boyfriend role."

"That wouldn't have been fair," Tom said. "I understand why you did what you did and how betrayed you felt by me not being completely honest with you. I couldn't have punished you for that. I just wanted to stay in your orbit, give you all the space you needed, and hope that one day you might find it in your heart to forgive me. To move past who I used to be. To move forward together. It was a lofty ambition, but I've always been fond of those."

Maya's hand was still in Tom's, but she wasn't letting herself get any closer to him. Not yet. Not until she'd said what she needed to say. "I've been learning a lot about forgiveness lately," she said. "And I'm starting to understand it now. I know it's unfair of me to hold the person you used to be to any kind of standard, even one that the person you are today lives up to so easily. I think it just rocked my world to learn that it's not just terrible people who do things like that, get behind the wheel drunk and endanger the lives of others. To learn that even someone

I love did something like that, it just…it messes with my whole narrative about good and evil, honestly. It reminds me that even the person who caused Nina's death…even that person was made of all the same stuff that you and I are. He may have even been a very good person who made a very bad decision. Or suffered from a very bad illness called addiction. And I know now how unfair it is for me to judge people who experience addiction just because I never have."

"That's a lot of excellent revelations you've had, Maya," Tom said. "Though I have to admit I got a little hung up on one of them…did you say that even someone you *love* could do something like that? Are you…were you talking about me? Do…do you love me Maya?"

Maya felt her face burning bright crimson as Tom's eyes bored into hers. "I think that just slipped out. I…I don't know…I…maybe we make too big a deal out of using the word love, you know? Maybe I just meant it like how I love chocolate or when a kitten falls asleep on my lap or…"

Tom stopped her with a soft touch on her cheek as his thumb came to her bottom lip. "I love you, Maya. And I don't just mean that like the way I love coffee or going for a run. I mean I love you. I've been sick feeling like I messed up everything between us, like I lost you. You're a very special person, Maya. So sharp and so soft, so capable and so tender, so smart and funny and beautiful. You're the rarest of gems, and I love you."

Maya felt his words washing over her and sinking into her psyche. She savored the moment, wanting to remember every detail about it at the same time she felt the butterflies in her stomach turning into adrenaline coursing through all of her limbs, too. "I love you, too," she blurted. "I didn't know how to say it, so I wanted to soften it. But yeah. I definitely love you. It scared the crap out of me and I didn't want to do it anymore. I wanted to take it back, to run away from whatever we could have built together. But I'm pretty sure I love you more than I'm scared of what it means to love you, and that's at least a really good start."

"That's a perfect start," Tom smiled. "Now that we know we both love each other, it seems like the only natural thing to do next is to kiss and make up, right?" He was staring at her lips as his tongue darted out and moistened his own.

Maya nodded wordlessly. She leaned in and Tom met her in the middle, his bottom lip fitting perfectly between her lips as his top lip kissed the bow at the top of her mouth. He groaned as if a tension that had been building inside him for weeks was finally easing. The two of them stood there kissing each other tenderly, saying all the unspoken things between them without using any words. Maya's hands were messing up Tom's hair, and he had one hand at the base of her neck while the other caressed her cheek. All the tension that had been coursing through Maya's body only minutes ago was dissipating with every gentle kiss, as if she were coming back home, back to normal in Tom's arms.

After what felt like twenty minutes, Maya stepped back to take a breath and pulled away from Tom when she realized they were standing in the middle of the departures lobby at the airport. Glancing over Tom's shoulder, she saw Declan looking in their direction, a smirk pulling up one corner of his mouth.

She looked up at Tom. "Whoops," she said. "I think we got a little carried away in the middle of the airport."

Tom groaned again. "I'm kicking myself now for not begging you to have this conversation with me at your apartment."

Maya laughed. "You'll be back in, what...two weeks? I think waiting until then will be the most delicious kind of torture."

"Total agony," said Tom. "I'm tempted to walk over to that counter and change my return flight right now. I could turn right around and take the next flight back. I don't even need to leave the airport in Dublin."

Maya was already shaking her head. "Your brother needs you, Tom. The time will fly by, it really will. And I promise not to freak out about how scary it is to love someone while you're gone."

"You'll save that until I get back?" he asked. "Until I'm within arm's reach and I can help walk you through it?"

"I promise," she said, taking his hand in hers. "Come on, let me walk you two to the security gate. We can't have you missing your flight."

Twenty-Seven

“I honestly don't know how it's possible that you're my daughter,” laughed Janice over the video call. “I should have taught you how to make coffee when you were a child. That might have made those early school morning wake-ups a little less painful.”

“I'm pretty sure you did teach me,” Maya said, pouring boiling water over the filter full of ground coffee beans. “But like any other skill, if you don't use it, you lose it.”

“Is that why you're practicing making a cup right now?” Janice asked. “Just so you'll still remember by tomorrow morning when you're making it for Tom?”

“Of course!” Maya answered, wrinkling her nose. “You don't expect me to drink this, do you?”

“Never,” her mom replied. “But I'm glad to see you've mastered the pour over method. If you want to branch out into other coffee making methods in the future, I'm sure we can get you a book or something.”

“I can buy you an espresso machine for your birthday!” Maya's dad suddenly appeared behind Janice, a huge grin spreading across his face.

Maya laughed. "That's really okay. Thanks, Dad. It's really just about the gesture I want to make for Tom, not about becoming a barista or anything like that."

"Understood," said Bill. "How long has it been since you saw him again?"

Janice answered the question before Maya could. "It's been two weeks since their dramatic goodbye in the airport. I wish I could have been there!"

Maya's cheeks flushed at the memory. "Um, no, you don't, Mom. The whole thing was awkward enough with his brother watching us and it only would have been more awkward if you'd been there, too."

Janice waved a dismissive hand at her. "I'm not saying I wanted to watch you smooch your boyfriend or anything like that. I just wish I could have seen you letting your guard down. Pouring your heart out. You know, the good stuff."

"You do see that, though, don't you? When is my guard ever up with the two of you?"

"Of course it's different with us, sweetie. It's just a special thing to see you with a special someone in your life. That's all."

"Well, *that* you will see for yourself in real life soon enough. You two are coming to Chicago for a long weekend next month, right?"

Janice's eyes brightened before Maya's eyes. "We are! How could I forget? Will we get to meet Tom then? It's not too soon?"

Maya laughed. "No, it's not too soon. He's heard all about you, you've heard all about him...it just makes sense to make the introduction in person. We could do brunch, maybe. With Andie and Luisa, too!"

"Oh, I would just love that!" Janice said, turning to Bill and swatting him on the arm. "Why can't it be next month yet? I want to go see my daughter!"

Bill grabbed Janice in a bear hug and squeezed her tightly. "It'll be here soon enough, my dear. We don't want to crash Maya's reunion with Tom, after all. Let's give the kids some time to themselves before we descend on them."

"That's fair enough," said Janice. "Okay, hon, we'll let you go. Great job with your coffee lesson, even though it's causing me physical pain knowing that you're going to pour that beautiful cup in the sink as soon as we hang up."

"I sure am." Maya smiled. "But I promise that the next cup I make will not be wasted and will be fully appreciated."

"That's all I can ask," Janice said. "We love you."

"I love you both, too," said Maya.

When the call ended, she did exactly what her mom had predicted and poured the practice cup of coffee down the drain. Tom's plane was arriving in the late afternoon, and she still had a few more hours to get everything ready for that time. She was surprised by how physically uncomfortable the anticipation was, and she was glad to have a few more distractions lined up before it was time to head to the airport.

Maya had planned to meet Andie and Luisa for a late lunch downtown, and she would head to the airport after that.

Chicago traffic could be a beast in the late afternoon hours, and she didn't want to risk being late for Tom's arrival. In the time he had been gone, they had been talking on the phone every day and texting any time they were both awake. She was enjoying getting to know him in a different way—without even the possibility of physical contact, they had shared a lot of conversations, both of the deep variety and of the inane variety. She had met both of his parents on their video chats, and he'd even shown her a little bit around Dublin. The city looked beautiful, and Maya had already begun to dream about traveling there together someday.

Most of all, she was enjoying the regular check ins with Tom because they had helped her stay focused on what she really wanted: him to come back to Chicago and the two of them to be together for real. That was an idea she knew would have terrified her into inaction just a month ago, but things had changed. She was determined to give this relationship the best of her, and she knew that the only possible way it could be a failure was if she let her fear of being close to someone stop her from ever giving it an honest try.

She had a feeling Tom was thinking the same thoughts. That he was holding her tenderly from afar, not too tightly to scare her away and not so loosely that she would think he didn't care. It was a delicate dance, of that Maya was certain, and he had done it well. After all, here they were a mere four hours away from his arrival and she was not only scoping out the traffic situation on the way to O'Hare airport but she had also washed her sheets, stocked up on groceries for the weekend, and even learned how to make a decent cup of coffee. In all the conversations they'd had about Tom's impending arrival, they had both agreed that uninterrupted time alone in Maya's apartment was what they both wanted most in the world. Sure, exploring the world—or heck, even just exploring Chicago—together would be nice, but that could wait until they'd had some time to themselves. After all, it had been two long weeks since their airport kiss, and a lot of anticipation had built up in that stretch of time.

Maya was meeting her friends at a restaurant called Juice, which naturally had a rooftop terrace overlooking the lake. A lake view was always their number one priority in a place to eat, a consideration they valued even more than the quality of the food, and Juice was no exception to that rule.

Maya was the first to arrive, so she claimed the table they had reserved, then sat down to wait for her friends. She reached into her purse for her phone and took the opportunity to make sure all her clients were set for the next few days. The more time she had to spend giving Tom her undivided attention, the happier she'd be.

She scrolled through her emails and was pleased to see there was nothing urgent demanding her attention. In the time since she had left Andersen Consulting, she had taken on three new clients, in addition to Tom. Two of them were people she had met at the entrepreneur's event she had attended with Tom, and the third was a referral from one of those. In just two short weeks, it had become clear that the unique selling point Maya—and her new brand as a solo marketing expert—had to offer was a mission-focused dedication to helping non-profits and social enterprises get their message out and create their impact on the world. And it wasn't just that those were the clients that were convenient to her—no, Maya had found the job satisfaction she had always been missing at Andersen Consulting. Or at least, she had been missing that satisfaction until she started working with Tom, until she had seen her hours of work directly translate into impact in communities that most needed it. With her three new clients, the daily metrics she was tracking went beyond ad impressions and click-through rates. She could also track the number of scholarships funded, microloans dispersed, and water filtration systems produced. It was fulfilling beyond anything Maya could have ever imagined marketing work to be.

"Heads up!" Luisa's voice broke through Maya's thoughts as her purse landed on the table next to Maya. "How are you feeling? Stressed? Excited? A little bit of A, little bit of B?"

Andie had walked in behind Luisa and took the seat opposite her. "Hi Maya." She smiled. "I'm so excited for you!"

Maya put down her phone and smiled at her friends in turn. "I'm excited too. And really glad to have a little friend time before I head to the airport. I think I've already cleaned every square inch of my apartment at least twice. It's like I'm going stir crazy. I sit down to read a book and I can't focus on the words in front of me, so I just reread the same paragraph over and over again."

"Did you try working?" asked Luisa. "That always takes my mind off things. There's nothing like getting immersed in a project—ooh, or some client drama—to get me out of whatever is stressing me out and just totally back into the zone."

"I got everything done, actually," said Maya. "And yes, it did help...until there weren't any more client deliverables to create or emails to respond to. Then it was just me and my feelings again. All that excitement and anticipation just filling my stomach full of angry butterflies."

"There's nothing wrong with sitting with the feeling," said Andie. "I know some of us—" She looked at Luisa with a raised eyebrow. "—like to find new ways to distract ourselves. But you can lean into the feeling, too, you know? Sit with it...enjoy it if you can. Whatever the feeling is, it's fleeting. It might not come back again. So enjoy it for what it is. The next time you pick Tom up at the airport, it might feel like just another Tuesday. But today it feels like Christmas morning and the first day of summer vacation all rolled into one. That's sweet."

"It is," agreed Luisa. "I never thought of it quite like that."

Maya shook her head. "Me neither. And that helps. I was feeling silly for being so excited, but it's actually a pretty special thing."

"Feeling silly for a feeling—any feeling—is just old programming," said Andie. "It's that same old voice that tells you not to cry or someone will see. Not to smile too much or someone will notice and take away whatever's making you so happy."

"But there's nothing wrong with being happy *or* with crying," said Maya. "And life or the Universe or God isn't just waiting until I get too happy to do something terrible to me. That's not how it works."

Andie was silent, but she was smiling. "Exactly. I'm really proud of you for getting that. It's not an easy lesson, especially after the hurts you've experienced."

"Thanks," said Maya, feeling a lump of emotion travel up her throat. "It's getting a little easier to live my life without waiting for the other shoe to fall. And to remember Nina with joy and love and not only with sadness. I'm sure I'll have sad days again. I'm not naïve enough to think those ever really go away...but I think there will be a lot more happy ones. And I know she would want me to be happy. To love. To have all the experiences she didn't get to have. I don't need to deprive myself of these fundamental parts of life just because I won't get to share them with her."

"You're so right," said Luisa. "And that's really beautiful. Thanks for sharing that with us, Maya."

After they had gotten the deep spiritual truths and heavy emotions out of the way, the three friends enjoyed their late lunch. The meal was tasty, but it was the laughter, the comradery, and the support they shared that made the moments together fly by far too quickly. Before she quite realized what was happening, Maya's plate was being cleared away, the check was being split up between the three of them, and they were saying their goodbyes in front of the restaurant.

"Have fun tonight," said Luisa. "And give Tom our best."

"I'm so proud of you," said Andie. "And I know Nina is, too."

Maya hugged Andie while Luisa squeezed her hand. When they all pulled back and separated, their smiles were wide and Maya's eyes were shining. "Wish me luck," she said, before climbing into the taxi waiting nearby.

The closer the airport got, the harder it was for Maya to sit still in her seat. She was fidgeting around, opening her phone only to close it again after she realized she hadn't received any new emails in the last twenty seconds, and overall finding it impossible to contain her excitement. She managed to stop herself from spilling her life story to the cab driver, but that was only because there was a lot of traffic and she knew his energy was better spent on keeping both of them safe on the road.

Finally, they arrived in front of the domestic arrivals, and Maya was exiting the car. Tom had texted during her meal with Andie and Luisa to let her know he was boarding the flight from New York, and in between checking her empty inbox she had been refreshing the web page on her phone that had the latest update on his arrival time. His plane had landed just a few minutes before Maya arrived at the airport, practically bouncing up and down with excitement.

After thanking and tipping the driver, Maya tried to find a place to wait for Tom where she'd be able to keep an eye on every single exit from the airport. He was going to have to go through the baggage claim area, and since she didn't know which carousel he'd be at, she figured the best plan was to stake out a meeting place and then text it to him. It was more exciting and romantic to just trust that they would be magnetically drawn to each other no matter where she stood, but she wasn't interested in taking any chances.

She sent Tom a message. "Hey, I'm here. I'm not sure where you're going to exit, so I'm waiting under a giant sign that says 'Meeting Point A.' It would be some kind of cruel joke if they had more than one of these, but that would also be completely illogical. Anyway. I'm here. Come find me. I'll be looking for you."

His response arrived within seconds. "We're still taxiing up to the gate and it feels like it's taking an eternity. I'll be there as soon as I can, so don't you go anywhere."

"Welcome back. I'm really, really glad you're here."

"Me too. Can't wait to see you xx."

Maya smiled at the "xx" at the end of Tom's message. Those same letters had caused her no small amount of stress just a few weeks ago, but now they brought her comfort and reassurance about where she stood with Tom and how he felt about her.

Maya bounced on her toes, eyeballing every new batch of people that came through the exit doors. She saw people who'd clearly been traveling on business, dressed in suits and uncomfortable shoes, and she saw families coming back from vacation—or arriving in Chicago for a fun time. Whether they were coming or going, the families with young children looked simultaneously worn out from the journey and relieved to be on the ground again. The parents were tired, and the kids were wired. She smiled at a young mom who glanced her way, then went back to staring at the departure door.

Tom hadn't texted again to say that he was off the plane or that he had picked up his suitcase, and Maya was resisting the urge to ask for moment by moment updates. Instead, she kept her eyes glued on that door and bounced higher on her toes whenever someone stepped in front of her and threatened to block her view.

It was only when she felt a large, warm hand on her lower back that she remembered there may have been more than one exit from the baggage claim. But who cared about that? The pressure on her back and the electric signals that were zapping all up and down her spine quickly dissolved any lingering thoughts.

She turned and faced Tom, looking into his eyes for the first time since they had both been in this same airport together just a couple of weeks ago. He had somehow gotten more handsome since then, but it was possible she wasn't the most objective judge of his attractiveness.

"Hi," she said, feeling the smile break open across her face as all the excitement she'd been feeling drained right out of her body and into the tiled floor.

"Hi," he smiled back. He pulled her in for a hug, clinging to her like she was solid ground after a month at sea. Maya felt her anxious heartbeats calm down and return to normal, only to accelerate again with something else—a different kind of anticipation that was a lot more fun. No more worrying about traffic delaying her arrival or a dead cell phone keeping them from finding each other...now all she wanted was to take this man with her back to her apartment, lock the door, and not think about the rest of the world until Monday morning at the absolute earliest.

Tom finally broke the hug, sliding his arms up from Maya's waist and resting his hands so that one sat on the back of her neck and the other cupped her cheek. Anticipating his next movement, she reached up to grab the front of his shirt, leaned forward, and kissed him. She kissed him like she had been missing him every moment since he left, and he kissed her back like he wished he had never gone. And again, this moment like a bookend of the last one they had shared in the flesh, they stayed pressed into each other, oblivious to the world around them, while the hustle and bustle comings and goings of a major airport circled around them.

Eventually, when they both needed to come up for air and remember they were in public, Tom stepped back, holding each of Maya's hands in his. "Thank you for the warm welcome," he said, smiling. "But I think it's about time we got out of here. What do you have in mind?"

Maya dropped one of his hands, tugging the other one to get him to follow her. "You're all mine now, Mister. I've got everything we need in my apartment for at least the next 48 hours. You should probably text your parents to let them know you landed safely, but for the rest of the weekend, you're all mine."

Tom grinned back at her. "I really like the sound of that. Though if I'm being honest, I'm all yours for a lot longer than just this weekend. In fact, I don't have any intention of being anything other than yours."

After he said that, Maya had to kiss him again. "Good," she said, when the kiss ended. "I'm all yours, too. Now, let's get out of here."

Author's Note

This story has been the hardest to write and the hardest to put out into the world for a lot of reasons, yet here we are, together, on the very last page. If it touches even one heart, helps even one person understand their own grief, I will consider it a great success.

Thank you for reading Maya and Tom's story. Luisa and Andie will each be getting a book of their own, so if you're curious about what the future holds for them, then please make sure to subscribe for updates.

If you enjoyed this book, please consider leaving a review, as that is one of the best ways to support indie authors like me. Reviews left on major retail sites (wherever you bought this book is a great start!), The StoryGraph, GoodReads, and BookBub will help other readers discover this book, too.

To stay updated on other works in progress, please visit my website at kcmccormickciftci.com and subscribe to my newsletter. I send out monthly updates on upcoming releases, books I'm loving, and other recommendations.

About the Author

KC McCormick Çiftçi is an English teacher turned romance writer. She spent the majority of her twenties living and working abroad, collecting the experiences that inform the stories she tells. She enjoys telling multicultural and international love stories through romantic comedy and women's fiction. She lives in Turkey with her husband and a herd of cats.

Prior to diving into the world of romance, KC published two self-help books for intercultural couples, *Loving Across Borders* and *The K-1 Visa Wedding Plan*. Both are available wherever books are sold.

For updates on upcoming releases, behind the scenes news, and all my favorite book recommendations, visit kcmccormickciftci.com (or just point your phone camera at the QR code below).

Books by KC McCormick Çiftçi

Austen in Turkey

Pride, Prejudice, & Turkish Delight

Sense, Sensibility, & the Mediterranean Sea

Home (Abroad) for the Holidays

Christmas on Inishmore

Intercultural Relationship Self Help

Loving Across Borders

The K-1 Visa Wedding Plan